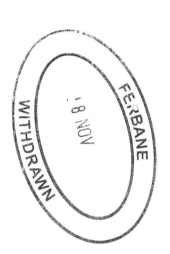

Writers'
Garage

SERVICES AND RESOURCES FOR INDEPENDENT WRITERS

Rosaleen Flanagan

UNDERCURRENTS

*The second instalment in the
detective Cathy Spragg series*

Rosaleen Flanagan
Dublin, Rep. of Ireland
www.rosaleenflanagan.com
rosaleen@rosaleenflanagan.com

Visit my website for details of my previous book Missing Links or for updates on my next book:

www.facebook.com/rosaleen.flanagan.7

twitter.com/rosannaflan

UNDERCURRENTS is the second book in the detective Cathy Spragg series, it is a follow on from MISSING LINKS.

Cover photograph by Philomena Brady.
Layout design by Francesca Giannotta

© 2019 Rosaleen Flanagan
Paperback: ISBN 978-1-9161306-0-9
Ebook: ISBN 978-1-9161306-1-6

Acknowledgements

My sincere gratitude to those who helped me better hone in on the script, in particular, Helen Ryan, Mary Kelly and Cathy Leonard Doyle. This book would have remained just a script if not for the tireless work of Francesca Giannotta and Gian Luca Tapinassi of Writer's Garage whose support I so appreciate. And again, a big thank you to friends and family for your encouragement.

Friday - 29th May

12.50pm

Sergeant Matt Bracken was working at his desk when he heard the commotion. Arriving onto the street he found Brian Enright and Pat Lynch shouting abuse at each other. Now Pat hadn't what you would call good social skills. Since he had been made redundant from his job his fastidious behaviour had caused a stand-off with more than one of his neighbours.

Brian was by his van and turned as Matt approached.

'He now thinks he has a say in who parks in front of his place.' Eyes wide in disbelief. 'And he doesn't want me parking here.'

Pat's house was next to the river. He stood by his front door hyped up with eyes skittering everywhere and nowhere.

'His van blocks the light into me front room and he leaves it here for hours, sometimes overnight.' Shaking his head continually he added, 'It takes up two car spaces and anyone comen to see me has nowhere to park.'

There was a shave of a laugh from Brian. 'And who might I ask would you be expecting to call?'

'That is none of your, none of your business,' replied Pat full of gusto as he tilted his chest toward Brian.

The village of Carrabhain was normally quiet at that hour, but today was no normal day. Hogan's pub was organising a weekend singing competition that had revellers arriving from early morning to pitch tents in the limited space by the river. Then at the grand age of a hundred and one, Una Foy had died. Her ten children, extended relatives and friends were at the graveyard, burying her. Matt had been warned about one of her sons who had previous convictions for assault. And on top of all that, it was the start of a bank holiday weekend and the tenth hot day in a row.

Brian's house across the street was one of the few that had a wide enough side entrance to take a van.

'Why don't you park at the rear of your place?' asked Matt.

Pat beat Brian with the answer.

'Because,' his upper lip curled. 'Because he's hiren out spaces in his backyard for them with a tent comen for that singen competition. That's why.'

Matt scanned the parked cars across the street, sure enough, two belonged to Brian's sons, another to his wife and the fourth was Brian's own Toyota.

'You can park here for an hour but you better move it after that.'

Satisfied, Pat lifted his head off his shoulders. 'I'll be timen ye, one hour, no more.' He folded his arms.

It wouldn't surprise Matt if Pat was to remain there to tick tock away the hour.

'That fella's cracked,' said Brian crossing the street after clicking his van shut.

'Don't you make things worse,' Matt sounded sharp.

There were three cruisers docked on one side of the bridge and two on the other. One couple was stretched out soaking up the sun to the sound of The Eagles taking it to the limit. The parched heat had Matt's shirt sticking to him. He made his way back to the station with that tune playing around in his head. When his mobile rang, he didn't recognise the number.

Although the voice sounded familiar but speaking at such speed Matt couldn't catch a word spoken, leaving him to ask, 'Who is this?'

'Detective Finnegan here.' The words were clearer second time around. 'A woman's body has been found at the marina in Doonaleigh. Reeves is away. I'll need you on this for now; see you there in fifteen minutes.'

The previous year Matt had worked with Finnegan on a double murder case but he hadn't heard from him since. And he wouldn't have if Reeves was on hand. Those from the funeral were returning to the village. Cars were now stretched from beyond the community centre to as far up as O'Mara's pub.

He could refuse. He didn't have to be obliging.

Sounding unusually affable Detective Finnegan said, 'Superintendent Clarke has asked for you to assist me.'

With the crowd expected over the weekend, the station would remain open throughout; the reason Matt was working the day shift with a new recruit, Garda O'Hara, from Athlone. But O'Hara was competent enough to handle things until he returned. Doonaleigh with its fine marina was only a seven-minute drive further down the river.

'Right, I'll see you there.'

1.45pm

A group had already gathered by the marina entrance.

Sergeant Ryan was on the gate.

'The body was discovered by the caretaker Jimmy Abbot. Neither of us recognise her,' Ryan whispered as Matt was admitted.

Detective Finnegan then pulled up. Once through the gate, they both made their way towards the Forensic Team at the far end of the dock.

Tom Gilligan was on his hunkers by the corpse which had been placed on plastic sheeting. 'Not a pretty sight, but that's to be expected after being in the water for some days through this unnaturally warm spell.'

The body was of a woman of medium height. Matt guessed she was in her forties. Her slime waxy face had open blisters. Some scalp was missing large clumps of hair. Her wrists were tied in front of her with narrow orange rope. Her left foot was partly eaten away and deep lacerations were obvious around her right ankle. The heavily blood-stained right shoulder of her jacket was almost in tatters. Emanating from her was the smell of sludge and decay.

Matt approached the caretaker Jimmy Abbot.

'Those two were heading out earlier when they complained of a smell.' Jimmy nodded to the couple huddled together on the nearby bench. 'I found a week-old carton of milk floaten by the side of their cruiser.' He glanced at the carton by the bollard. 'When I went to lift it out, there she was bobben away next to it.'

'Did any other cruiser leave here today?' asked Matt.

Jimmy shook his head and pointed at the cruiser *Lir*. 'No, theirs was the first headen out that early.' He frowned.

'This can't stop the rest of them from leaven?' His shoulders dropped. 'It's our first busy weekend this year.'

Matt went to speak with the couple. Colin Dunne explained how he had planned the surprise weekend for his girlfriend Deirdre. Not what he had bargained for as Deirdre sat dazed clutching a flask that smelt of brandy.

He returned to hear Detective Finnegan advise Gilligan to sweep through the interiors of every cruiser there.

The detective then checked his watch. 'The pathologist is on leave but her assistant has agreed to carry out an autopsy at Tullamore hospital tomorrow.'

A forensic photographer was taking close-ups of the body as Matt turned to trail the detective back to his car.

Finnegan opened his car door.

'Check out all reports of missing women. I'll meet you at the hospital tomorrow at three. When our sub-aqua unit arrives, get them to thoroughly comb this place.' The detective threw his jacket onto the passenger seat before sitting in. 'Reinforcements are on their way from Athlone, I'm sure you know the drill. Forward me your report this evening.'

The familiar chime of an ambulance siren cut through the air. There was the clanking of a stretcher and that purposeful stride of paramedics as they gained access through the gate and made for the corpse. Matt returned to the scene as her body was zipped up in a body bag. After lifting her onto the stretcher, she was wheeled back to the ambulance. Onlookers stood by anxious for a glimpse but there was none of her on view.

No sound from the siren as the ambulance drove off.

The weather-beaten caretaker explained that the cruiser *Lir* had been docked at the marina since Wednesday. Yes, he got the whiff of something the previous day. No, he didn't think anything of it with the water temperature warmer than usual he'd guessed it was a dead fish or rodent. Yes, he had the details of everyone who had hired a cruiser in the last two months as well as those with cruisers docked there on a permanent basis.

They headed to his office.

When reinforcements arrived, Matt described the woman before directing a house-to-house inquiry to be carried out. Although Sergeant Ryan believed the victim wasn't local, with her in such a state he could easily be mistaken. The scene needed to be manned. The remaining two guards would accompany Sergeant Ryan to the station to compile a list of hotels and letting accommodation within a thirty-mile radius. Inquiries were to be made of all bookings in the last four weeks that included a woman who in any way matched their victim. He guessed a four-week span would cover all possibilities.

'Check for anything suspicious. A woman on her own or a couple who left earlier than planned, if there was an obvious tension between guests, or if any of them had hired a cruiser or had a cruiser docked here,' he had concluded.

Two jeeps arrived. A diving crew of five pulled on wetsuits and dragged cylinders from the rear of the second jeep. Matt outlined Detective Finnegan's instruction to the bald-headed supervisor Tom Foy. He passed him his mobile number and asked to be contacted if anything was discovered. As he was about to drive off, he noticed Colin Dunne packing the boot of his car. Matt already had their contact details; they were free to leave. Deirdre was in the front seat and although the heat of the afternoon was stifling, she appeared to be shivering.

6.10pm

The most recent report of a missing woman was a twenty-five-year-old from Westport but she'd been caught on CCTV the previous Wednesday in Castlebar. The closest to the victim's age was a missing woman from Limerick, but she was dark haired, overweight and taller than their victim. On the off chance that her Missing Person's Report had not yet been uploaded onto the Pulse System, Matt contacted each Divisional Headquarters, but he had no luck there. He sat for a minute thinking of their victim. What kind of life had she lived? Had she siblings? Was she married? Did she have children?

The previous case he'd been involved in, the victims were his locals. Their demise happened on his watch, leaving him with a more personal connection. With no link to this woman, he felt somewhat detached. She might be a criminal for all he knew. Was it possible to remain determined to solve a murder if the victim were a devious deceitful human being? He knew, in theory, it shouldn't matter but he imagined it did. Then again, she might have been a decent salt-of-the-earth kind of woman. Regardless of the life she lived, she didn't deserve to be thrown into a river with hands so tightly tied leaving it impossible for her to break free. But perhaps she was already dead at that stage. If so, what was the reason in securing her hands at all?

He checked the list of those who had hired cruisers. Thankfully there weren't many as the season was only starting. The first couple was from London. It would be unlikely that the victim was a foreigner. *What was he thinking!* A perfect way to dispose of her body. Treat her to a surprise holiday and dump her overboard in a country where no one knows her. But if that were the case then what excuse could there be for her disappearance! Unless she didn't have a caring family or friends. Perhaps she was so free-spirited nothing she did would surprise any of them?

His call to London was answered by Laura, Adam's wife. It had just been the two of them on the trip. No, she or her husband hadn't noticed anything suspicious from anyone they'd met. She gave details of their flights to and from Dublin. They checked out.

The last to have booked the cruiser *Lir* was an antique dealer from Dublin. Jonathan regularly cruised the river along with his partner Simon. When asked if there had been any women on board, the answer was a resounding, *No*. Likewise, they hadn't noticed anything suspicious from anyone. Simon, in the background, reminded Jonathan of the trouble they had pulling away from the dock at Carrabhain the previous Wednesday morning. But Jonathan replied that the problem was Simon's in not allowing the engine time to warm up before accelerating too quickly.

Matt was halfway through the list when he noticed the time.

He phoned Sergeant Ryan for an update.

Ryan sounded hesitant as he said, 'I had a call from Detective Finnegan. He instructed me to forward anything to do with this drowning to him and him alone.' He paused before adding, in that heavy forlorn voice of his, 'The supervisor of those divers was told the same thing.'

Matt could feel his blood boil. He was useful for the donkey work but no more than that. Although he as a sergeant was higher ranked that Detective Finnegan, for all the years Finnegan had managed the Divisional

Investigation Team in Athlone as a senior detective, he had earned himself some serious clout. If Matt wanted in on this case then he would have to keep his mouth shut.

At ten o'clock, Garda Deegan arrived to start his night shift, another recruit from Athlone was on her way to assist him. He had heard of the find from the evening news. He didn't imagine the victim was anyone they knew. If so, they would surely have heard something by now.

Matt emailed his short report before sorting arrangements for the following day. There was a ban on overtime but Deegan agreed to cover for him in the afternoon. He had just married and was working on building their house when it suited him; he'd take time off in lieu of what he was owed.

Driving home, Matt thought of DI Spragg. She had led the previous investigation he'd worked on. Since then he had met her occasionally in the village. Superintendent Clarke had stressed how highly she had rated his input in the case while discussing Matt's request for a transfer to the Divisional Investigation Team. At first, the Superintendent had been sympathetic in admitting that with a shortage of sergeants, such a transfer would be problematic. He then outrightly blamed Matt for not realising when first recruited to the force that criminal investigation was for him. It would have been a straight-forward transition, start at the bottom and work his way up. But as a sergeant of a station that left detectives cautious, unsure whether to consider him one of them.

'Detective Finnegan is back at the helm. He assures me that he and Reeves, with whatever rank and file they require, can handle the workload. That is precisely what those at the top want to hear,' the Superintendent had emphasised. 'But be assured, your efforts didn't go unnoticed.'

Heading home after that meeting, Matt was reminded of his days in school and that poster of a woodland scene plastered on the corridor wall with the words, *Two roads diverged in a wood and I took the one less travelled by, and that has made all the difference.*

Well, Matt had absent-mindedly headed down the most travelled road.

As for Detective Finnegan, Matt had noticed how he had filled out in the face and lost his previous gauntness. According to Deegan the word around Athlone Station was that he had all but resigned before his tumour reduced. For now, he was in remission.

Matt drove up the driveway and parked in front of the house. He'd give anything for a second shot at working a murder investigation, but he'd never be considered a true player. Finnegan, and Reeves when he returned would make sure it remained that way.

It began to rain as he stepped out of the car. Warm rain that felt good on his face.

Saturday - 30th May

2.50pm

Overnight, heavy wind-swept rain crossed the country. Matt had woken to the sound of it lashing against the windowpane and had felt the cool dampness in the air on arriving for work at eight that morning. Deegan, when he turned up to start his afternoon shift described crossing the bridge to the sight of what looked like a tent sailing down the river.

When Matt stepped out of the car in the hospital car park, it was the start of another downpour. The rain soaked through his jacket by the time he made it through the hospital doors.

No nod of recognition from Detective Finnegan when he turned up, late. Once through the second set of doors at the far end of the corridor, Matt noticed the fully gowned men at work. One was hosing down a flat basin of blood. The other was working on the corpse lying on the table in front of him. He turned towards them when they entered.

'Perfect timing. I've just finished stitching her up.'

Her body was lean with a deep open wound to her right shoulder. The blisters on her face were cleansed of slime and less obvious while her tanned textured skin left the usual prominent autopsy Y-shaped incision somewhat dimmed. She had been an attractive woman with strong cheekbones and blonde shoulder-length hair.

The assistant pathologist introduced himself as Tony

Andrews, his technician was a Greg Keogh.

'That cut to her shoulder might have been an attempt to remove a birthmark or tattoo, would you think?' asked Matt.

Tony Andrews nodded. 'It appears to have been a clean-cut wound which occurred prior to her drowning and would have caused her to immediately bleed out.' Moving to the other side of the table, he raised her left hand. 'See the slight indentation under the knuckle of this finger; to me that suggests she wore a wedding ring.'

That made her husband number one suspect for he hadn't reported her missing. Then again, she could have been widowed or recently separated.

Tony spoke in that matter-of-fact tone of his. 'Difficult to be precise as to when she was drowned but a week to ten days is as accurate as I can be.' He was gentle in the way he handled her as he moved down along the table. 'Both her ankles were tied with a rope of similar width to that used on her wrists. That rope was attached to a heavy weight of some kind.' He beckoned them to come closer. 'The weight broke the talus bone of her left ankle which then forced itself out through her skin. That allowed the flesh of her foot to be eaten away by fish, rodents, who knows?' Her foot resembled a ragged-edged stump of a tree. 'They'd have fed off her shoulder too if it hadn't been protected by her jacket and shirt but they were almost there.'

Moving around her as though she was his property, Tony continued. 'Her lungs were half-full of water and there was swelling to her brain. The reason for that.' He dropped the sheet over her body and moved to the counter where he picked up a slim narrow instrument holding a piece of plastic. 'This caught in her throat which blocked her airways. With airflow constricted, the flow of blood through her system pumped more rapidly which caused her brain to swell.' His mouth tightened. 'She was alive on entering the water.' Placing the instrument back on the table he returned to view the corpse. 'There is heavy genital bruising. But what's even more disturbing is that an object such as a heavy bar was inserted up through her cervix with such force it twice punctured the wall of her vagina.'

Matt heard himself inhale. What sick human being would have brutally tortured her like that? As if it wasn't bad enough that she was left to decompose at the bottom of the river.

Tony moved away from the counter. 'Her last meal was a burger and chips, eaten about five hours before she drowned. It will be a week before I have the results of her toxicology report.' He left the file on the counter. 'What she was wearing I've placed in those bags; they are to be passed on to Tom Owens in Athlone. One of her shoes is missing.' He nodded towards the bags on the side table. 'She had a good bone structure, teeth that have been extensively worked over, hair recently dyed, nails manicured and her breast implants are relatively new, say within the last eighteen months but alas no registered identification.'

'A woman who took pride in her appearance,' suggested the detective.

'Yes. Tony nodded. 'Her fine tanned textured skin would imply she was someone who enjoyed the sun but knew to take the appropriate precautions.' Approaching the smaller basin, he removed his gloves and began scrubbing his hands. 'Oh, and she had a botch termination when she was young. The scarring from that prevented further pregnancies.'

Matt lifted the bags from off the table before turning to take one last look at the woman who from all accounts appreciated the life she had lived but someone had stopped appreciating her.

As they left, Detective Finnegan handed Tony his card asking him to forward his completed report ASAP.

Returning along the corridor the detective held that swaggering stride of his while swinging his arms as if he were holding a weight in both hands.

Matt walked beside him.

'Any leads yet?' Matt asked.

The detective continued walking.

'No,' he replied.

Whatever he knew he was keeping to himself and to avoid being questioned further he quickened his step and was out the door and gone.

///////

4.45pm

Cathy Spragg had arrived at her holiday home in Carrabhain two weeks back. She sat in her living room listening to music with Truman stretched on the mat in front of her. A book on positive living lay shut beside her. It had suggested the need for emotions to be clearly labelled in order to own them, work through them and then move on. Working through boredom was doable. But comparing her present lifestyle to what it had been ten years back and realising how drastically it had shrunk was the problem. Back then a bank holiday weekend stretched out like an elastic band with shopping, cooking, watching movies, feeding her daughters and their friends if there was a sleepover and if not, then taxiing them to where they needed to go. Plenty of fun-screeching-laughter or fused accusations when emotions dipped low over something considered a full-blown catastrophe. Little or nothing could swing those moods either way. That was all part of her life back then. Now she had a problem filling her day, alone.

She needed a routine to keep her mind focused, if not, according to what she had read her free time could eat her up and spit her out into a fog of depression. She would be forty-nine in September. What scared her was the idea that she had reached the expiry date for life's thrills. It could be downhill from here on.

Since arriving down, she had worked in the garden. An apple tree, pear tree and a gooseberry bush had been planted. It was the wrong time of year to be planting anything but she had watered them every morning and evening. The present heavy rain would help them survive. *What's next?* She had asked herself more than once.

She shuffled a pile of recipes on the coffee table in front of her. Of course, if she hadn't been suspended, she might not be feeling so flat. A heated argument with her boss, Detective Superintendent Gavin got out of hand. The case she had been working on was possibly one of domestic abuse. Theresa, along with her partner Brendan lived with her mother. The elderly emaciated woman had been found dead in an upstairs bedroom. She hadn't eaten in days and had multiple bruises to her body. Theresa was her mother's carer. She had admitted that in recent months her mother had been confused, was on medication for depression, and had lost her appetite. They had locked her bedroom door at night for safety reasons as more than once she had wandered out onto the street while they slept.

Theresa was a large unkempt woman in her thirties who spoke with a deadpan voice and had herself been diagnosed with depression. Cathy couldn't be sure if Theresa understood that her mother had deserved better care or if she were in fear of Brendan who continually spoke for both of them.

When her boss had recommended that a charge of manslaughter against Theresa be presented to the Director of Public Prosecutions, John Collins, Cathy lost it.

'I have no intention of presenting this to him.' She had shouted. 'We don't have enough evidence against Theresa.' She knew the time and effort it would take to make such a case and not forgetting that with John's office inundated with prosecution files he would likely view the case as she did. But if the case did go to trial, her money would be on an acquittal. Hampered by such tight budgets and with no overtime allowed her team was expected to be doubly resourceful. Another blow to their morale was the last thing they deserved. Already one of her team, Eileen, had been prescribed anti-depressants, while Ken, who'd worked with her for fifteen years had applied for early retirement.

'It would be a waste of time. Assault, even neglect would be dodgy when we can't finger the culprit. Brendan could have wanted her dead for all we know,' she had argued.

Her boss, with that sly grin of his, had replied, 'Don't forget yourself, DI Spragg. I have the final say in what is forwarded to the DPP.'

When she made no response, he remarked how she had become too *softly softly* of late. That was what really riled her.

She had shouted that the bureau would be better served with additional staff to help support their findings rather than expecting them to plod along on a wing and a prayer.

That, in turn, rattled him. His response was that her overly sensitive moral conscience was more at fault than anything to do with the bureau.

'Who the fuck do you think you're talking to?' she shouted. 'This,' she held up the case file, 'Is not being sent to the DPP. Not by me at any rate.'

When he calmed down, he had the audacity to state how he wasn't obliged to tolerate her insolence. She had been suspended with immediate effect.

From where she sat, she noticed the light on the cooker's panel had gone out. The oven had reached the required temperature. Cathy moved off the sofa and made for the kitchen. She had invited her neighbour to dinner the following evening. An overdue thanks to Molly for keeping a close eye on the place when she wasn't around. She rolled some cooking apples from the bag onto the table. Searching the cutlery drawer, she found the peeler. At least the apples were juicy. She hated dried up apples in a crumble.

Last week she had forwarded an account of that day's incident with her boss to headquarters as requested. He would have made a similar submission, no doubt exaggerating her outburst. It would be her word against his. Fortunately, her colleague Philip had been handed Theresa's case with instructions to be thorough. A neighbour who had previously refused to talk to them admitted she often heard Brendan shouting and sometimes there was the sound of furniture being thrown around the place. Learning of the possibility of Theresa being charged with manslaughter, a cousin was quick to admit how she herself had witnessed her aunt flushing her dinner down the toilet. But most importantly, what had not been written up in the autopsy report was that the victim's liver was seriously diseased which would have caused her to bruise easily. Philip had phoned her with the news, John Collins was considering a charge of negligence against the couple, although he'd need to study the facts more closely before ever agreeing to bring it to trial.

That was something. But having to defend herself as if her years of handling some of the worst criminal cases stood for nothing was hard for her to accept. Not to mention that her suspicions that day had been somewhat accurate.

The peeling of the apples stopped when she heard that familiar voice of Detective Finnegan or Jeff as she knew him. She raised the volume of the radio.

This woman's body was found at the marina in Doonaleigh. We would welcome anyone with information on her identity to come forward. She was in her forties with shoulder length blonde hair, sallow complexion, medium build and approximately five foot four inches in height. If you know anything that might help us identify her please contact the following dedicated phone number...

On switching off the radio Cathy wondered how long the woman had been in the water.

The recipe book sat open on the counter. Baking wasn't her thing but if she were to put effort into making a dessert it had to be something she enjoyed and she was partial to apple crumble. She'd been eating nonstop since she arrived down to Carrabhain. So much so that her clothes felt tight and now the flesh under her arms wobbled when she jogged. But it was a holiday weekend and with such a drab change in the weather, she'd wait until Tuesday to start a healthier eating regime.

With the apples cut into chunks she again read the recipe to find she should have first started by making the crumble topping. Sugar, flour, butter, oat flakes, and spices were measured and mixed in a bowl. The apples were browning fast; she sprinkled them with sugar before covering them with the topping. The dish was placed in the oven.

There was nothing in what Jeff had mentioned or in his tone to suggest the cause of death might be suicide. The evidence pointed to foul play.

If only she knew the full details.

///////

7.55pm

A group, organised by a Neil Harris had hired a cruiser two weeks previously. Neil was an arrogant git who in a loud voice requested Matt's full name and rank before announcing in an even louder voice that his fiancée, Jennifer, was the daughter of DI Spragg. Matt didn't consider him a suspect and decided not to call him back after he'd abruptly hung up. He wondered what DI Spragg thought of her prospective son-in-law. No, he couldn't imagine her ever *bonding* with the likes of Neil Harris.

He switched on the kettle and watched the ginger-haired Patrick Fowley across the street in conversation with Mrs. Lynch. He was Tess Fowley's son, home again on holidays. He had left the village after finishing school over twenty years back. It was Tess who tracked him down in Vancouver and paid for him to visit her around Christmas. Matt had taken holidays at the time and hadn't met him. When he returned, Tess had popped into the station with a photo of Patrick with his wife and two teenagers.

'He phones me now at the weekends.' Words uttered with

pride.

At Sergeant Larkin's retirement do the previous November the news was out that Tess's son was returning home for a visit.

'When he was at school he was as rowdy as the rest of them but there was no badness in him,' Sergeant Larkin replied when Matt made inquiries.

Matt, still curious had asked, 'But why didn't he return before now?'

Richie swayed from having drunk too much. 'I don't know. Tess was fierce upset when he left, that I remember. But she refused to discuss it with anyone. She'd get so annoyed if ya even mentioned him.' He had then glanced over his shoulder before adding, 'I heard he never attempted to contact her in all those years and probably never would have if she hadn't tracked him down. It's all very secretive if you ask me.'

Matt returned to his desk. Drawing a line through the name of Neil Harris it struck him how little he knew of DI Spragg's personal life. Yes, he knew she had two daughters and that her ex-husband was a solicitor. Jackie had mentioned that her eldest daughter, Jennifer, was a doctor. He hadn't known that, or that she was engaged to be married.

The last group on his list was from Stepaside in Dublin. The organiser, Peter Lennon had sounded irate and refused to name the women in his group. Matt thought he was on to something but was assured by the sergeant at Stepaside station that Peter was sound; even he knew about their week on the river and could list the names of the women in the group.

'There's none of them missing if that's what you're thinking. They had a great time. Peter suggested for me and the wife to try it out sometime.'

Garda Deegan arrived as Matt finished his last call of the day. He felt tired. That morning he'd covered five miles in the rain and was now feeling the worse for wear. Jackie hadn't phoned him all day, no doubt due to their argument the previous night. How did she expect him to react on hearing she had invited no less than fifty to the twin's first birthday party? Knowing her the number was closer to seventy, mostly locals. She hadn't considered that if it rained, they'd be crammed into the living room like sardines or if they drank too much, he couldn't allow them to sit into a car and drive home. He believed in being friendly with locals but at a distance, otherwise, it made things awkward if in the future he would be obliged to arrest one of them. Jackie had refused to see things his way. She had no intention of backing down. They were all welcome, whether he liked it or not.

Deegan sniffed the air. 'What the hell is that smell?'

To his dismay, Matt spotted the bags of the victim's belongings under his desk. Damn! If Detective Finnegan hadn't rushed off as he had, Matt would have handed him the bag for delivery to Tom Owens. It was too late to drive to Athlone. Anyway, with a ban on overtime and it a bank holiday weekend it was possible that her belongings wouldn't be missed until Tuesday. With a pen, he carefully pulled open the bag. The jacket collar sat ripped as if it had been caught in something. The label read *DL Gasur*. Not a brand he was familiar with. Expecting the smell to get even worse he locked the bags in the cabinet of the back office.

On leaving the station he stood on the step and slowly inhaled as he got that sense of stillness in the air you get after rain. There was something calming about it.

'Hi, stranger.'

He turned to find DI Spragg walking towards him with Truman by her side. She usually walked on the opposite side of the street.

'Hi ma'am, how are you doing?'

'Fine.' She warmly smiled.

With his head bowed, Truman appeared unusually lethargic.

She stopped and patted Truman's head.

'I heard about the woman who was found drowned in Doonaleigh. You probably don't know much about it?' She glanced at him before casually tilting her head in the opposite direction as if not overly interested in the details.

But she didn't fool him.

He leaned against the squad car and filled her in on what he knew. It was good to talk it over. There was no one he would trust with such information as her. Much and all as he and Deegan hit it off, Deegan was still close to those in Athlone where he'd been stationed before his transfer to the village. He had mentioned once how Detective Finnegan could seem distant to some but to those who knew him, he was sound. He'd said it in such a respectful way that Matt knew to keep his opinion of the man to himself.

He watched her grimace on hearing how the victim had been tortured.

She removed her cap and jammed it into her jacket pocket before settling her hair. 'That sounds brutal. As if she was meant to suffer.' She waited as Gerry and Margaret Grehan greeted and passed them. 'Was there anything to point to her identity?'

He shook his head. 'Nothing in her pockets, no rings on her fingers. Either they were removed or they're lying somewhere at the bottom of the river. There was one worn walking shoe and as for her clothes, forensics haven't got them yet, but her jacket has a *DL Gasur* label.'

She slowly nodded. 'A woman with expensive taste if she was wearing that brand of clothing.'

That pleased him. From his full day's work, he had nothing, until now.

'Look,' her voice softened. 'If you do get involved in this and need a sounding board, call out to me. I'm around for a while.'

'Thanks.' No point pouring over how his involvement was minimal.

'I better keep going,' she pulled on Truman's lead. 'He'd prefer if we turned for home. He's getting too lazy for his own good.' She moved off.

Opening the car door, a thought suddenly struck him. He quickened his step and caught up with her. 'We're having a birthday party for the twins tomorrow week and we were wondering if you'd like to come along.'

She tucked her hair behind her ear. 'That would be lovely. What time?'

'Any time after three.'

'I'll look forward to it.' She smiled before continuing on her way.

Dropping into the car seat he imagined Jackie would be pleased he'd added her name to the list of guests.

Tuesday - 2nd June

8.28am

Things returned to normal in the village. The busy weekend had included three arrests, two for the possession of drugs and one for disorderly conduct.

It was Garda Deegan's day off; the station belonged to Matt.

The previous Sunday, after obtaining a photo of the victim from Tony Andrews, he had driven to Doonaleigh. The divers were packing up to leave. The supervisor Tom Foy was quick to scuttle around to the rear of the jeep out of sight once he noticed Matt arrive.

Jimmy Abbot examined the photo.

'She looks different from when they dragged her out of the water. But no, I never saw her before.' He had sounded certain. 'I'm good with faces, names I forget but not a face.'

All those with cruisers docked at the marina or had hired one that season had been questioned and were no longer of interest to him. That being the case and in need of clarification on what next to check out, Matt had attempted to contact Detective Finnegan but found his mobile had been switched off. He had then phoned Athlone Station and had spoken to Garda Coyne who didn't think they had gotten anything worthwhile from their public appeals for information to help identify their victim. Matt didn't know whether to believe him or not. He had a curt way of answering as if he were being careful with his words leaving no opening to be questioned further on the matter.

The foul smell had seeped through to the front office. He went to pull the bags from the filing cabinet. He then locked up, dropped the bags in the boot and headed for Athlone. Reaching the station, he was surprised to find Tony Andrews stepping out of his car. He approached Matt and sounding high-spirited explained how he and his girlfriend were heading to Sligo for a couple of days. He had a problem with Detective Finnegan's email address. Twice he'd tried to send his report but, on both occasions, it was automatically bounced back to him. Since he was passing that way, he'd decided to drop it off himself.

'But here.' They had reached the steps when Tony stretched the envelope towards him. 'You give it to him. I hope you find the bastard or bastards who did this.' He turned to rush off.

Matt was escorted down the stairs to Tom Owens in his large office which seemed dimmed by the lack of natural light. Tom was in his fifties, thin-lipped, eyes haggard but not hollowed as once was the case. Matt had worked with him when just out of training and stationed in Longford. Tom had suffered a nervous breakdown before Matt had left for Dublin. When he eventually returned to work, he had accepted a transfer to Athlone. His job entailed listing and tracking every item that left the station pertaining to a crime, in particular items for forensics. Before he took up the position, the station had come under notice on numerous occasions when items were either mislaid, misfiled or misappropriated. But not anymore.

With his large plastic gloved hands, Tom flicked through the rank clothing. Every item she'd been wearing looked expensive, her jeans and shirt were of the same brand as her jacket. The top right shoulder of the shirt was in tatters.

But the one shoe was well worn.

'Forensics were on earlier to know when to expect this lot.'

Matt pulled the large envelope from under his arm; it wasn't sealed with the flap neatly turned inwards. A phone on the desk the other side of the office rang. When Tom finished the call, he seemed surprised to find Matt standing in front of him.

'You wouldn't mind if I used your copying machine?' He wasn't sure if he could trust Tom whose eyes were on Detective Finnegan's name printed on the front of the envelope. *Peculiar*, was how Deegan had described Tom, it was how others at the station also viewed him. Matt hoped there was still an understanding between them from their days in Longford. If he was wrong, he had seriously overstepped the mark. Garda Coyne had been vague when Matt had inquired as to when Reeves was due back to work. It was possible Matt might remain on the case until it was solved. Even if he was just a floater, he'd accept that, but not without the opportunity of proving himself. To be on a level par with those on the investigation team, for he was sure at that stage a team had been set-up, he needed to be familiar with the details of that report.

Tom glanced at him steadily. 'You better be quick, Finnegan is on his way down here.'

Matt pulled the report apart and rapidly ran each page through the copying machine while Tom sat calmly tapping away on his computer. When Detective Finnegan came through the door, Matt, with his back to him was re-organising the report and slipping it into its envelope.

'What are you doing here?' the detective sounded alarmed.

'Just delivering the victims belongings.' Matt turned to face him. 'Oh, and I met Tony Andrews on my way in. He mentioned how he had a problem with your email address and asked me to give you this.'

Finnegan grabbed the envelope and removed the report. His eyes fixed on certain pages, others quickly scanned over.

Tom glanced at the tray holding the copied report before returning his attention to Detective Finnegan. 'I'll show you what we have so far.' He sounded amiable, pleasant even. Stretching out his arm he directed the detective to move across to where her belongings remained on display.

Before following, Matt scooped up the copied report and stuffed it into his inside pocket. He turned and watched the detective who seemed only interested in the ripped label of her jacket with its loose threads. When Tom Owens began tagging each item Matt and the detective left him to it.

'Who else is involved in this investigation?' Matt asked as he climbed the stairs.

The detective rushed ahead of him.

'No one you would know. I heard you were looking for me on Saturday. If you would re-check all accommodation booked in the area, that would be a help.' At ground level, the detective continued up to the next floor without so much as glancing back at Matt.

At the security door, the duty officer buzzed him through. He was outside and had almost reached the squad car when he thought he heard someone call his name.

'Sergeant Bracken.' The voice was louder this time.

He froze before turning to find the caller. It was Superintendent Clarke on the front steps beckoning Matt towards him.

'Were you here for the briefing?' he asked as Matt approached.

Matt sounded surprised, 'No Sir, I wasn't.'

'Follow me.' The Superintendent with a purposeful stride entered the station. Once through the security door, he headed up the stairs and along the corridor before opening a door without knocking.

From the doorway, past the Superintendent's burly figure, Matt felt himself standing tall as he viewed Detective Finnegan sitting behind his desk.

'Is Sergeant Bracken working this case or not? I had insisted on his involvement yet he tells me he hasn't attended today's briefing.' The Superintendent stood with a look of frustration.

A cautious expression ran through the detective's features. 'I explained to him that if he's late, I'd fill him in on what's been discussed. He can remain at the village station instead of here; it worked well for us the last time.' He lied so easily.

The Superintendent shook his head. 'Remaining at the village station isn't a problem. But he needs to be here with the rest of the team for each briefing.' He stressed the word *briefing* as he took the chair opposite the detective. 'This morning was your second briefing and he attended neither of them?' Still a strong whiff of anger in his voice.

Detective Finnegan slowly nodded. 'I'm afraid he was busy at the village over the weekend.'

The Superintendent turned to Matt; his face tight in a frown. 'You get yourself here every morning for nine.' He spat out the words before his attention returned to the detective. 'Now perhaps you can enlighten us both on what you have so far.' He glanced at the chair next to him and half-turned. 'Don't stand there like a statue, man.'

Matt took the chair.

Detective Finnegan focused only on the Superintendent as he rhymed off the details from Matt's reports as well as what he'd picked up from Tony Andrews. Matt noted that he withheld the fresh details of the pathologist's report itself. Not prepared to discuss them in front of Matt, not until he knew more, until he was another step ahead of the posse.

'What about that sub-aqua team, did they find anything?' asked the Superintendent.

Finnegan sat back in his chair.

'There were threads on a loose nail of the cruiser *Lir*. I noticed similar threads on the label of her jacket which is on its way to forensics for comparison. The sub-aqua unit has finished in the marina. They intend inspecting other locations further upriver.' The detective enjoyed being the man in control of what the Superintendent was to be told, of what the public was fed, the one out to ensure that Matt's involvement was minimal. Any commendation for solving this investigation would be his and his alone. Did Finnegan actually think Matt couldn't see that? Or did he just not care?

'The clothes she was wearing were expensive.' Matt couldn't stop himself. He had nothing to lose. The Superintendent wanted him involved. And if he were involved then outlining what he had discovered was his job.

The Superintendent perked up. 'How do you know that?'

Matt outlined the brand of clothing and where such clothes could be purchased. Jackie had rhymed off the precise stores the previous night. It was enough to wipe that smug look from the detective's face.

The Superintendent cupped his chin. 'That backs up your opinion that she was someone used to the high life.' His attention was on the detective and following a slight pause, he asked, 'Have you checked if these stores hold records of their customers. Do they have any idea who might have bought the items, that kind of thing?'

Matt was in like a shot. 'I'm looking after that, Sir.'

The Superintendent, with little enthusiasm, said, 'It's a bit of a lead, I suppose. At least it's something.' With the support of the armrests, he rose from the chair. 'Right well I'll leave you both to get on with it.'

A quick knock on the door was followed by an officer entering to inform the Superintendent of a call from headquarters.

On passing the officer, the Superintendent said, 'Will you show Sergeant Bracken out?'

They were on the stairs when Matt inquired from the officers as to when Reeves was due back to work.

The code was punched into the keypad of the security door as the officer replied, 'He broke his leg playing soccer and won't be back for another four weeks at least.'

As Matt left the building, he felt his inside pocket; it was there, safe and sound. Walking towards the squad car, he controlled the urge to smile.

///////

10.55am

Tess was standing in the doorway when Matt returned to the village. She beckoned him over and introduced him to Patrick who was packing the boot of the hired car.

There was firmness in the handshake. 'I heard it was you who found Tess lying there freezing in that shed.' There was a light twang to his accent.

Matt nodded.

'I'd never have been forgiven if anything had happened to her.'

Whenever he thought of how he'd found Tess just in time after she'd got tangled up in their murder investigation, it left him with a sense of relief that luck had been on his side that day. It was also the reason he found himself closer to her than to others in the village.

Tess glanced at Patrick. 'His wife is Jackie; remember we met her in the supermarket yesterday with those gorgeous twins?'

'Oh right, she is your wife?' He sounded surprised. Folding his arms, he added, 'I hear you are friendly with Gerard Higgins.'

Gerard was Matt's running mate. It was short-sighted of him not to have figured out that with Gerard and Patrick both locals and of the same age, they would have known each other.

'Yeah, Gerard is married now with three kids.'

Tess stepped out from the doorway to allow a teenage boy to pass with his head dropped as low as possible without him falling over. Behind him came an older girl who walked with a stride of her own, red hair falling around her face, iPhone in hand connected to her earplugs. She'd no interest in anyone and pushed in next to the boy before banging the car door shut in a typically teenage fashion.

Matt smiled as Tess rolled her eyes.

'You'll have the chance to catch up with Gerard at the party on Sunday,' he said as he moved to leave. It never came easy for Matt to talk small talk.

But then Patrick's wife Melissa arrived out, that involved another introduction. Thin with thick hair turning grey she looked like a hippy in a cheesecloth skirt and flat sandals. Her strong eyes were evident when she smiled. She was older than Patrick who was explaining that Matt was Jackie's husband.

She made for the front passenger seat. 'We're looking forward to the party on Sunday.'

Patrick took the driver's seat and waved as he pulled away. Matt and Tess watched them go.

'He did well for himself, has his own garage and employs two mechanics. Melissa is a teacher, the solid kind. She has the patience of Job with those kids.' Tess chuckled.

'How long are they staying?' Matt asked.

'They're here until the beginning of August. I'm hoping Catherine will come to visit him while he's here.'

It was strange how before that day Matt had never met either of Tess's children. It was stranger still that he'd never heard of her daughter visiting her since he'd arrived in the village almost three years previously and she only a flight away in London.

Tess sighed as she said, 'Terrible about that woman found in Doonaleigh. Hard to believe no one knows who she is or where she's from.' Her attention was then drawn to the noisy exhaust of Brian Enright's van pulling up outside the supermarket.

'Sure is.' He headed across the street.

'See you Sunday,' she called after him.

7.25pm

Cathy was pleased to find him at the door. Her curiosity had gotten the better of her after their Saturday's chat, so much so that on Sunday she drove to the marina in Doonaleigh. Jimmy Abbot bragged over finding the body. He moaned about the hassle caused for someone no one knew. But he wasn't surprised that the divers had found nothing in the marina.

'If she got hooked up to that cruiser it must have happened further up river and not here.' He then squeezed his eyes shut. 'Who is to say she was ever next or near this place when she was drowned?' With a burst of energy, he added, 'Who's to say she was ever on a cruiser? It could be that she was thrown in off a bridge and once she was about to surface, she got tangled up by a loose screw or a trailen rope. They were fierce interested in the hull of *Lir*. I'm sure they took somethen from off a rusted screw.'

Knowing the river better than most, she knew to value his opinion.

She and the sergeant made for the kitchen.

'It's the pathologist's report,' he said on handing it over.

That sure as hell pleased her. She was quick to find her glasses on the worktop beside the bread bin and began reading its contents. Most of the details were as the sergeant had already mentioned to her. An eaten away left-foot and clean-cut wounded shoulder. The account of how the wall of her vagina had twice been punctured by the insertion of a heavy type bar as well as the scarring from a previous termination made for interesting reading. The assistant pathologist was clear in explaining that the uterus was one of the last organs to remain undisturbed, which was why such scaring was obvious.

Unless she was told otherwise, she'd assume it was the work of a man. That wasn't to say a woman wasn't capable of such torture but there was something essentially male about it. Not a man with psychopathic tendencies for he'd have enjoyed watching the life being sucked out of her and drowning would have provided him little satisfaction. More like a man out for revenge. Perhaps she couldn't be forgiven the lie of a secret affair or, for some reason, he'd come to hate her and wanted rid of her. But one thing was for sure, her drowning was no spur of the moment craziness. It had all the signs of being premeditated.

Cathy had scanned the internet for information on death by drowning. What she had picked up was that a body didn't automatically rise to the surface but could remain on the river bed for at least two weeks until the required gas had formed to inflate the body tissue. Even when freed of whatever weighed her down, she should have remained there on the river bed for longer. What Cathy couldn't discover was whether the cling film caught in the victim's throat had trapped enough air in her lungs to prematurely raise her up or if the warm temperature at the time had helped quicken the process.

The sergeant's elbows rested on the table as he explained his first phone call to DL Gasur Ireland. 'The assistant manager needed a style number for each of the items. I got that from Tom Owens. The second time around she confirmed that those items were from Spring of last year's collection, but the shirt was never available in Ireland.'

Now that was interesting.

'So, she was either foreign or she bought the shirt abroad or online.'

He shook his head. 'It was never available online; there were only a few orders of the blouse dispatched before they discovered a flaw in the fabric. I was assured that any order that left the factory was flawless. The blouse would have sold quickly in the shops as it was an essential item in one of the best storylines of that season.' He read his notes as if he didn't rightly understand them. 'She agreed to contact head office in France and will email me the list of stores where the blouse was sold.'

The sun was streaming through the patio door. 'An attractive woman in her forties who dressed of the best,' she found herself saying.

'And her flat lace-up walking shoe was well worn.'

Her eyes narrowed against the light. 'She was someone stylish as well as practical in knowing the benefit of comfortable shoes.'

'She might have been a well-healed prostitute,' said the sergeant.

She smiled. 'I've never heard of a prostitute in flat lace-up shoes before. But if she wore them in her private life, then she wasn't working at the time she was drowned.'

This drowned woman intrigued Cathy. At least focusing on her freed her from boredom. Her first thought that morning when coming into consciousness was an imaginary vision of the victim. She was smiling, little or no make-up, hair just right, earrings matching her necklace. She wore a thin-strapped summer dress. A perfect shot for a selfie.

If she were Irish how come no one had reported her missing? And if not Irish then why drown her here? That was what puzzled her.

If there was any inkling that the woman was foreign with no links to this country, she believed Superintendent Clarke would have no qualms in allowing the case to drop to a cold case. She could even imagine him shout how *our budget doesn't stretch to spending unnecessary hours cleaning up crimes relating to another jurisdiction.*

Considering Jimmy Abbot's theory and knowing the river as she did it made sense that if she were thrown off a bridge by those with even half a brain then she'd have entered the river close to the centre for her to remain undisturbed. But even if they could pinpoint exactly where she entered the river, so what? If, as the sergeant had mentioned they had no joy in their enquiries to hotels, guesthouses or airbnbs within a thirty-mile radius then where did she come from? To Cathy, tracking down her identity from her clothing was the sergeant's first priority.

She fidgeted with her hands. 'Get what you can from every item of clothing she wore. Find out where each brand was available. Compare that with the location of DL Gasur stores who sold that blouse.' She tapped the table. 'See if you can obtain a list of their customers. If you could try to pinpoint where she lived, now that would give you a serious lead. Chances are there is a missing person's report on her somewhere unless she lived like a recluse, which I doubt.'

Watching him she imagined the wheels of his brain turn at a greater speed than when he arrived.

She took her time. 'Be careful with Jeff Finnegan. Don't go barging in with what you're thinking, you will only make enemies for yourself. Just calmly outline what you discover. Jeff is cute enough to know that what you tell him can't be ignored.'

He thanked her for her advice as he went to leave.

After he headed out the gate, she checked Truman's bowl. He was drinking plenty but didn't seem to have much of an appetite. After pouring herself a glass of wine she headed out through the sliding door onto the patio. From there she stepped down onto the lawn where she slipped off her sandals and walked in bare feet. A chapter in that book she'd read suggested the need to connect to all the senses and feeling her feet being tickled by the grass felt good. When she returned to the patio, she sat on the swing chair. It was ever so peaceful to just view the river glistening in the evening sunshine while the reeds by the water edge swayed in the breeze.

Wednesday - 3rd June

8.55am

Three sets of eyes fixed on him as he made his way to the empty chair across the conference room. Apart from Detective Finnegan, the other two were younger than him. One he didn't recognise, the other was Garda Fallon who had on one occasion worked a shift at the village station. His sniffling and snooping to avoid having to actually work had bugged Matt no end. And here he was part of the investigation team.

Once seated he found himself close enough to the case board to study its information as well as the photos of their victim. Detective Finnegan remained at the front of the room. No formal introductions seemed necessary as he turned to the young man on Matt's left.

'Cummins, have you anything new to report?'

Wide-eyed, the young man replied, 'Unfortunately, I don't.'

The detective turned to McFadden. 'What about you?'

McFadden sniffled. 'I've someone helping me check CCTV footage from both Dublin and Cork airports for the week before she was drowned, but there's no sighting of her yet.'

The detective rolled his eyes. 'What the fuck is wrong with you? You've been working on that for two full days. Have it completed by tomorrow morning?' He then turned to Matt. 'And you, did you discover anything?'

'Her shirt wasn't purchased here. It was sold last year at stores in Paris, London, Liverpool, Edinburgh, and Munich. They will send me a list of those who purchased it by credit card or cheque but they have no way of knowing who paid for it by cash.'

The detective paced the floor. To McFadden, he said, 'Pay special attention to flights arriving from those destinations.' He headed back to the top of the room and pointed to the photo of the victim. 'I've sent this to our colleagues in Northern Ireland, unfortunately, they have no Missing Person's Report that's a match to her.'

'She could have arrived here by ferry,' said Matt.

Cummins flicked his pen. 'I've got those three new recruits checking out CCTV footage from all ferries in that same time frame.'

Cummins had McFadden tossing him a startled glance when he mentioned how her breast implants were untraceable.

'She must have had the job done on the cheap in the Czech Republic or Hungary or some country like that.' As if reading Matt's mind, he added, 'She might have been a high class prostitute.'

Detective Finnegan waved his hands in front of him. 'Let's not lose the run of ourselves here. We stay with the facts and not wild assumptions.' He again viewed her photo. 'She was the kind of woman who would have worn valuable rings. Now someone might have tried to pawn those rings or any other jewellery she was wearing.' He returned his attention to Cummins. 'Check out pawnbrokers in Dublin. Start with those who don't ask too many questions. See what you come up with.'

Cummins pulled his jacket from off the back of the chair.

Detective Finnegan headed for the door. The briefing was

over. Short and sweet. Just as Matt had expected.

Cummins introduced himself while stuffing his arm through the sleeve of his jacket. He explained how he had come from Divisional Headquarters in Cork and before that from the National Criminal Bureau in Dublin. He was broad shouldered with a look of being committed to the job.

McFadden remained where he sat. 'Garda Deegan seems settled in the village.' He made it sound as if it were a near to impossible occurrence.

When Matt made no reply, McFadden was quick on his feet to escort him down and out through the security door. Leaving the station Matt couldn't help thinking how McFadden with nothing to recommend him was part of the investigation team. Yet he, due to a shortage of sergeants, couldn't be plucked from the village even with his previous involvement and somewhat success from working on a case of double murder.

If the case could be solved prior to Reeves returning, then Matt's request for a transfer couldn't be ignored, either in Athlone or further afield. Investigative work gave him a buzz. It was where he believed he belonged.

////////

11.02am

The previous night Cathy had ignored Lucy's first call. She didn't have many friends. There was Molly next door and Martina, her neighbour in Dublin. Then there was Lucy whom she'd known from her school days. But Lucy could sound so overbearing at times that Cathy often felt the need to distance herself from her. Their conversation two months ago was when Cathy had mentioned that she was considering buying a cruiser.

'Something small, that I can dock at Carrabhain and take out whenever I'm down.' She loved being on the river but hadn't ventured out since her father sold his boat long before he had died.

'What, are you crazy!' Lucy had balked. 'That will only give you more of a reason to bury yourself down there. Why not head to the Mediterranean and enjoy a real cruise. You'll end up a recluse if you don't watch it.'

Cathy hadn't spoken to her since.

But when Lucy rang a second time, Cathy had felt obliged to answer.

'Hi.'

'Finally, you answer.' Spoken with determination.

Cathy made no response and Lucy had continued. 'Just so you know, I fell in the supermarket and badly sprained my ankle. I only returned to work last week.' She sounded in sympathy with herself and hardly had time to take a breath. 'I've been on a cocktail of painkillers and anti-inflammatories. But thankfully the foot is beginning to feel part of me again.'

'I'm sorry. I should have called to see you.'

'Yes, you should. I've lost count of the number of times I've phoned you. For some reason, I couldn't even leave a message on your mobile. Talk about keeping the outside world out,' she said with more than a flicker of frustration.

Lucy had been part of the original team to set up the DNA department at the Forensic Science Ireland Laboratory. The lab was understaffed and had access to nothing as progressive as the British DNA profiling system, or so Lucy kept telling her.

'I've had a lot on my mind,' Cathy had replied.

The good thing about Lucy was that she never held a grudge, just wanted always to remain in contact.

'I'm off to Vienna on Saturday. Tomorrow I have a day off for some shopping. How about the two of us catching up over lunch?'

'That sounds like a plan.' For the most part, Cathy enjoyed Lucy's company. As she had to collect post from the house, she had decided to make a day of it.

'Say, the Shelbourne Hotel for half-past one.'

It had been settled that quickly.

The traffic was heavy on the M50. Still in a rush when she reached the house, she gathered up the post and crammed it into her bag. With the place feeling stuffy, the windows were opened wide. The garden was flourishing after the heavy rain. A pink clematis she thought was dead had reappeared along the fence above the white campanula. There were four messages from Lucy on her landline, but that was it. No one else to check in on her, no one. She grabbed some sweatshirts and a rain jacket to take with her. All windows were shut and the alarm re-set before she headed for town.

Fortunately, a couple was just moving from a table by the window as she entered the hotel foyer. Cathy ordered a coffee that arrived as Lucy showed up. She was tall for a woman and had a way of standing back to view what surrounded her as if weighing up whether to stay or not. That expression was there even with her array of shopping bags and her walking stick for support.

'You can see why I'm late.' She dropped the bags under the windowsill and threw her walking stick on top of them.

Cathy stood to hug her. 'Sorry, you've been through so much.'

Lucy dropped into the chair.

'I saw a crotchety old witch looking out at me from a shop window only to realise it was me.'

'Don't exaggerate,' quipped Cathy.

After they had ordered, Lucy sounded cross when she said, 'You never told me that Jennifer got engaged to that young man, Neil, is that his name?'

Not something Cathy had warmed to, never mind wanted broadcasted.

'There's not much I can do about her hooking her star to his wagon.' She recalled the excitement of her daughter when she extended her hand to flaunt her engagement ring. Cathy had congratulated her. Wasn't that what she was meant to do! Neil had lost his job the previous September and hadn't secured another. It wasn't a problem for him to live off Jennifer. Whenever he smiled, Cathy imagined he was out to make her think he liked her, but he didn't fool her. Even her ex-husband Dan worried at how Jennifer weakened to Neil's every whim. The difficulty for Dan was that for years it was he she had doted on, but not anymore. Inquiring over how Neil was doing on the job front, you got the same curt response from Jennifer, *He's trying his best; the state of the economy doesn't help.* Yet the worst years of the recession were behind them.

Lucy settled herself right back in the chair, which made her seem even taller. 'You have to let her go. Just be there for her if she needs you.' On a lighter tone, she added, 'I think you forget how you felt about Dan. That's how she feels about this Neil.'

Yes, Cathy had loved Dan, pregnant when they married; he was everything she had wanted. He worked hard and would have done anything for her in those first few years of their marriage. When he began to wear expensive shirts, unusual ties and was never without the scent of aftershave she knew he was having an affair. When he came clean about it there was no surprise. It wasn't that she didn't feel deeply hurt but she knew herself that what they'd once felt for each other had dried up. She wasn't the kind to lay down and plead for him to stay. It was over. She needed to move on even if she dreaded the idea.

Her coffee was now cold.

'If Neil didn't lean on her as he does, I'd be less critical.' Arching her eyebrows, she added, 'I'd bet it was she who bought the engagement ring.'

With a nod, Lucy frowned. Cathy shrugged back at her. It wasn't something any woman would want for her daughter. Changing the subject somewhat, Lucy gave a rundown on how her sons were fairing out and how her daughter-in-law couldn't have been more helpful when she couldn't put her foot to the ground. When lunch arrived, Cathy mentioned in return how she hadn't heard much from her younger daughter Sinead since she'd returned to Australia with her boyfriend, Malcolm. But at least she'd be home later in the year for good.

'Those dreadlocks of his were something else.' Lucy's whole mouth dropped. 'Hair roped like twine with fuzzed ends, ridiculous.' Her face stretched as she laughed. 'Will he be coming home with her?'

'I don't know. Malcolm's visa isn't up until next February.' The matter was a sore point with Sinead who hoped he'd be leaving with her. 'Can you believe she suggested staying with him illegally until February.'

What was it with her daughters! Neither of them had chosen partners Cathy would consider solid marriage material but then neither of them was yet married. She was reminded of that saying of her mother's, *Many a slip between the cup and the lip.*

Lucy chatted on about her upcoming trip to Vienna, how it was a group holiday that included a night at the opera. With those sharp eyes of hers, she said, 'You've put on weight. You have a narrow frame which emphasises it too easily. It doesn't suit you.'

'That's from eating too regularly.' She explained about her suspension.

When the waiter arrived to remove their plates, Lucy ordered dessert, Cathy declined.

'Good for you, Cathy. If you didn't show your teeth to him, he'd walk all over you. He's got a name for being a bully. That's not to say some of your colleagues might like to see the back of you.' She made a face. 'But that comes with every job these days.' Her expression was serious. 'You have to stand your ground, or you'll do an injustice to all women in the force.' There was that *women's libber* voice of hers, the one that left men scared of Lucy.

'Thanks for that.' Since Cathy's suspension, Lucy had been the first to stand firmly behind her. The general feedback from her colleagues was that perhaps she'd been too aggressive, too outspoken, and too expressive with her opinion. Ok, she'd accept that she shouldn't have shouted at him, nor should she have used foul language but that was all she'd admit to.

It was after three when they finished their cappuccino. Lucy gladly accepted the offer of a lift home and allowed Cathy to gather up all the bags from around the table.

She drove out onto the street and stopped at the traffic lights.

'You know about the woman found drowned at

Doonaleigh?'

Sounding tired Lucy replied, 'I thought you weren't working.'

The light turning green had her pulling off. 'I'm not.' Her attention remained on the car in front. 'There is nothing much to go on I understand.'

The traffic was light.

'No, there isn't.'

Lucy couldn't tell her anything if there was nothing to tell. She needed to back off. 'How is work since you returned?'

'OK,' Lucy replied, still sounding tired. 'There are a couple of students working with us at the moment. I have them checking through the DNA from our database of unidentified victims. I've asked for a report of all DNA that was entered into that database over the past ten years. They then have to compare a victim's DNA against the DNA of those who had presented themselves as a relative, especially those who turned out not to be related. It is the only way they'll learn the ropes and grasp what exactly the job requires.' She glanced out the window. 'They're so eager, they remind me of how interesting I found the job when I first started out.'

Cathy drove along Earlsfort Terrace, around onto Hatch Street stopping at the lights and then on through Ranelagh. When she pulled up outside the house, she helped Lucy in with her bags but dismissed her friend's offer of a coffee.

'I need to beat the traffic.'

Lucy stood in front of her as she was about to leave.

'I worry about you spending so much time on your own in Carrabhain. Apart from your job you don't seem to do much with your life.' She made it sound lonely.

Cathy crinkled up her nose. It was bad enough knowing you were living a boring life. Perhaps even becoming a bore. But being challenged to turn your life in a different direction as if it were as easy as clicking a switch was too big an ask.

'Heading off somewhere on my own wouldn't be my thing.'

Lucy's eyes opened wide. 'I'm not heading off on my own, it will be a group of us.' Then sounding even more encouraging she said, 'There are plenty of holiday packages out there to suit you.' She lay her hand on Cathy's arm. 'If you didn't put effort into solving a case would it get solved?' Their eyes locked. 'No, it would not. It's the same with planning your life outside of work; you need to stretch yourself more or life will pass you by.' She removed her hand from Cathy's arm. 'There I go again, telling you what to do.'

Cathy hugged her. 'You have a great holiday.'

She waved at her friend before driving away.

///////

3.55pm

When Matt looked up from his desk, he was surprised to find Cummins entering the station.

'So, this is your man cave.' Cummins checked the place over.

Thankfully, Deegan had just finished his shift.

Cummins leaned against the counter. 'I understand you worked closely with DI Spragg last year on that case involving Ned Cunningham.'

It had to be McFadden who had filled him in.

'DI Spragg worked from here. The daily briefing happened here,' replied Matt.

Cummins ran his hand along the countertop.

'I've worked with her twice; she can be tough.'

'But fair,' came Matt's rapid response.

Cummins, still leaning on the counter turned sideways to face the front window.

'I suppose you heard she's been suspended, lost the head with her boss. They say she's finished.'

The last thing Matt had expected to hear. He re-read an email to blank his surprise. If he had been aware of the situation, would he have shared with her what he had regarding the case? But having being suspended, there wasn't much she could do with the information. He was conscious of this athletic, fit detective's attention on him.

He glanced up at him. 'Why are you telling me this?'

'I heard you two were tight.' He half-smiled. 'I was just wondering if she mentioned anything to you? Has she had a belly full of it at this stage?'

The man had some nerve.

'What, her and I *tight?* That's total bollocks. I'm no way privy to her way of thinking. Time will tell what she decides.'

Cummins raised himself from the counter. 'If she's out then I won't be the one sent to any division in need of detective support. That'll be down to the newcomer.' He stepped away from the counter. 'I never know where I'll end up from one week to the next.'

Matt glanced at the young, ambitious but naïve Cummins who preferred the bright lights of Dublin. He wasn't the only dissatisfied floater around even if he thought he was.

'Right,' Cummins distanced himself further from the

counter, their session of small talk over with. 'The divers were delayed; they've just arrived.' He turned to leave. 'Why not join me, watch them at work?'

Some fresh air would do him good. Since arriving back from the briefing that morning he'd spent the day at his desk and his head felt as heavy as a stone. He locked up.

It had turned into a dull mild afternoon. When they approached the bridge, Matt noticed the divers' jeep by the side of Hogan's pub. Cummins left him to talk to Tom Foy. There was the sound of voices coming from one of the three cruisers docked, but no one on deck. Matt walked along the narrow path of the bridge and took in the fine breadth of the river. In the distance, he could make out a cruiser heading downstream. The traffic passed behind him. He considered the possibility of the victim being thrown from close to where he was standing. He checked the railing. At one spot the wire sat low as if it had been stretched. He had no way of knowing what had caused it or when it happened. It could have been that way for ages. If she had been thrown in from here then it occurred in the dead of night to avoid being seen. But if it were premeditated, then why choose such an unsuitable location? Athlone with its wide-path bridge or Mulladoon or even Croon where there is little or no traffic to contend with would have been a more suitable location for such a crime.

He recognised Tess's grandchildren close to the divers. The girl's voice carried as she inquired as to what they were up to. Her brother headed along the bank with his head down, searching. He picked up a stone and threw it low and with accuracy, it re-bounded three times before skidding along the river surface and disappearing. The girl remained close to the divers as they strapped cylinders to their backs. They sat along the dock and secured their mouthpiece before dropping into the water. Moving in closer to the edge of the river the girl shouted to her brother to come to have a look but he ignored her and headed further down along the river bank.

Cummins approached him. The water glistened when the sun made an appearance as they waited for the divers to re-emerge on the opposite side.

The last diver out shook their head towards Cummins. They spoke among themselves before again disappearing. It was just in front of the cruisers where they re-appeared. In a shot, the girl was there asking questions. *Had they found anything? What exactly were they looking for? What lay on the bottom of the river?*

The divers moved closer to the bridge and again disappeared.

'They'll reappear on the other side of the bridge,' said Cummins.

Crossing to the path on the far side of the bridge Matt noticed a cruiser pulling in and wondered if that was where the cruiser *Lir* had been docked. Five minutes later, a diver surfaced. He waved his arm in the air. A crew member steered the dingy towards him. Matt and Cummins hurried down to investigate. The dinghy's position was close to where Matt had been standing on the bridge. The girl also noticed the commotion and ran across the street and down onto the far bank shouting at her brother to follow. He had returned by then but remained perched on a boulder smoking a cigarette.

Something was lifted into the dingy. When the dingy returned to shore it held a slab of granite wrapped in narrow orange rope.

The girl was next to him.

'What did they find?' she asked.

'Look, you need to move back, it's nothing to worry about,' said Matt wanting her out of their way.

She was slow to move.

Thursday - 4th June

8.53am

From her large handbag, Cathy retrieved the post she'd collected from the house the previous day. She still couldn't believe how stupid she'd been in not fixing her renewed tax disc to the windscreen of her car. There had been a check-point before she reached the M50 on her way down. Her expired tax disc was two months out of date. She was instructed to produce her up-to-date tax disc within a week at Athlone Station. She didn't have her ID on her at the time, not that that would have made a difference but she imagined the guard's tone might have been less gruff. And he certainly wouldn't have grinned as he dismissed her suggestion that she surrender such documentation at Carrabhain Station instead.

Over a mug of tea, she read the postcard from Sinead. She and Malcolm had moved to Fremantle which was on the coast west of Perth. The weather was cooler now and the store where Malcolm worked wasn't that busy. Not surprising when they stocked surfing gear.

There was a bill from her dentist, a notice from the residence association regarding planning permission and a glossy circular from the county council. Caught up in the circular was a heavy white envelope. Her heartbeat quickened as she opened it. The letter was signed by Assistant Commissioner Adam Keegan and recommended that she contact him by the 4th June to arrange a meeting to discuss the matter in hand. Placing the letter on the table, she watched it automatically draw itself back into its folded position and realised that today was the 4th June.

She had decided against reporting the incident to the Association of Garda Sergeants & Inspectors. If she had and they got involved, trenches would be dug deep on either side. It could take a year before the matter was resolved and for all that time, she'd be out of work and more bored by the day. Although she was prepared to fight and prepared to take a stand, she knew it would be an uphill battle. His word against hers, no witnesses. She just hoped she was doing the right thing in going it alone and that the outcome would not damage her career. Of course, she knew she could depend on Dan's legal advice and support if needs be.

She unfolded the letter and finding her mobile she punched in the relevant phone number. When answered she stated her name after she had requested to speak with Assistant Commissioner Adam Keegan. She then waited.

'Good morning DI Spragg.' His voice sounded efficient, warm even. 'Thank you for your call. I appreciate your willingness to try and have this matter resolved informally. How about dropping in to see me some day next week?'

'Fine,' she replied. 'I'm free any day.' She found it hard to cool that burning anger running through her.

'Let me check my diary.' He could be heard turning pages. 'Wednesday is good for me, say eleven o'clock.'

'Yes, Sir. That fine with me.'

'Fine, I will see you then.'

When the call ended, she stared at her mobile. The tension within her began to dissolve. Dan always preached about the importance of showing a clear line of communication in such cases. Finding her computer, she checked the letter for the assistant's email address. She tapped away until she was satisfied with what she'd written confirming the time and date of their agreed appointment. She then pressed *send*.

///////

9.20am

Matt and Cummins had worked late into the night running through all suppliers of granite in the country. The closest to the slab found in the river was a Roadstone product.

Detective Finnegan examined the brochure he'd been handed.

'It's not the same size and even the texture seems different,' he said.

He was right. The recovered slab had been used to drown her, as not only was the attached rope a match to that tied around her wrists but they had also found her missing shoe close by.

Finnegan dismissively dropped the brochure back on the table.

'Are you telling me that slab isn't available to buy here in Ireland?' He glanced at Cummins and then Matt.

Cummins replied, 'It's not available now. But who knows, it could have been taken off the market some years back?'

Matt raised the Roadstone's brochure from off the table. 'This is the closest match to what any supplier here ever had. There's no knowing who produced the slab of granite or where it was picked up. It could have been imported by a developer during the boom. If the developer has since gone bust and sold it on for cash, we have no way of knowing who bought it.'

'Always the one to smash our endeavours is our Sergeant Bracken.' A mixture of sarcasm and fun in Detective Finnegan's voice.

Sadly, Matt had no counter-argument.

Their promising lead had rapidly evaporated.

When McFadden admitted that he still hadn't completed his check of CCTV footage from both airports, it was enough to tip Detective Finnegan over the edge.

'What the fuck is wrong with you?' he yelled. 'Do you think detective work is some kind of leisure time where you can work at your own pace and do as you like. Is that it?' No response. 'You know you're as useless as a one-legged man at an arse kicking contest.' He finished by demanding that McFadden have a completed report for him by lunchtime. 'Taking account of her age, height, and description of the clothes she wore as well as those specified routes you've been told to consider, it shouldn't be that difficult a search to finalise.'

Still in fighting mode, he turned again to Matt. ''You've checked everyone who hired a cruiser?' Every word emphasised. 'I know you and Cummins think she was thrown from that bridge but before we commit to that theory, we need to rule out any possibility of her being on a cruiser.'

The only group Matt hadn't fully flushed out were those who had accompanied Neil Harris. He'd get onto it if only to cover his ass.

Everything about Finnegan's stance told you this investigation wasn't going his way. They should have known more than they did.

He turned to Cummins.

'How did you fare out with those pawnbrokers?'

Cummins shook his head. 'Nothing so far.'

When Finnegan again paced the floor, Matt read from his notebook.

'The brand of underwear she wore was *Marine Mabson*. They have stores in cities where DL Gasur sold that blouse. I checked their website, the bra alone costs £290. They also sell online.'

Cummins made a whooshing sound. 'Another dead end,' he said as if out to antagonise Finnegan even further.

The mood around the room was edgy serious and yet with those words, it flipped that seriousness totally on its head. For a split second, there was nervous fun there leaving Matt with an urge to laugh. He checked his notebook, his head bowed.

Then sounding like the one responsible to lead the way regardless of the challenge, Finnegan said, 'Right let's keep going on this. Cummins, you get one of those new recruits to check if she arrived here via Belfast or Knock airport.' He focused on McFadden. 'You better have what I need by lunchtime and then take charge of checking out those arriving into the country by ferry and have that completed by tomorrow morning. No more excuses.' He turned to Matt, not bothering to disguise his smirk. 'That doesn't leave you with much to bother about.'

He left the room.

4.55pm

Neil Harris sounded groggy on answering the phone. It didn't take long for his arrogance to kick in.

'What do you mean you want me to answer some questions? I've told you everything you need to know.'

'Is your address, Apartment 14, The Elms, Willow Park Lane, Swords?'

'What if it is?'

'Mr. Harris if you prefer, I'll have a squad car call to you within the next hour to ask you these same questions.'

A short silence followed.

And then in a meeker voice, Harris asked, 'What do you want to know?'

He then rhymed off the names of those who had accompanied him the week he'd cruised the river. All of them, apart from him, worked at Beaumont Hospital, which was a help.

'And yourself, where do you work?' asked Matt.

'I'm unemployed at the moment.'

Matt then contacted the hospital's HR department. They listed two of the group as nurses, two doctors, and a physiotherapist, all of them had worked in the last week.

A walk around the village was what he needed to stretch his legs. He recognised DI Spragg as she left the supermarket to head home. She always kept to herself, not the kind to divulge much to others. So why should he feel annoyed that she hadn't mentioned to him her suspension? If he were in her position, he wouldn't be rushing to mention his predicament to anyone either. It really wasn't any of his business.

Glancing towards the bridge he noticed Pat Lynch

sweeping the path in front of his house. He was another individual who had difficulty opening up, even slightly.

Matt made his way towards him.

'How are the skies looking these nights?' he asked.

Astrology was Pat's obsession. He could talk at length over the patterns imprinted on the night skies or be excited for weeks over an upcoming eclipse. It had been a pastime of Matt's late father. He'd mentioned this to Pat when he first arrived at the village. Although Matt himself had no interest in the stars or the planets floating around the universe it had been a means of connecting with Pat and was the reason Matt could more easily reason with him when others couldn't. That was as much the work of a sergeant as anything else.

To his surprise, Pat replied, 'Come in and I'll show ya what I've got.'

Pat had told Matt that from his redundancy money he'd bought himself a more up-to-date telescope, computer, and camera. So Matt wasn't surprised to arrive into the kitchen and find Pat lifting out one of three albums of recent photos. Matt told himself to show some interest, to say something encouraging at least. He took the album from Pat and began scanning photos of the moon at all angles. There were others of brilliantly bright stars on a clear night. All of them dated and timed.

'This one is good enough to be included in a magazine.' Matt was surprisingly impressed. The photo of the moon falling back into the horizon was better than anything he had seen before, almost mesmerising.

'I think the same,' said Pat with no trace of modesty. 'And I've entered it in a competition. If I win, I have to write a piece for *Astrology Magazine*.'

'I'd be surprised if you didn't win something.'

Pat pouted. 'No point comen second or third. It has to be first place.'

Matt browsed through the second album and tapped at a photo of the river. 'Why did you take this shot?'

Pat studied it for a minute. 'I heard a splash and turned me camera to see what was goen on. That's what I got.' He went to remove the photo. 'I meant to delete it, shouldn't have bothered printen it.'

But Matt stopped him by pulling the album towards him when he noticed the time and date the shot was taken. Friday, 22nd May at 3.45am.

The photo was of the far side of the river where two men were close to a dark coloured car.

'What did you see exactly?'

Bristling, Pat looked uncomfortable. 'I'm not a peepen Tom or anythin like that. The splash sounded clear as if I was standen on the bridge itself.' No eye contact between them as he continued. 'The winda was open and I turned to see what was goen on, without thinken I'd taken the shot.' He examined the photo. 'Two men runnen to the parked car the far side of the bridge.'

'Did you recognise them Pat; had you ever seen them before?'

Pat shook his head. 'I only saw the back of them, that's all.'

'Did you get the car registration or the make of the car?'

Cars were a lesser obsession with Pat, but an obsession all the same.

His eye flickered. 'I zoomed in with me camera. It was a navy battered station wagon with a yella number plate and a GB sticker on the rear winda.'

Matt could hear himself exhale but knowing to keep his eagerness at bay he casually said, 'You'd be helping me no end if you could drop into the station to give me a full account of what you remember from that night. Those men shouldn't have been dumping anything into the river.'

Pat's eyes shifted close to where Matt was standing. 'I'll go with you now before I have me dinner.'

'Fine.' Matt smiled. 'Just fine.'

Friday - 5th June

9.30am

In that flat-pan voice of his, McFadden confirmed that there was no sighting of the victim arriving into the country from either Dublin or Cork airport. He was still working on the CCTV coverage of Dublin port but could confirm she had not come through the port at Rosslare or Cork.

Cummins sounded more energised. 'The check on Belfast and Knock Airport gave us nothing either.' He then made for the case board and added the name, John Curley.

He turned towards Finnegan. 'He's a pawnbroker who had a wedding and engagement ring brought in by two foreigners. Now, this was Wednesday last. They were quick to accept €2,000 cash but the rings were worth at least ten times that. He has no contact details from either man.' He grinned. 'He tried to convince uniform he had no reason to believe they were stolen. However, he wore gloves when examining the rings so they can be checked for fingerprints. He also has a signature on a receipt although I doubt it's legit. The men did mention how they were originally from Libya. And there's a camera on the door which should give us their description.'

Finnegan smiled. 'That, is the kind of lead that makes my day.'

Cummins lapped up the approval even though Matt didn't consider it a significant lead. Those rings could have been stolen from anyone, anywhere.

Matt's turn to add to the pot. 'I spoke with Pat Lynch from the village. He's into astronomy.'

Still, in somewhat of a jubilant mood, Finnegan remarked, 'What, I suppose he saw her in the stars and she told him she's happy and doesn't want anyone charged over what happened to her?'

His attempt at humour wasn't lost on the others.

But after Matt read from his notes, no one was smirking.

'A British number plate,' said Cummins with a burst of enthusiasm. 'No wonder we can't trace the slab of granite.' He shook his head. 'The pawnbroker did mention how one of the men asked to be paid in sterling.'

A detail Cummins should have known to mention.

'Of the five cities where that shirt was sold, three of them are in Great Britain. It might be an idea to run her details past their Missing Person's Bureau to see if they have anything on her,' said Matt.

Finnegan gave it some thought. 'You have a contact in London.' He clicked his fingers. 'That detective that helped us solve that case from last year. What was his name?'

'DI Andy Scott,' replied Matt.

'Give his contact details to Cummins here. It would be weeks before a request would be sanctioned and dealt with. But if Andy Scott could do a quick check on missing women in London that would be a big help.'

It was DI Spragg who was acquainted with Andy Scott. Matt had the impression there was some personal history between them, not something he wanted Cummins to discover. Knowing Andy, he would inquire as to how she was doing and Cummins in that laddish way of his would mention her suspension and perhaps other information she'd prefer he didn't hear about. Matt wasn't so confident that Andy would be willing to help out. Having someone run through files of missing women in London was a huge ask.

'I'll contact him. At least he knows me. He can be tetchy at the best of times, and as he's not obliged to lift a finger to help us, we don't want the door slammed in our face straight off.'

Cummins nodded at Matt. 'Yeah, I see where you're coming from.'

Outvoted, Finnegan nodded in agreement before his attention returned to Cummins. 'According to the toxicology report, there was benzodiazepine in her system, suggesting she was doped.'

Cummins chewed his bottom lip. 'She could have been drugged, kidnapped and stuffed into the boot of a car then ferried here without being observed. I've seen for myself how the boot of a car is seldom checked.'

Detective Finnegan glared at him. 'You make it sound like these criminals were most intelligent in carrying out their crime. Well, you better prove you're just as intelligent in catching them.'

Matt scanned his notes.

'We have two men running from the bridge in Carrabhain on a night within the timeframe of when our victim was drowned. If they are the same men who pawned those rings, then how come they haven't returned home by now?' asked Matt.

No one responded.

Detective Finnegan straightened his tie while directing his attention on Cummins. 'You head to Dublin. Have those rings checked for fingerprints? And get the best shot of the men from what CCTV is available. Have uniform check out all accommodation around the city where they might likely have stayed around the time she was drowned.

They might still be there.'

Cummins, all fired up, left the room.

In a strong voice of authority, Detective Finnegan instructed McFadden to contact all ferry companies for a list of British registered vehicles that had arrived here in the last month and to mark off those that had since left the country. 'It's those who are still here that we're interested in.' He walked out of the room but then came back. 'Also check for cars that might have left about three weeks ago and returned in the last week.' He turned to Matt. 'You check if these men booked accommodation around here in that same time frame.'

He then walked out.

//////

12.40pm

When there was no reply, he left a message. It was over a year since he had last spoken to him. On that occasion, Andy had asked for DI Spragg to give him a call. She had reacted so dismissively when he'd relayed the message that he didn't think she'd made contact, which was why he wasn't sure how Andy would respond on being asked to help out yet again.

Jackie phoned.

'How is your day going?'

'Fine, what are you up to?'

'I've planted up the flowerbeds. They look great.' She sounded pleased with herself.

He grinned. Jackie was on the go non-stop. Everything in the house had to be spotless, the sheets on the bed were changed every third day. His shirts were hardly off his back before they ended up in the washing machine. The twins couldn't dribble or they were immediately changed from top to bottom. Every room had been re-painted in the last three months. There was the constant smell of *Dettol* in the house and every surface continually wiped down. Now she had moved out to the garden.

'How are the twins doing?' he asked.

'Fine, I have them in sun hats even though there's not much sun but you can't be too careful.' There was the loud sound of a power hose. Then silence. Jackie had bought it to wash down the driveway. He'd promised he'd do the job when he got in from work that evening. Obviously, she decided to do it herself.

'I met Molly Molloy in the supermarket; Cathy Spragg's dog had surgery this morning. Don't ask me what's wrong with him. You should call into her this evening; just to make sure she's alright. Molly said she was very upset. That dog means everything to her.'

On hearing the beeping sound of another call holding, he was quick to finish the call. The moment he dropped the handset, the phone rang.

'I never thought I'd hear from you again.' Andy sounded jovial.

'How are you keeping?' asked Matt.

There was traffic in the background. 'Oh, you know, crime keeps us all busy. So, what can I do for you?'

Matt outlined some details. 'I'll send you her photo. If you could check if she's on any missing person's file in London, it would be much appreciated.'

A cry of protest from Andy. 'But she could be from anywhere.'

'I know.' Matt wasn't one for pushing things. If Andy wasn't biting then he'd nothing to force his hand.

Someone loudly called Andy by name.

'I need to go. Send me what you have and I'll see what I can do.'

The call finished.

///////

7.45pm

Cathy had picked over the dinner Molly placed in front of her.

'He's survived this length which is a positive sign,' said Molly in that comforting tone of hers as she dished out some bread and butter pudding.

Truman would remain overnight at the veterinary surgery. Once they had carried out the operation, the no-nonsense vet had requested that she leave. On arriving home, she had phoned on the hour. On her third call, she was told Truman had woken and was naturally groggy. The vet had explained that if Truman made it through the night, he could be collected the following morning. 'But don't phone here again, please. We're too busy to be answering the phone. If his condition deteriorates, we'll let you know.'

She almost cried that morning when she'd found him in his basket drooling, his eyes shut, his belly swollen and him moaning in pain, unable to move. It had her flapping around like a headless chicken. She ran next door for help, but found only Molly's son Adam finishing a bowl of cereal at the kitchen table. He was quick to follow her back to her place and with the help of a blanket, he lifted Truman gently out of his basket and into the back of the car. He also insisted on accompanying her to the vet. Truman had Gastric Torsion or in layman's terms a twisted stomach. Cathy had frozen on hearing the words *a life-threatening condition*. Truman was her only responsibility and yet she'd ignored his symptoms of being tired all the time and drooling more than usual, symptoms obvious to anyone with a brain that something was wrong. But not to her. She had concentrated too much on being bored. Well, bored was nothing to the fear of losing Truman, of finding herself without him. She had welcomed Molly's dinner invitation. It gave her somewhere to be and someone to talk to. When her mobile rang, her stomach sank at the thought of Truman having given up the fight. Was she about to hear those dreaded words of sympathy?

Viewing the screen, she sighed with relief. It was a Dublin number.

'Hello,' she whispered.

'Sorry to be ringing you so late but I'm still here at work and I've been dithering on whether to phone you at all if I'm being honest.'

On recognising Lucy's voice Cathy couldn't help but spew out the details of Truman's condition.

'Oh, poor you.' She replied in full sympathy. 'But you're lucky you got him to the vet on time. Gastric Torsion can be so serious.' That was Lucy for you, a font of knowledge on most matters. 'I won't hold you up then but I just wanted you to know that those students I mentioned did some work on that victim's DNA.'

'Right,' replied Cathy as she tried to think clearly.

'Believe it or not but we got something of a hit.'

Molly was now at the sink washing the dishes.

Cathy didn't quite understand what Lucy meant. But pulling her brain back into working mode she moved out to the quietness of the hallway.

Lucy continued. 'It was Mark. He's the brightest of them. Remember I mentioned how they were working on all DNA entered into the database of unidentified and missing persons over the last ten years?'

'Yeah,' replied Cathy.

'Well, that included the victim's DNA. Mark then began to compare all DNA held in that database against each other, including those whose DNA had been entered as unidentified but had since been identified. Two profiles kept coming back as a close near match. I couldn't believe what he found and to be honest I was as excited as him when I examined his findings. One of those profiles is the recent victim herself. It turns out the other is a close relation, I'm talking close as in brother. She's related to an unidentified man previously found in a field in the north of the city with a bullet in his head. He was later identified. You'll never guess who he was?'

Cathy's mouth was wide open. 'Lucy, just tell me.'

'Ken Rogers. Martin Rodger's brother.'

Cathy leaned against the hall table. She remembered the case of Ken Rogers. He had been found with serious syringe marks along both arms. He'd lived in England for years and hadn't been known to the guards. They hadn't a clue who he was when he was found shot through the head in a field near Navan. Afterwards, he had been identified by his brother, Gerry. The story was that Ken owed a drug dealer serious money. That was more or less confirmed when the following month that very drug dealer and the man suspected of pulling the trigger were found hanging from trees in that same field. There was nothing to point to those involved in their murder. But that was how Martin Rodgers worked, mercilessly and secretively. Those in the force knew it. But they could pin nothing on him.

'Lucy, thanks for the heads-up on this.'

'I knew you'd find it interesting. To be honest, the chances of any of the DNA in our unidentified database ending up related to another's DNA in that same database is one in about a billion. But we hit the jackpot.'

Cathy was still finding it hard to take it in as Lucy continued. 'The findings have been forwarded to Superintendent Clarke. And those responsible for her drowning won't sleep too soundly if Martin Rodgers has anything to do with it.' There was a slight pause. 'Now I have to go, hope Truman will be back to himself soon. I'll contact you when I get back.'

'Thanks again, Lucy.'

Returning to the kitchen, Cathy was swamped in her thoughts.

'Is everything alright?' Molly asked hesitantly as she held a drying cloth in one hand and a dinner plate in the other.

'Yeah. No, it wasn't the vet.' Cathy shook her head. 'It was a friend and ah, yeah, everything is fine.' A mug of tea was waiting for her on the table. She returned to where she'd been sitting.

'You haven't forgotten the twins' party on Sunday?' Molly also returned to the table.

Cathy wasn't fully listening but agreed with Molly to contribute to a gift voucher as a present. She even handed over an amount of cash from her purse without bothering to count it. Part of it was handed back. With the tea drunk, she thanked Molly who tried to persuade her to stay a bit longer, but Cathy needed what she'd been avoiding all day, space by herself. With an excuse of being exhausted Molly seemed to understand.

Walking back to her place with head bowed she almost bumped into the squad car parked in front of her gate.

'How is Truman?' the sergeant asked in a concerned-sounding voice.

She tried to smile.

'If he lasts the night, he should be fine.'

They both entered the house. In swept a soft breeze when she opened the patio door. She pulled a bottle of whiskey from the cupboard. The sergeant declined her offer but she poured herself a large one. Sounding like a robot she answered his questions on Truman's condition all the time asking herself if she could keep what she knew to herself.

He caught her staring at him.

'What is it?' he asked.

'I know the identity of the victim.' She savoured her second mouthful of whiskey. 'She's Martin Rodger's sister.'

He took his time in asking, 'How did you find that out?'

She explained the DNA comparisons that had been undertaken and that a trusted contact from the lab informed her of their findings. She avoided mentioning Lucy by name.

When the sergeant made no reply she said, 'Martin Rodgers was once the country's most prominent drug dealer. This was about twenty years back when our drug squad was ill-equipped to deal with the likes of him. After CAB was established, I imagine the idea of having his bank accounts frozen or his assets removed was what triggered his *Damascus* moment. The word is he no longer deals with drugs but he's got serious contacts in the criminal world and has been tentatively linked to a series of bank raids. But he's intelligent enough to cover his tracks. He uses his betting shops as a respectable front for laundering money.' She folded her arms.

'Would he have been behind this?' he asked.

She considered the question.

'No. He's known to be a family man. The word out there is if you touch any member of his family, you'll be lucky to live to regret it.'

'Then how come he doesn't know his sister is missing?'

'Maybe she hasn't been living here. Like her brother Ken, she might have gone her own way or disowned the family way back.' It was hard to imagine that two siblings ended up murdered while their brother was such a tough nut. 'I doubt he's responsible for this. Even if she seriously pissed him off, he'd never have allowed her to be tortured as she was.'

The sergeant updated her on the sighting of the men on the bridge. He also mentioned their lead regarding the pawnbroker. Add that to the victim's identity and the case was moving along nicely.

But the sergeant sounded bewildered in asking, 'Why murder her here? I mean if she is Martin Rodgers sister then she has no connection to the village. We'd have known by now if she had.'

She couldn't answer that. So far, her involvement in the case was at a respectful distance. Truman's recovery was now her top priority as was her upcoming meeting with the Assistant Commissioner. The last thing she needed was to be tripped up in any way by her involvement in this. Time to back off, to allow the team to finish the job. No harm done.

She took a deep breath.

'Did you hear I was suspended?'

He nodded. 'Cummins happened to mention it.'

She managed a weak smile on hearing that. How eager Cummins was to get his feet under the table with a more permanent position at the bureau. But according to her colleague Philip, the rumour sweeping through their department was that if her position did need filling, Jeff Finnegan was first in line. That would leave Cummins in the same position he presently held. Jeff certainly had the experience but more importantly he was friends with Detective Superintendent Gavin from way back.

'By the way, I spoke to Andy Scott earlier today.'

He had to have noticed her jaw drop.

'You didn't mention anything to him about my suspension?' Oh God, was the desperation she was feeling audible?

'Of course not.'

She moved to rinse her glass at the sink.

'I don't want him to know my business.'

He stood to leave.

She stepped towards him.

'When Finnegan outlines the identity of your victim you behave as if it's all new to you. Please.' Her tone was firm. 'And whatever you do, don't check out Martin Rodgers on your computer.' She paused. 'Jeff would hate to think he was being undermined by either of us.' She imagined that Jeff would have guessed that the sergeant was in touch with her and he might also be aware of her closeness to Lucy at the lab.

He nodded.

At the door, he turned. 'See you Sunday at the party.'

'Yeah, looking forward to it,' she said and she miles away.

When he left, she headed upstairs, plugged the bath stopper in place and poured in plenty of *Radox*.

She had met Andy while working a case in London at a time when budgets covered such travelling expenses. It had been madness to have gotten involved with him and him five years younger than her and married. He'd phoned her many times since then but she'd ignored his calls. Their relationship better fitted a distant memory.

The last thing she needed was a sympathetic *poor you* message from him.

Sunday - 7ᵗʰ June

3.30pm

Molly's son Adam sat sprawled across the sofa watching *Sky Sports*. He had happily agreed to stay with Truman for the afternoon. Cathy had no interest in the TV. It was on Jennifer's suggestion that she not only had one installed but had signed up to the sports channels. Her daughter was concerned that Neil should have something to occupy his time when he came to visit. Not that they came too often. It still irked her at how easily she'd been swayed into doing anything for Neil's sake.

At the door, she again explained to Adam the times for Truman's feeds of liquidised food and antibiotics. She returned to move Truman's basket into a position that would make it more comfortable for him to view the TV.

She and Molly travelled together in her car. Taking the turn off the main road she found cars parked tight to the hedge on either side of the narrow road and the gate posts smothered in pink and blue balloons. A bouncing castle stood to the side of the house. The screams and laughter from the children were more audible when she stepped out of the car. It left her asking herself if perhaps, she had made a mistake in agreeing to come. She was never what you'd consider *comfortable* with children. Lucy put it down to her logical practical way of thinking. She had made it sound as if it was next to impossible for Cathy to unwind and engage in fun things. Maybe Lucy had a point.

Cathy nodded back at those sitting around the bench in the front garden. There was an obvious glow about Jackie when she appeared out from the house to greet them while holding a whimpering blonde-haired Ella in her arms. When Cathy first knew her, she had short hair. Now it was to her shoulders, softer, which suited her better.

'I think she's scared of everyone, she's not used to crowds.' Jackie bounced along with the baby. She seemed pleased when told that Truman was over the worst. But frowned when Molly handed her the gift voucher.

'You didn't need to bring anything, it's just an excuse to have everyone here for a party.' Holding it she added, 'but thank you both,' and she smiled.

She returned inside with Molly following behind. Cathy approached retired Sergeant Richie Larkin wearing a hat that shaded part of his face. He was enjoying a drink by the side of the house while watching the kids on the bouncing castle.

'I have my daily routine, a good walk, some fishing when the weather is fine, no point fishing in the rain. The odd night I'll head to the pub for a drink.' He sounded happy with his lot. 'What more can a man ask for?'

He introduced her to Matt's friend Gerard Hogan. But just then a boy by the bouncing castle began crying on being pushed. Gerard rushed over to deal with him.

Matt as everyone there called him, arrived out with beers for those sitting along the garden bench. Cathy watched as he welcomed Mrs. Lynch who thanked him for inviting Pat but she explained that unfortunately parties weren't his thing.

He moved from Mrs. Lynch towards her.

'Glad you made it.' He smiled.

'It's a great turn out.' She sounded upbeat.

A teenager with ripped jeans and a mop of red hair rushed through the door holding a baby. 'He won't stop crying.'

'This is Aiden.' Matt lifted the baby from the teenager and talked baby talk until the child stopped crying.

Cathy watched how easily he handled Aiden. This softer side of him was as natural as the serious him. Not what she had expected.

'Who have we got here?' Richie Larkin inquired as the teenager was about to head back indoors.

'I'm Heather Fowley.' It was said with a bucket load of confidence.

Tess had mentioned how Heather was a top-class swimmer. She had won a scholarship to some university in Vancouver. Watching her chat with Richie, Cathy couldn't help but notice her profile, high cheekbones and wide mouth she got from her mother, her hair colouring came from her father.

'Is your grandmother here?' Cathy asked when Richie went in search of another drink.

'Oh yeah, we were the first to arrive, Gran would hate to be late.' She grinned and walked into the house straight-backed with her head held high.

Cathy followed. There was a large vase of flowers in the hallway and the fresh smell of paint. The closer she got to the kitchen, the louder the chatter. Women sat around a table covered with a tablecloth edged in pink and blue ribbons. Cathy helped herself to sticks of carrot and celery and a generous serving of some blue cheese dip. Bottles of wine, prosecco, orange juice, tonic, whiskey and gin were pooled together in the centre of the table. Everyone was helping themselves.

Tess, who was sitting next to Mrs. Lynch beckoned Cathy to come to sit next to her. Once seated, a woman in her seventies wearing garish lipstick and an expensive dress offered Cathy a sandwich before introducing herself as Dorothy, Matt's Mum.

'If it weren't for Jackie, I wouldn't know what he was up to.' Then leaning across the table, Dorothy lowered her voice. 'The experience of working with you last year helped build his confidence no end. He's inclined to be shy and although he was bright at school, he refused to consider college.'

Jackie arrived with an apron for Dorothy who insisted her daughter-in-law was fussing. Nevertheless, she pulled it over her head and firmly tied it at the back.

The chatting around the table was non-stop.

Mrs. Lynch mentioned how she'd recently had a cataract removed. 'Afterwards, I was so disappointed to find my favourite skirt wasn't brown but red. Imagine!'

They seemed amazed over Eileen Grace losing four stone in weight from her herbal diet.

'She had to do something, she'd got as big as Birr,' remarked Tess.

The others were in full agreement with that.

Cathy poured herself a glass of wine. The sound of hungry children clambering through the patio door raised the sound level by about ten notches. Paper plates were handed around as aproned Dorothy explained to the kids that the potato wedges just lifted from the oven were too hot to serve. But wedges were what they wanted.

Aiden, sitting on Matt's hip chewed away on a crust of bread held in his chubby fist while his father poured drinks for all the kids. A young boy began crying when a girl knocked over his plate of food. He was the same boy who had cried earlier by the bouncing castle. Again, Gerard led him to the table to fill another plate with whatever he wanted. Nancy from the supermarket was making tea. More trays of food arrived, devilled eggs, mini quiches, stuffed mushrooms, spring rolls and some cooked salmon. Cathy filled her plate.

After she had finished pouring tea Nancy pushed in between Tess and Mrs. Lynch. Dorothy looked more than a little hot under the collar as she divided out the last of the wedges. Cathy was enjoying her delicious salmon when Nancy asked Tess if she'd heard anything from Catherine recently. She hadn't. And then Tess did something completely out of character by turning her back on Nancy.

Noticing Cathy's attention on her Tess casually said, 'There are also steaks being barbecued out on the patio.'

Nancy, looking snubbed, stood up to help Dorothy who was holding a tray of sausages that needed sharing out.

The high-pitched screams of children began to grate on Cathy's nerves. After finishing her food, she strolled out through the patio door. The large barbecue had six steaks on the go. She was told it would be another five minutes before they were ready. But she'd had her fill of food.

To the back of the garden was Melissa relaxing on a lounger, her head wrapped in a scarf which gave her face a more elongated appearance.

As Cathy approached, Melissa whispered, 'I'm really not good in crowds; it all becomes a bit of a blur after a while. I stand there on being introduced while my brain shouts, *I've better things to do than remember names of individuals I'm not likely to connect with again.* It goes right over my head. You probably think I'm unsociable. Maybe I am and my brain knows it.' She began to laugh.

'I know what you mean.'

Once comfortable in the lounger next to her, Cathy sipped some wine. From the sweet-scented smoke of herbs and spices, it was evident those in charge of the barbecue knew what they were doing. There was music coming from somewhere. The sound of Adele's voice bellowed out *Set fire to the rain.* When the song finished, Cathy could see Molly by the patio door and hear her laughing at something said in a male voice which she believed was Richie's. The atmosphere was just right for a party. Sitting back to view what was going on in front of her was enough for Cathy.

She turned to Melissa. 'Are you enjoying your holidays?'

Melissa nodded. 'Yeah, it was important for Patrick more so than for us.' In that restful voice, she added, 'But I think we now need to focus on the kids. They've been great really.'

When the sun made an appearance, Cathy closed her eyes. Even though she had slept soundly for eight hours she still felt sapped of energy from the high emotions of the previous day. Another glass of wine would go down a treat, but she couldn't risk it as she was driving. Though it wasn't much of a distance to walk home and she had a pair of walking shoes in the boot of the car. But Molly wouldn't be keen on walking. What remained in her glass would have to do.

'Do you know Patrick's sister Catherine?' Melissa asked.

Cathy opened her eyes. 'No, but I saw a photo of her last year at Tess's place. An attractive woman wearing large sunglasses on a yacht with her husband's arms around her and the blue sea stretched out behind them.'

Melissa looked aghast. 'You must have a photographic memory?'

'I think I remember it because it had everything you'd want from a holiday photo.' It had to be the wine that had her opening up. She'd only met Melissa once before in the supermarket. 'I used to come here as a kid. My father lived on his own and apart from Molly, I didn't know many from the village. I'd have seen Patrick and Catherine at Mass on Sunday but wouldn't have known who they were.'

'You know they're adopted?' Melissa asked.

'Yeah,' Cathy replied.

A girl of about four tripped as she rushed out the patio door. With knees grazed, she howled as if she'd been stabbed through the heart while Matt attempted to console her.

'She was so manipulating.'

With her attention still on the child, Cathy turned and sounding confused asked, 'Who?'

'Catherine.' Melissa then bowed her head.

It was then that Heather arrived out from the house and approached them.

'Mum, how much more of this do I have to take?' She sounded just like Jennifer at Heather's age.

'Oh, come on it's not that bad,' her mother quipped.

'But it is.' Heather stood with arms stiff and hands facing the ground.

Melissa explained how Patrick and Brandon had gone to a hurling match and now Heather regretted not joining them.

Heather focused on Cathy.

'Brandon and I watched those divers at work the other day, Matt was there so it was police work, right?'

Cathy watched her come sit next to her.

'They're not police here, they're Gardai and I suspect it might have had to do with the woman they found in Doonaleigh.'

It was what everyone around the village was saying, yet the interest in her identity was fading as she wasn't local. An article in a Sunday paper had even hinted that she was here on holidays.

'I told you, Mom.'

Melissa spoke in a disapproving tone, 'She's hoping to work in the police force back home and spends too much time watching those crime programmes. I've tried to warn her off. I mean it can't be good for the soul to have to deal with those in a society whose minds are deranged or have an addiction of some kind.' As if realising that was exactly the work Cathy did, she reached over and placed her hand on Cathy's arm. 'The crimes in Canada are much worse than what you'd have here, believe me.'

Cathy didn't believe her. She wondered how Melissa would have handled hearing of the torture their victim had endured before being drowned. But those details were too morbid for the day that was in it.

Melissa was hungry and sent Heather to plate up some fish with plenty of vegetables and a little potato. When Heather left, Melissa went on to describe her job as a Special Needs teacher. She asked Cathy if she had children.

She described them both.

'You must be proud of them.'

'I suppose I should be,' replied Cathy.

'I think we as parents forget that today's world holds so many obstacles for our children,' said in a teacher's voice.

Patrick and Brandon arrived as Heather returned with Melissa's plate of food. Brandon was typically non-verbal, hair falling over his eyes. At least he nodded when asked if he had enjoyed the match.

Matt hadn't expected that by holding a baby in his arms it would draw everyone towards him as if he were Santa Claus. Their open expression of joy on describing Aiden's large blue eyes or his great smile or even the way he frowned like a little old man was novel.

He was enjoying his second beer when he noticed them heading up the driveway. Watching them approach he imagined the effort it took for them to come. Jacinta walked next to Chris who firmly held Josh's hand. Even as the young boy pleaded to join the others by the bouncing castle, he was being held tight. The memory of DI Spragg telling them how they had found their daughter Aoife's body was something that would stay with him forever. They had both aged greatly in the last fifteen months but thankfully they had Josh to keep them busy. The boy suddenly wrenched free of Chris to run towards the other kids. It left them standing as if stripped of their crutch.

Matt went to greet them. 'Glad you could make it.' He smiled.

'Isn't he just a dote?' said Jacinta stroking Aiden's arm.

Aiden hid his face in Matt's chest. He was sleepy and getting cranky. Matt prayed that he wouldn't cry, wouldn't scream or make strange with Jacinta, or anyone, but especially not her.

'You've come just as the second round of food is being served.' Jackie arrived out and automatically hugged Jacinta.

Matt went to grab Chris a beer and returned to find him by the barbecue chatting to Gerard and Patrick who had almost glued himself to Gerard as soon as he had arrived.

They were discussing those who had lived in the village twenty years ago and trying to figure out where they had ended up. After about five minutes Matt left them to it. He might have been mistaken but he'd felt Chris had clamped up with Matt there.

It was after eight when he headed up the stairs with Aiden asleep in his arms. He dressed him and settled him in his cot. From downstairs came the sound of someone laughing and his mother's clear voice asking if there was anyone else for cake.

Jackie arrived in. 'You beat me to it,' she said as she lay Ella down to be changed. 'She's exhausted.'

With Ella settled, Jackie stood next to him by the window. 'It was a great day, wasn't it?'

He pulled her to him. 'Yeah, perfect.' He kissed her.

They returned downstairs as Deegan arrived. DI Spragg and Molly were leaving. Molly thanked him for a great afternoon as Jackie hugged DI Spragg. Their attention turned to Richie Larkin who had become rowdy. His wife was fit to kill him. She was anxious to leave but the local taxi driver, Lucy O'Brien, was telling her she had a number of bookings to deal with first. It would be forty minutes at least before she could accommodate them.

'I'll drive them home.' Insisted DI Spragg.

Problem solved.

DI Spragg then stood in front of him. Before Matt knew it, she was half-hugging him.

'Matt, enjoy rearing those beautiful twins. You only get one shot.'

She pulled away but held that intense expression of hers.

'I'll do my best.' He nodded.

The four of them walked towards her car.

Monday - 8th June

9.10am

In an attempt to appear indifferent to what was about to go down, Matt was late for the briefing. He apologised, mentioned how it was due to a lengthy phone call regarding a robbery.

Detective Finnegan was by the display board, file in hand. He waited for Matt to be seated before he removed two charts from the file and stuck them to the board. Then pointing to the top chart, he said, 'This here is the victim's DNA profile and this.' On to the second chart. 'Believe it or not, is a copy of Ken Rodgers DNA profile.'

'What's that drug addict got to do with our victim?' asked Cummins.

Finnegan cocked his head. 'It seems some intellectual student at the forensic lab found such similarities between both their DNA profiles to consider them to be brother and sister.'

Both Matt and Cummins stepped forward to study the charts.

'This is unbelievable,' cried Cummins.

Matt was unsure of how to react. Should he appear to be as astonished as Cummins? Or as lost as McFadden who probably hadn't registered the connection to Martin Rodgers or perhaps didn't even know of him?

He returned to his seat.

Detective Finnegan drew his attention from the charts to Cummins.

'If our victim is the sister of Martin Rodgers then it's time for us to show that compassionate kind-hearted side of the force.' He turned around to face them. 'A touch of sympathy and support for a brother who has lost a sister before gently inquiring as to why none of the family reported her missing. And he'll also need to be aware that he and his associates will be closely watched.' He grinned at Cummins. 'We don't want those responsible for this ending up with a bullet to the head.' He nodded. 'Let's get to him first before he has a chance to hide behind that well-experienced solicitor of his.'

'His reaction to this will be something else.' Cummins was totally in tune with Detective Finnegan's way of thinking.

That quick glance of theirs, two minds as one. They were running the show. Matt and McFadden were only spectators.

He was about to ask why they were focusing on Martin Rodgers as he wasn't the only family member not to have reported her missing. But in hesitating, Detective Finnegan beat him to it.

'Where might we find our Martin Rodgers?'

Cummins had the answer.

'Drogheda. I staked out the residence once. It's just outside the town.'

Detective Finnegan stood with hands on hips. 'You can do the deed along with McFadden. Unfortunately, I have an appointment to keep.'

McFadden looked scared. 'But I've to be in court for eleven.'

Matt watched McFadden with some remnants of uniform work still attached to him. Following up on assaults by drunks or druggies, pinpointing thieves, fingering road users who broke the speed limit suited McFadden perfectly. He didn't belong on this or any other investigation. Dealing with the likes of Martin Rodgers was way out of his league.

Cummins grabbed his jacket and headed for the door. It felt like they were rushing things based on so little information, they didn't even have her name for God sake. But Matt wasn't about to stand up and challenge their decision. He couldn't have them suspect that her identity was something he had mulled over all weekend. His only option was to play it safe and go along with them.

At the door, Cummins turned. 'Can't Sergeant Bracken accompany me?' But as if noticing the frown on the detective's face he lightly added, 'If that's alright with you?'

With no other option, Finnegan agreed. He then raised his hand. 'Phone me after you've spoken to him. I want to be in the picture straight away.'

'Will do,' replied Cummins all hyped up and ready for battle.

///////

9.55am

She arrived at Athlone Station sooner than she expected. Adam was with Truman. The only other task she had set herself that day was to dye a pair of faded trousers. Nothing more exciting than that. But she wasn't complaining.

The public office in the station was empty. She handed over her up-to-date tax disc at the front desk. When the young officer went to write it up, she made for the Notice

Board. There were the details on the new legislation regarding penalty points, next one over was a poster with information and a helpline number on drug abuse. She heard someone come through the security door and felt them stand and almost breathe on her.

She turned to face a grinning Jeff.

'Well, well, what a surprise.' He looked older but had filled out since they'd last met. Smartly dressed in a crisp shirt, sharp tie and, she imagined, his best suit.

'And a good morning to you Jeff.'

When the young officer returned Cathy proceeded to join him at the desk.

Jeff followed. 'I was sorry to hear about your suspension. A difficult one that.' He stood, holding out his chest with a smugness that made her skin crawl. Another of the arrogant shits in the force who thought he could talk to her as he pleased even though she was senior to him. But she'd been suspended. He believed he could say what he liked.

'Terrible.' His voice loaded with sarcasm.

'Thank you, officer.' On gathering her documentation, she noticed the officer smirk. From what she'd provided him with he had her name. It wouldn't take much to make the connection as to who exactly she was. That's if it hadn't already registered with him. Jeff was well considered not just by those at that station but throughout the force. For that reason alone, his comments would be around the station by lunchtime and scurrying out from here in every direction by the end of the day with Jeff viewed as being clever and sharp-witted, all at her expense.

Jeff moved to the door and stood rattling coins in his pocket, waiting for her to pass, as if enjoying the idea of her squirming.

Well, she wasn't about to satisfy his chip on shoulder big as a plank begrudging nature she told herself as she packed everything into her bag.

On passing, she turned to face him full on.

'I hear you're hoping for a transfer.' She too could be sarcastic. Her voice was loud enough to be heard by the officer at the desk. 'Or was that just a rumour?' She raised her finger to her mouth as if not sure if she were mistaken.

The muscle across his left cheek twitched.

She smiled on stepping away from him thinking how well Sergeant Bracken had the measure of him.

///////

10.45am

Cummins again mentioned how he didn't know of anyone at the bureau who had ever questioned Martin Rodgers. What concerned Matt was that they were wasting their time. The chances of even getting past the gates of the residence were close to zero.

From the M50 they took the turn for the M1. Drogheda was only forty minutes from the border with Northern Ireland. The town had strong links to the North which was part of Great Britain. A number of IRA members lived along the border, making it easy for them to tip in and out of the North without much fuss.

Cummins watched for his reaction as he asked, 'Have you any idea who Detective Finnegan is meeting in Dublin?'

'I'd be the last he'd confide in,' replied Matt in a chuckle.

Sounding inquisitive Cummins added, 'It must be important.'

Matt agreed. As a senior detective what could possibly override his obligation to face down the likes of Martin Rodgers? It struck Matt as they drove through the town of Drogheda that perhaps Cummins who remained hyped up at the prospects of such an encounter wasn't as confident as he portrayed, or even experienced enough to deal with such a man.

They arrived onto an impressive leafy residential suburb.

'Why live in Drogheda when he's originally from Dublin?' asked Matt.

'They say he's nothing to do with the IRA but by living here he's either letting them know he's not afraid of them or he wants those he's involved with to think he just might be connected.' Cummins turned into a driveway. A pair of large metal-sheeted gates faced them. 'It seems his father was a member way back but there was a serious falling out. He ended up with a broken arm, some teeth missing and he was shot in the knee. He warned his children against ever becoming members.' Cummins stepped towards the gate and pressed the intercom button; Matt couldn't hear the conversation but he was gobsmacked when the gates opened. They passed manicured lawns that sloped down to a gleaming white house surrounded by an array of flowering shrubs shaded by a row of black stemmed bamboos.

As the car came to a halt at the front of the residence two growling Rottweiler's baring teeth sprang forward from the side of the house and pranced against the driver's door.

Cummins held the door out in front of them as a barrier. The sound of a whistle had the dogs standing to attention. Then came a softer sound which had them leaping back around the side of the house out of sight.

Cummins swept his hand over his jacket to remove anything that shouldn't be there.

At the front door, a hollowing ding-dong of a bell repeated itself. When the door opened, Cummins did the talking, producing his ID to the woman whom Matt guessed was foreign and appeared a little confused. But she nevertheless escorted them to a large marble-floored room. The cream covered chairs seemed uninviting, the hangings on the walls impressive and the rug on the floor too plush to be walked on. They stepped across to the window that gave them a view of the tennis court. A fit blonde-haired woman played against a teenage boy, watched by the dogs lying quietly on the path.

Martin Rodgers arrived in, casually dressed, in chinos and a short-sleeved shirt. This was the closest Matt imagined he'd ever get to the man. He was of medium height, fit, with hair perfectly dyed black.

He shot them a look of total confusion before asking, 'What the hell are you two doing here?'

Obviously, they weren't whom he'd been expecting.

Cummins straightened himself. 'Thank you for taking the time to see us, Mr. Rodgers.' He raised his ID and announced his rank as well as Matt's. 'Unfortunately, we're here to inform you that the woman drowned in Doonaleigh has been identified as your sister. We'd like to extend our sympathy to you and your family at this time. We'd also like to ask you a few questions in order to discover what we can about her and to stress how anxious we are to find those responsible for this.' He sounded relieved to have gotten that off his chest.

The man's eyebrows dropped before they spread across much of his forehead. 'What makes you think she's my sister?'

'The DNA from Ken Rodgers and our drowned victim confirm they were closely related as in brother and sister. I can understand how distressing this must be for you, but it's important for us to learn what we can about her. Such as her name, where she'd lived and whether she was married?' Matt rhymed it off.

Rodgers smiled. 'Is this some windup? No, it's too late for an April fool's joke but it is a joke, right? If it's not then someone is out to make idiots of the two of you.' Then pointing his finger at Matt, he added, 'But you're not believable. That's your problems. You should have done your homework first. This is the most ridiculous intrusion from your lot that anyone could have thought up.'

Matt was about to answer when the attractive blond woman they had watched playing tennis entered the room. With a towel around her shoulders and a jar of cream in her hand, her eyes were on Cummins.

'Martin, is everything alright?' Hers was a strong confident voice.

'They want to connect me to this woman drowned in Doonaleigh.'

She went to stand by him. 'I'll have a serious word with Laura. She doesn't understand that just because someone announces themselves at the gate, they should be automatically allowed entry.' She sighed. 'What is the point in having gates at that rate?'

Martin studied them both with amusement.

'Tell my wife what you've just told me,' he demanded.

After Matt repeated himself, she glanced at her husband with a look that said, *Are they for real!* She too laughed, not a fake laugh but one of those full of fun laughs. After scooping cream from the jar, she rubbed her hands vigorously.

Cummins in an effort to inject some formality into their claim said, 'Her DNA was compatible with that of your brother's Ken Rodgers.'

Martin's wife answered, 'Mistakes are easily made.' As she closed over the jar of cream, she frowned. 'What reason was there for Ken's DNA to be checked against that of your victim's?'

It wouldn't do to explain that some students attempting to familiarise themselves with the workings of DNA decided to make comparisons.

'We don't need to explain that to you,' was Cummins response.

Rodgers was by the table, that smile continually tripping off his lips.

'Have you any idea how ridiculous you sound.'

His wife chimed in. 'You remind me of a couple of sheriffs from a Wild West film. All I can say is God help this country of ours if we're to depend on the likes of you to solve our crimes.'

They both laughed.

Then Rodgers shook his head. 'According to the papers, this poor unfortunate woman was in her forties.' When Cummins went to reply, Rodgers cut him off. 'Well gentlemen I've only one sister in her forties and she was here with us over the weekend for a barbecue.'

There was dead silence.

Then his wife threw a shrewd glance towards Cummins. 'This could be construed as harassment, coming here like this attempting to connect your victim to my husband with this cock and bull tale of yours. I have a good mind to contact our solicitor. Now if you wouldn't mind, it's time you left.'

Martin was enjoying every minute of this.

'Well gentlemen if you don't want to end up with your balls in a wrench, you better do as the lady asks.' He opened a drawer and searched until he found what he was looking for. 'I am a reasonable man,' he stretched his hands out in a mocking gesture. 'If you need to question me it cannot be for something I know nothing about. This is my solicitor's contact details.' He handed Cummins his card. 'If you ever need to contact me again, I suggest you do so through him.' He then pointed towards the door.

They found their own way out.

Cummins furiously pulled his mobile from his pocket. Matt could catch the high-pitched voice of Finnegan on the other end of the line asking what Cummins meant that Rodgers wasn't related to the victim.

'He's given me his solicitor's details. There's nothing more I can do here.' Cummins fidgeted with his tie while listening to the detective's continual barrage before he broke in by saying, 'The man is adamant he's not related to her. That should have been checked out before we headed up here.' After a minute of listening to the detective's response, Cummins rolled his eyes. 'Sorry, I can't hear you the coverage is bad. The line is breaking up.' He pulled the phone from his ear switched it off, opened the car door, got in and once Matt was seated beside him, he drove away. 'Finnegan is off the fucking wall. Why wasn't he here instead of you?' This was followed by a heavy sigh. 'He needn't blame me for this cock up. We looked like right idiots in there talking through our arses.' He waited at the gate. When they opened he drove out and away at speed.

Matt remained silent on the return journey. There were the obvious questions but no answers as to what had just gone down. It felt like he'd landed two steps further back in line for a transfer, the last place he wanted to be.

The upstairs room to the back of the house was where she kept the treadmill. It gave her a fine view of the river. Since she'd started her 60-minute workout, two cruisers had passed, but moving at a snail's pace they'd be lucky to reach Croon before dark. Clouds were settling along the horizon. Above them, the sun's reflection was mirrored by the river as it deepened to the colour of salmon pink.

Truman barked at the ringing of the doorbell. Fearing he might do himself harm on becoming too excited, she rushed downstairs to investigate.

After the sergeant made for the kitchen, she guided Truman to the living room. 'Good dog, yeah, you're a good dog.' She rubbed him down.

Back in the kitchen, the sergeant paced the floor.

'Martin Rodgers isn't related to our victim.'

'I don't understand,' she said, automatically dropping onto the nearest chair.

He ran his hand through his hair.

'Cummins and I will be the laughing stock of the force when it gets out.' There was such anger in his voice.

More confusion as she imagined she hadn't heard him correctly. No, she rewound what he'd told her, she wasn't mistaken.

'Are you telling me the two of you went to question Martin Rodgers without first carrying out the simplest of enquires such as talking to neighbours of the family from when they grew up?' She attempted to control herself but couldn't. 'To discover her name for a start.' She made a whooshing sound of a sigh. 'Cummins should have known that much.' She grabbed a towel from the utility room and patted her face. 'I told you there was the strongest possibility he wasn't responsible for what happened to her.' Her eyes bore through his. 'Even if he was, you'll find it impossible to get anything from him or any of his family after today's episode. What the hell were you thinking?'

His knuckles whitened as he held the back of the chair.

'Just what did you expect me to do? What?' He flung his arms out in front of him. 'Stand up at the briefing and say something like *I think we should at least know her name, where she had lived and if she'd been married. It would help to know that much before charging up to question her brother.*' His voice was loud enough to have Truman barking. 'You had Cummins like a jack-in-the-box gagging to get going.' He jerked his head toward the ceiling. 'And Finnegan heading to Dublin for some important meeting. Neither of them concerned over how little we had.' He released a sigh. 'My opinion is the last to be considered.' He faced her. 'Haven't you copped on to that yet?'

Cathy lowered her head. It wasn't the time for arguing. They both needed to calm down.

She got up to switch on the kettle.

'Tea or coffee,' she asked.

'Nothing thanks,' he hissed.

His stare swept across the table. 'Finnegan is convinced those from the lab got it wrong. The head of the department is on holidays. The report was down to her. She'll have some explaining to do when she gets back.' He rubbed the back of his neck as if attempting to release its block of tension. 'Fuck sake, talk about a total mess-up.'

It was hard to say who annoyed her most, Lucy for allowing those students to experiment on the victim's DNA if they weren't proficient enough to know exactly what they were doing. Perhaps that student, Mark, wasn't as bright as Lucy had imagined but knew enough to pull the wool over her eyes. Then there was Jeff. What was he thinking sending Cummins along with the sergeant to deal with the likes of Rodgers? His slip-shod way of passing the can to Cummins was a big mistake, but typical of Jeff. However, Cummins was his own man, he too had good contacts in the force, no way would he take the blame for this. Backed into a corner Jeff would focus on anyone to blame for this mess other than himself. That put Lucy front and center in the firing line.

Cathy made some tea. 'Anyone check out the family's background?'

He was by the sliding door, facing the river. He didn't turn around. 'Cummins did. There were ten of them; one died as a child, Ken some years back. Martin now has six brothers and a sister married in Cavan very much alive according to the sergeant there.' He was calming down. 'That wife of his is as sharp as a razor.'

Cathy looked up. 'Madeline. She's his second wife.'

She stopped at that. It wasn't a secret but she had no intention of bladdering on how Madeline had started off as a promising barrister and a close friend of Cathy's ex-husband, Dan.

In the early years of their marriage, Madeline was someone they had regularly socialised with. But that doggedness of hers in challenging those whose opinion on a point of law differed from hers was relentless and irritated Cathy no end. Dan, on the other hand, wallowed in hearing how good he was at dealing with clients or how well he knew when to keep his mouth shut. Madeline made him sound superhuman.

The story went that Madeline's drinking got in the way of her career. She had met Martin Rodgers when attending

Alcoholics Anonymous. It was common knowledge that he had once been an alcoholic. What few knew was that, back then, Madeline was suicidal with mounting debts she couldn't afford. Dan hadn't a clue about the situation when she had invited him and Cathy for dinner to a fancy restaurant, saying she wanted them to meet someone special. Cathy had stood with her mouth open when she saw Martin Rodgers at the table. Surprisingly Dan hadn't recognised him but then Martin had always maintained a low profile, not even his name had registered with Dan. Cathy had trouble shaking his hand. Madeline in her tight fitted black number and heavy jewellery casually mentioned that Martin was a bookmaker as if that was where he made his money. She had sounded excited when she suggested for Dan and Martin to go sailing some time seeing as it was something they had in common. Cathy picked at her food knowing she was being a hypocrite in pretending everything was fine. Eventually, she eyed Dan to follow her out as she excused herself from the table. He almost didn't believe her, found it difficult to think that Madeleine would be stupid to think that he, as a promising solicitor, would ever want to be in such company. Ultimately, Dan, full of charm returned to the table to apologise, lying that Cathy had a migraine and was anxious to head for home.

As a couple, *they helped each other through their demons,* was what Madeline told Dan the following week. He tried to advise her against associating herself so closely with Martin, but it was no use. Madeline believed everything Martin told her, which was incredible twaddle from a barrister who knew that without viable evidence she should never believe anything as being the truth. There were rumours she was responsible for mislaying evidence on a case again Rodgers. That destroyed her fine reputation.

Again, Martin came to her rescue and provided her with an apartment. He had been married at the time. There was no question of him leaving his wife but she unexpectedly died of a brain tumour. Cathy cringed on remembering opening the invitation to their wedding. She had since heard they had two boys, now teenagers. Martin had four children from his first marriage, all married with children of their own.

Matt broke the silence. 'The Superintendent was like a raving lunatic when he heard what happened. Martin Rodger's solicitor contacted headquarters to advise that there should be no further contact with his client.'

He went on to mention what he'd got from Cummins regarding Martin's father, Dick Rodgers and his association with the IRA. Cathy recalled another rumour that had surfaced around the time Martin and Madeline had married. Up to that moment she had forgotten about it, a rumour that suggested Dick as being a womaniser. She couldn't fully be sure of the details. She had preferred to blank out anything to do with Martin Rodgers if she could help it. Any case that held a whiff of his involvement she avoided, for fear of her colleagues discovering how they knew each other.

She poured milk into her tea. 'Even if there's been a mistake, the victim was closely related to him.'

'But she's not his fully-fledged sister.'

She drank some tea.

'Dick Rodgers was a tyrant of a man. He had ironclad control over his children. He lived off the state and knew everything he was entitled to. He even led a picket on Leinster House over his squalid living accommodation after which his family moved to one of those flats on Holles Street.' She felt she was talking to herself when she noticed the sergeant staring out at the river, in another world.

She leaned forward.

'You should check through the Register of Electors in that area. Dick would have made sure all of his children were registered to vote. Find out the ages of each of them, see if his mother is still alive and while you're at it, Martin's mother had a sister who lived in the same complex. Find out the ages of her children and where they are now.'

He turned to face her. 'You weren't there to see the fun in his face over how ridiculous we sounded.'

Cathy took her time. 'You find leads. You check them out thoroughly. You eliminate those that are not relevant. That's what you call *proper procedure.* Before eliminating this lead, convince yourself it's not relevant.'

She passed him, opened the sliding doors and headed for the large garden chair. There was the sound from a family of ducks by the edge of the river. That liquid gold sun tinged with red poured itself down over the distant landscape. She was glad when she heard the front door bang shut.

Tuesday - 9th June

10.30am

It was just after eight that morning when Matt had a call from Cummins telling him there wasn't going to be a briefing as he and Detective Finnegan were heading to Dublin. A hostel manager in the Christchurch area had two foreigners staying there three weeks back. They had complained about two rings of theirs that were stolen. A known kleptomaniac had a bed in the hostel that same night and the manager needed time to check his usual hiding places. Items he stole usually turned up a week after they'd been snatched, either in the toilet cistern, the freezer or even the bins. When the men returned last week, the rings had been found.

'We're hoping the manager will recognise the men as a match to those at the pawnbrokers.' And as an after-thought, Cummins added, 'I'll contact you if we need you.'

Matt was out of the loop. At exactly the time things were beginning to heat up. He decided that even if the victim wasn't a sister of Martin Rodgers, it would be a useful exercise to gather as much information as he could on the family. She had been a close relative which might be relevant further down the line.

After listing what he had obtained from both Cummins and DI Spragg, his first port of call was to his colleague Eddie, who worked at Pearse Street Station. Thankfully Eddie was on duty and yes, the Rodgers family had continued living in the flat on Holles Street. It was where Dick had died and where his youngest son Gerry still resided. Dick's wife Betty had a sister Nora. She had married Dick's brother Tom. They too had lived in that complex.

Eddie was a mine of information. And he had more to tell.

'From what I've been told, Tom wasn't the worst of them but he was afraid of his shadow and did exactly as Dick told him.'

'What about Dick's wife?' asked Matt.

'She's in a nursing home in Leopardstown. Your best bet would be to contact the parish priest at St. Andrews, Westland Row. The whole family was big into religion.'

Working on DI Spragg's suggestion, he combed through the Register of Electors for that area. If Martin and his sibling had been registered to vote at eighteen then he had their names and ages and there was only one daughter, not two. To have it confirmed he contacted the presbytery at St. Andrew's. The priest sounded cagey. He wasn't on for telling him anything and suggested that he call personally if he required such information. But Matt explained that wasn't possible as he was based in Carrabhain. The priest, a Fr. Cleary, happened to be a close friend of retired Sergeant Larkin and that changed everything.

'I remember you from his retirement do,' said Matt digging through his memories of the night. 'And didn't you sing a few bars of *Danny Boy*?'

'I did be dad and sure wasn't it a great night.'

When Matt again explained what he required, the priest mentioned that he'd only been at the parish for fifteen years and would need to check through the records.

Quicker than expected, an hour later, Fr. Cleary called

him back with the names and dates of birth of the ten Rodgers siblings.

'Now the eldest, Eamon, died from meningitis at age three.'

Their dates of birth tallied with what Matt had picked up from the Register of Electors as to their ages.

Fr. Cleary remembered Dick, a hard man for the drink who had wasted away from cancer. The priest still called out to see Betty in the nursing home.

'She likes to tell me that Eamon is waiting for her in heaven. She never mentions Dick. It's always Eamon and there's a Susan. She has a touch of dementia and can be confused at times. Susan might be someone she was close to in the nursing home who died. She wasn't told of what happened to Ken but she never asks after him either.'

'What about Betty's sister and her children?'

'Just hold on a minute.' The priest began a conversation with someone in the background. 'According to Fr. Grennan here, Betty's older sister Nora died of cancer when she was only thirty-five. Her husband, Tom, passed away ten years ago. Now I remember Tom. They had two children, Margaret and Tommy but Fr. Grennan thinks there was a younger daughter but he doesn't remember her name. I'll come back to you on that.'

'And I'll need their dates of birth if you wouldn't mind and if you know where they're now living that would be everything I need.'

'I'll see what I can do.'

Eddie emailed him with the contents of Dick Rodgers file. A note from 1962 about his organised march on Leinster House. Then a report from 1963 of his movements which would tally with his involvement in the IRA. A missing person's report made by his wife Betty in 1964, a hand-written note dated two weeks later stating that Dick had safely returned home. That certainly didn't concur with what Cummins had told him unless for some reason Dick wanted it kept quiet about how or why he'd been beaten up, most likely by members of the IRA itself. That would account for why Dick never wanted any of his family associated with the organisation.

But why was he beaten up was the question he'd like answered.

////////

2.15pm

Wearing rubber gloves and a long apron Cathy was by the sink. The shop assistant had explained her options. Option one, buy a sachet, pour it into the washing machine along with the item and allow the washing machine to do the job. Option two was to buy a box of dye, add the contents to a bucket of cold water, leave the item to soak and then rinse and re-rinse until the water ran clear. The task was meant for her, not for the washing machine. Her dyed trousers now looked new and so on to a blouse she'd prefer was navy. She stood over the basin, gathered the blouse in her hands and squeezed it tight driving the colour in deeper, at least that's what she told herself. After another minute's soak, she would begin the rinsing process. She cursed when her mobile rang, rubber gloves were pulled off as she went to answer it. At last Jennifer had decided to make contact. Cathy had left her three messages in the last ten days.

'I met Dad's new girlfriend Caroline for lunch. They have so much in common. Did you know he's back horse riding? The two of them spend Saturday mornings up in Carrickmines Equestrian Centre. He loves it.'

'Good. And how are you doing?' Cathy noticed the dribble of navy trickling down from her lower arm to her elbow. She pulled a sheet of kitchen paper to dab it away but the colour remained.

'Oh, I'm fine, why wouldn't I be?' Curt as usual.

'And this Caroline, is she younger than you?' Dan liked his women young. He had maintained a healthy lifestyle and looked ten years younger than his age.

'Oh no. She's more your vintage.'

'That's a surprise.'

'They are heading off to Italy next month for three weeks.'

Now that left Cathy with a tinge of envy. That was what she missed on being single. There was no one there to share a holiday or dinner or a family occasion. You were the odd one out instead of half a couple.

'Are you busy at work?' Cathy didn't want to dwell on Dan's happy personal life.

'Yes, it's hectic. By the way, Neil wrote a letter to the Garda Ombudsman complaining about a Sergeant Bracken. Can you believe he contacted him twice and demanded he answers questions about whom he was with when we were cruising the Lemoy River. He made Neil feel he was being interrogated even after he had mentioned you. Of course, he told him what he wanted to know. But there is no doubt he was harassed. I read his letter. One thing about Neil, he knows how to put his point across.'

Cathy could feel the heat rising from her neck and at speed, it reached her face. Jennifer, intelligent as she was had just made a major blunder.

'I never knew about you two cruising the river. When exactly was this?'

A pregnant pause followed before her daughter replied, 'Ah, well I had a week off and it was a last-minute thing with some of our friends.'

'Jennifer, don't bullshit me.' It was always an effort not to argue with her eldest daughter.

There was a brief silence.

'It's just that Neil never feels welcomed at your place. You make it obvious you don't like him. That's why we thought it best not to tell you.' The voice of reason.

Cathy counted to ten. She remembered the couple's last visit to Carrabhain. No, they weren't interested in going out to eat, leaving Cathy to slave over dinner on both nights without a *thank you* from either of them. And after dinner, they snuggled up in the living room watching TV without even an offer to clear the table, it had left Cathy feeling like a stranger in her own home.

She eventually found her voice. 'The sergeant had every right to question Neil. If I'd been dealing with the case and he wasn't forthcoming I would ask myself what exactly is he hiding, what does he not want me to know?' She felt like screaming. 'Don't you know it's a murder investigation the sergeant is working on?'

Jennifer was so insular, never bothering to read the papers or be interested to know what was going on in the world beyond the hospital. It was for Neil to enlighten her on what he considered relevant news. Neil's slant on things was what she got and his opinion was enough for her, warped and all as it was.

Cathy attempted to adopt her daughter's tone of reason.

'I can understand if Neil isn't aware of how we do our job, but *you* should have known to put him straight. Or are you afraid to tackle him on anything?' It was no good, her voice was running out of control, part of her brain was telling her to pull back, to stop, yet another part was urging her to gallop on. 'You cruised past this house without a thought for me. What is wrong with you?' Her temper was peaking. 'I'm not sure if you have a proper backbone when it comes to family or maybe you do hate me that much.' She was aware that Jennifer was still on the line when she added, 'You might like to inform Neil that unlike him, those in the force have enough to fill their day without dealing with his nonsensical letter.'

Jennifer's voice of reason was gone.

'There you go again. Neil will be family soon, the father of your grandchildren yet you would stand up for this sergeant before him? Don't you dare talk of family. Your work was always more important to you than us. You think only of you.'

Jennifer's attempt to send her on a guilt trip was pointless for she'd heard those *poor me* comments too many times before.

'You can put forward all the arguments you want with regard to me, but wait until you have children of your own before you deem me to have been so unloving and inconsiderate to your needs.'

When her mobile went dead, she felt like throwing it against the wall. Her whole body shook with temper. Then Truman looked at her with those sad eyes of his. She moved to where he lay, sat on the floor next to him and buried her head in his neck.

5.05pm

She only answered the phone after checking the caller ID.

'Hi,' she said in a croaky voice.

'Are you OK?' He sounded concerned. 'I called to the house earlier but there was no answer.'

She blew her nose. *Hold it together woman.*

'I'm fine, apart from a touch of hay fever; I was probably out for a walk at the time.' Of course, she'd heard the doorbell. It had been a job to keep Truman under control for she hadn't wanted to deal with anyone just then. Talking to him over the phone was as much as she could handle.

'I checked out the Rodgers family.'

She thought for a second before going in search of a pen and notebook.

'Go ahead.'

He filled her in on what he'd discovered. Apart from Martin, three of his siblings were living in Spain, one in Florida, a sister married in Cavan and Eamon and Ken dead. Gerry, the youngest still lived in the flat on Holles Street and Paul was a small-time criminal living in Cork. He finished up by adding that Martin's mother Betty was in a nursing home in Leopardstown.

What a coincidence! Her neighbour Martina had placed her mother in that same nursing home. Every September, the two of them attended their annual fund-raising sale of work.

She hadn't known that Dick's brother was married to Betty's sister.

'Just so I have this right, in 1964 which takes in the time Dick Rodgers went missing, Betty wasn't pregnant.'

'That's what it looks like,' the sergeant sounded more like his old self. 'But Betty's sister Nora did have a daughter in late 1964, Susan. The following year Nora died of cancer. Nora's two older children would be in their fifties now. They headed to the States in their late teens but Fr. Cleary has no idea where they're living. It is unclear what happened to Susan. There is no parish record of her making her communion or confirmation nor is there anything to indicate that she died. According to Fr. Cleary, Betty Rodgers often mentions a Susan, but he doesn't know if she's referring to Nora's daughter or someone from the nursing home.'

She was writing down as many details as she could when his next question sounded reasonable.

'Do you think Susan might be our victim?' he asked.

'She could be.' Two sisters married to two brothers, their children would be closer than just cousins, a double genetic link. 'Yes, she could.'

That was everything he had.

She completely changed the subject by mentioning the unmentionable. 'I understand you recently spoke to my not yet son-in-law.' She paused, then added, 'You were right to be firm with him.'

The sergeant was always fair and straight with those he dealt with. Part of her felt she was dishonouring her daughter by discussing it with him but she couldn't help how she felt.

'Yes Ma'am,' he replied in a way she knew they understood each other.

When the call finished, she mulled over all she knew of the Rodgers family while placing her blouse across the chair on the patio for it to dry. It was then time to feed Truman. After that, she contacted her colleague Philip.

'Getting bored with nothing to do? Let me tell you, your suspension sounds ideal while we have Gavin here almost afraid of us. The one thing he doesn't want is another internal complaint against him. I could tell him to fuck off and he wouldn't bat an eyelid. So, what can I do for you?'

After first discussing her meeting the following day with the Assistant Commissioner, she asked if he would make inquiries with his IRA informant on what he knew of Dick Rodgers. In particular, why he left the organisation.

'I'll see what I can do. By the way, we heard about the cock up with Martin Rodgers. Finnegan was here at a meeting with Gavin at the time.'

That had her smiling. 'Not the cleverest of moves.' It didn't surprise her that her boss considered she was all but gone from the bureau. Talk about a total dick head.

When the call finished, she suddenly felt a sense of appreciation in having Philip and the sergeant as colleagues she could depend on to watch her back. OK, so there was the odd misunderstanding that needed to be aired, but overall, they spoke the same language, aimed for the same results and understood each other. In contrast, her relationship with Jennifer often convinced her that she had no proper communication skills and no understanding of anyone.

Her meeting with the Assistant Commissioner was the following morning. She needed some fresh air to clear her head. A good long walk would do the job.

Wednesday - 10th June

11.03am

The Assistant Commissioner's secretary tapped away on her computer while Cathy sat opposite. *Cases are won on facts of law and not sentiment,* was a favourite saying of Dan's. She had often witnessed for herself how a judge zoomed in on the obvious points of law presented to him in a case. And of course, she knew to speak clearly with the minimum of words so as to portray herself as a rational human being.

She checked her phone before switching it off. Just before leaving the house that morning, she had a call from Philip. According to his IRA contact, Brian, he and Dick Rodgers had once been close. Both of them had joined the IRA along with Hugh Doyle. They were all neighbours, in and out of each other's flats on a regular basis. But things took a turn for the worse when Dick returned home one evening to find Betty having tea with Hugh. Dick was jealous if anyone as much as looked sideways at his wife whom Brian admitted was an attractive woman back then. A week later on his way home from the pub, Hugh Doyle had been badly beaten-up. According to Hugh's sister Laura, Dick had threatened to kill Hugh for getting his wife pregnant but Laura never believed a word of it for Hugh had a long-term girlfriend whom he later married. He'd no interest in Betty Rodgers. Hugh's cousins were senior members of the IRA. Dick and Tom Rodgers had been spotted that night close to where Hugh had been ambushed. They made it their business to handle Dick. Being the ringleader, he had paid the full price for the attack on Hugh while Tom wasn't touched.

'And what about Dick's affairs?' she had asked trying to line the facts up in her head, one, two three.

'Yeah, he was a womaniser alright, but Brian doesn't imagine he fathered a child with any of the women. If he had, Brian never heard of it and he would have heard back then. Dick's brother Tom was married to Betty's sister Nora. And according to Brian, Nora hated Dick for the way he treated Tom. It seems Nora and Betty were decent women. He thought it suspect when he heard that Nora had a child a year before she died as she was desperately ill with cancer at the time. Dick didn't leave the IRA; he was blackened by its members and that included Brian who had decided it was best to move to the North side of the city. He'd heard Tom had a nervous breakdown after Nora died. That's as much as he knows.'

The two facts that consumed her as she'd driven along the motorway were one, if Nora had been so ill, she'd never have had the strength to bear a child. And two, if Dick had been convinced Hugh Doyle had gotten Betty pregnant, then where was that child? There was no record of Betty having a baby in 1964. Of course, she might have miscarried. But coincidently, Nora presumably had a baby that year. That left her with a possibility she couldn't wipe from her mind. It was all she could think about. After the recent bungle, involving Martin Rodgers, she didn't think anyone would consider her theory as being plausible. Certainly not the sergeant, he'd see it as a stretch too far from reality.

The secretary answered the phone. Then with a smile, she escorted Cathy down the hallway where she knocked on a door, popped her head in and then stood back to allow Cathy the space to enter. Cathy held her head high as she walked forward, just as well as she was more than surprised to find it wasn't just Assistant Commissioner Keegan facing her. To his left was the Director of Communications Jerry Hynes. To his right, soon-to-be-retired Superintendent Grimes whom she had never liked. Although they all knew each other, the Assistant Commissioner did the introductions as she took a seat.

Superintendent Grimes began. 'I understand you were unable to control your temper while discussing a case with Detective Superintendent Gavin.'

That air of authority in his voice already irritated her.

She calmly replied, 'Yes Sir.'

He held a thin sweetly smile and glanced at her as if he had the means of cajoling her to his way of thinking.

'But surely you understand your behaviour cannot be tolerated. An overall apology from you would be a fair means of resolving this matter.' His words held a high degree of certainty. 'This is a force of over twelve thousand members. It is necessary for all of us to abide by the rules or we would have complete anarchy, wouldn't you agree?'

A sense of determination was building up inside her. She smiled as openly as she could. 'Yes, I do agree. But I also believe that if I am responsible for a case then my opinion on whether or not to have it forwarded to the DPP should be considered.'

He spoke with a slow sing-song voice while his Adam's apple bobbed up and down. 'There is nothing wrong with expressing your opinion if respectfully done.' He tented his fingers in front of him.

Without thinking, she said, 'And what if your opinion is well-founded?'

He attempted to sound rational as he replied, 'DI Spragg if we lived in a perfect world where everyone treated others with respect and courtesy at all times then having your opinion ignored would be a problem.' His eyebrows rose. 'But we don't live in a perfect world.' There was then an odd sound from him as he sat with his mouth pursed as if he were about to blow out bubbles. All huff and puff even though he was the least senior of the three of them. 'Not forgetting that according to what I've read, there is to be a charge of negligence brought against the couple.' He was having difficulty in not sounding sweetly triumphant.

She couldn't take any more of his sanctimonious attitude.

'That is a far cry from a charge of manslaughter. Having the couple convicted of negligence will be difficult to prove.' She watched him glance at her, totally taken aback by her directness.

There was a moment's silence.

It was refreshing to be asked by Jerry Hynes to describe her workload over the past year. Not something she had expected but as she ran through each case, even to her it sounded impressive. When asked, she filled them in on when she entered the force and gave dates of her promotions. Thankfully that was something Philip had suggested for her to check up on.

Then back to Superintendent Grimes who again suggested that her apology would resolve the matter. Again, she insisted that would not be happening. She viewed him as being a typical chauvinist who expected women to do as they were told. The sooner he retired the better, for all women in the force.

She found her voice. 'I have worked in the bureau for over twenty-five years. In that time, I have proved myself as a conscientious DI. At this stage in my career, I also deserve respect. It is not just those higher ranked than I who deserve it. We all do.'

The three of them scribbled on their pads before Assistant Commissioner Keegan leaned forward.

'What is your opinion on how this situation could be resolved?'

She took her time. 'Voicing my concerns to Detective Superintendent Gavin is part and parcel of my job. Yes, I did lose my temper, but my concerns on the matter were subsequently found to be justifiable. That should also be taken into consideration here.'

Director of Communications Jerry Hynes said, 'DI Spragg, you didn't answer the question. How would you suggest resolving this matter?'

She sat even more upright and looked at him without blinking.

'Sir, I believe I should be reinstated and my working record stand unaffected by this incident.'

Sounding cagey Jerry Hynes asked, 'Have you discussed this matter with the Association of Garda Sergeants & Inspectors?'

'No Sir. I was hoping I wouldn't have to.'

The Assistant Commissioner stopped writing. For some seconds his pen swung from side to side.

'Would you consider a transfer?'

It wasn't something she had thought about, nor did it require any consideration. 'No Sir, I would not.'

Another pause.

She noticed the Assistant Commissioner glance towards both men before he said in a light-hearted tone, 'Well I think that is all for now, DI Spragg. We will consider what you have put before us here today and will notify you of our recommendation as soon as possible.'

She thanked them before walking from the room.

Driving away, she felt as giddy as a goat. Perhaps she was wrong to believe she had argued her case positively. But one thing was for sure, she hadn't felt as good in ages. She deserved a treat. She headed for Grafton Street where she picked up a jacket and pair of sandals before walking through Brown Thomas where she allowed the assistant to wrap her favourite perfume in the pinkest of tissue paper. When leaving the car park, she checked the time. It was later than she would have liked. She ditched the idea of calling to the house.

One thing she knew about the nursing home, they were strict on visiting times. At the Leopardstown junction, she turned right. It had been *knowledgeable* Lucy who told her that Leopardstown was originally 'Town of the Lepers' from way back in the 14th Century. To avoid infecting others in the city, those with the disease were sent close to the Dublin Mountains where the air was fresher. Approaching the lights at the roundabout, she slowed down and noticed the Luas cross the elevated bridge in front of her. She drove onto the road shaded with trees with a sign directing her to her destination.

At the reception desk, she registered the name of Martina's mother, Ita Nolan, as the patient she was visiting. She was well familiar with the nursing home layout and knew to turn right at the end of the corridor. When a nurse went to pass, with a look of distress Cathy pretended to be lost, asked for directions, made the excuse it was her first time to visit Betty Rodgers. She wasn't sure if she had come the correct way and she had even forgotten the name of the ward.

The nurse in a hurry replied, 'No, don't worry, you're fine. She's in the second ward on the right.' She pointed down the corridor. 'St Helen's.'

When Cathy reached the ward, she buzzed to be admitted and found herself shuffling forward when the door sprung open. On her left was a row of beds back to back and beyond them, another that ran to the far end of the ward. Halfway up on the right was the nurse's desk. The nurse sounded busy on the phone reading details from a chart. She was foreign, Filipino most likely. Cathy moved along the row of women, the first was asleep, the name on her chart was Mary Colligan. Next to her was Betty O'Sullivan who was watching TV and ignored Cathy's inquiry on the whereabouts of Betty Rodgers. Cathy guessed the woman was deaf. The next bed was empty. In the last bed by the window was a bright-eyed woman fully clothed resting on the bedcovers and she watching Cathy with interest. Three vases of flowers filled the windowsill as well as an array of cards of an 80th birthday but no chart. The woman's bedside locker held two similar cuddly toys of a rabbit, one in pink the other in blue. Approaching the bed Cathy imagined the woman was alert enough to understand her.

'Are you here to bring me to the party?' The woman smiled.

Cathy had second thoughts about the woman's mental ability, but she couldn't roam from bed to bed without the nurse becoming suspicious for if she were a friend of Betty Rodgers then surely, she'd have recognised her.

'No, I'm afraid not.' Then leaning forward Cathy whispered, 'I'm looking for Betty Rodgers.'

The woman's smile widened, 'But that's my name. I'm Betty Rodgers.'

Cathy took in this small woman with a friendly smile, thin hair and clear blue eyes. The vases of flowers she reckoned were a week old. She moved to the locker and without permission lifted the largest card. The inscription inside read, *Love you always, Martin.*

'Are you alright?' the petite Filipino nurse asked from the high desk with her head stretched up from her shoulders in an effort to be seen.

'Fine, thank you.' Cathy then turned to Betty and asked, 'How are you today Betty?'

Betty hunched her shoulders with excitement.

'Did you bring me a present?'

Cathy rummaged in her bag, 'I just hope you like it.' She handed over the packaged perfume.

'I love perfume.' With a sense of eager suspense, Betty busied herself unwrapping the package. After spraying some she raised her wrist to smell it. 'It's lovely.'

The bottle was placed on her locker and she proceeded to lay the pink tissue paper flat on her lap. Her wrinkled hand gently ran along it removing all creases before it was neatly folded.

Cathy fought the image of herself as the wolf in sheep's clothing but she argued that it was her only way of discovering what needed to be known. She watched Betty work with the tissue paper that got limper with every fold. Then the blue cuddly rabbit was lifted from off the locker as the discarded tissue paper fell to the floor. Cathy found herself telling Betty of the rabbit she had seen that morning in the garden as she was having breakfast.

'What is his name?' Betty asked.

'Harry. I call him Harry.'

'Did he ever bite you,' asked Betty, ever so serious.

'No. He's very shy and runs off if I get too close to him.' Then Cathy asked, 'What is the name of your rabbit?'

'Bunnykins.' She softly rubbed one of his knitted ears. 'I've got two of them but he's my favourite.' The glance she gave the pink version sitting on the locker left you in no doubt that for some reason it wasn't to her liking. Betty listened on hearing of Truman's operation, of the bandage covering his stomach and how he was almost back to himself.

'How many came to your birthday party?' asked Cathy.

'They all came,' she smiled.

'Which of them is your favourite?'

'Martin,' said in a shot.

'How many children have you, Betty?'

She fidgeted with the rabbit's paw before her attention was drawn to the woman visitor buzzing the door open to leave. Either she didn't know the answer or she couldn't be sure how to answer.

Cathy remembered in time that Betty wasn't aware of Ken's demise. 'Eight boys and one girl and Eamon,' she prompted.

Betty nodded and then crouching inward on herself she said, 'Eamon is waiting for me in heaven.'

'And you had Colette but wasn't there another girl?' Cathy sat with that eminent look of confusion about her.

Betty whispered, 'Susan.' And then her hand went to her mouth. Through her fingers, she whispers. 'But Dick said she wasn't ours.'

Cathy came so close to her that their heads almost met.

'Was she born after Martin?'

The woman couldn't work out an answer to that. Instead, she replied, 'Dick said she wasn't ours. She was Nora's.' Betty then hugged Bunnykins and spoke to him. 'Then Nora went to heaven. She's there with Eamon, waiting for me.'

Cathy watched this woman talking to her Bunnykins as if he were real. Similar to her father, Betty was losing her mind but not so she couldn't remember key past memories.

Cathy guessed it must have been heart-wrenching for Betty to have her daughter taken from her and handed to her sister to be reared. To have been married to a controlling man like Dick Rodgers who believed what he said was gospel and no one dared argue with him. No one would have challenged him until Martin was old enough. How many beatings did Betty endure over Dick's mad certainty that she'd been unfaithful with Hugh Doyle! He would never have considered rearing a child that wasn't his but a child from the spawn of another man.

'Did you have a pet when you were young?' Cathy asked.

'No, we had no pets, but Martin had a guinea pig, called Ozzy.' Her voice was ever so soft. 'He was just like a rat with no tail but Martin kept him in his room away from me. He knew I didn't like him at all.'

The nurse arrived. 'Come on Betty we need to get you to the toilet.'

Betty allowed herself to be coaxed up from the bed. She took the nurse's arm and walked alongside her.

Cathy quietly checked her watch. 'I must be going now Betty. Visiting time is almost up.' She moved ahead of them and then turned to face her. 'Now you look after yourself.' She hugged her.

'I will, I will,' smiled Betty before asking, 'Won't you come again?'

Cathy nodded.

4.45pm

Once in the car, she switched on her phone. Three missed calls from the sergeant. She rang him.

He quietly asked her to hold on. She imagined him stepping out of the station on not wanting to be overheard.

His voice was above a whisper. 'Unlike Nora's first two kids, her daughter Susan wasn't born in the Maternity Hospital across from the flats but in the flat itself, which sounds odd with Nora ill with cancer. What's even more strange is that there's nothing on Susan after she was christened. I mean nothing.'

Another piece of the jigsaw. Another reason to believe that Susan was Martin Rodgers sister. Cathy figured that for Dick's plan to work with no questions asked the baby had to be delivered in the flat before being handed over to Nora. Betty had probably been hidden away for a couple of months before the birth. Ill as she was, Nora possibly went along with the plan for fear of what would have happened to the baby if she didn't. Even if neighbours suspected the truth, they weren't likely to blab knowing what Dick was capable of. But when Tom lost Nora to cancer and suffered a nervous breakdown, well he'd have had no interest in rearing Betty's child, nor would Dick consider taking her back.

It took her by surprise when the sergeant said, 'There is something else you need to know. Martin Rodgers has given an interview to a newspaper journalist about being harassed in his own home on false evidence. It's to headline one of the Sunday papers.'

That made up her mind on what needed to be done. The sergeant went quiet when she requested directions to Martin Rodgers residence.

In a tentative tone, he asked, 'Do you think that's a good idea, Ma'am?'

'Don't worry about me. Just give me the address.'

When the call finished, she drove from the Nursing Home out towards the M50. *Was she out of her cotton-picking mind!* There she was risking her career after defending her dedication to her job so admirably that morning. Was it all about to blow up in her face? Perhaps she was at that stage in her career where she was beyond abiding by rules. And there was that trace of excitement running through her from earlier that day. She would do what she'd planned before it completely evaporated. What the sergeant didn't get was that Martin Rodgers could help solve this case. He just needed to be convinced of it.

With the help of the sat nav, the address was easy to find. At the gate after pressing the button on the intercom system, it sounded strange to hear that voice from the past.

'Hello.'

'Madeline, it's Cathy Spragg here. I'd like to talk to Martin.'

The gate was buzzed open.

Madeline was waiting for her by the front door when she pulled up. With her flawless skin and shapely figure emphasised in fitted blouse and navy cropped trousers, she perfectly belonged in such a lavish house.

'I hope you know what you're doing coming here like this,' Madeline said with a look of indifference almost. 'But,' she smirked, 'If you want to make a fool of yourself, I won't stop you.' She led the way indoors. 'Funny, you always considered it beneath you to accept our dinner invitations and yet here you are. Uninvited.'

Cathy guessed that Dan had known not to mention to her such invitations. Even after all these years it still struck her as unbelievable how Madeline handled being married to a criminal. But that wasn't why she was there.

There was fun in Madeline's eyes when she said, 'You probably heard about Martin's interview with the journalist. I'm sure it will make for a great read. If you think you can persuade him against having it published, you won't.' She opened the door into a study. 'Look who the cat dragged in.'

Martin looked bemused when he glanced up from his desk.

'I can stay if you like,' said Madeline, to him.

'No need. I doubt Cathy has come to make trouble. I don't think even she is that dumb.' He continued to smirk.

Thankfully, she had come alone, no sergeant to react to Martin addressing her so familiarly.

Madeline left the room and closed the door behind her.

'What exactly do you want?' He was watching her closely.

When she wasn't offered a seat, she sat into the leather chair opposite him. The words rolled off her tongue. 'I know the woman who was drowned was your sister.'

He chuckled to himself. 'I'll add this accusation of yours to that piece for the papers.' He screwed up his face. 'What is it with you lot? Your fairy-tale way of trying to stitch me up over utter nonsense?'

She took her time. 'You had a sister; she came between you and Billy, but your aunt Nora pretended she was hers. It happened because your father believed your mother had an affair with a Hugh Doyle who got her pregnant. You probably never heard of him.' She reconsidered that last remark. 'Or maybe you did? Probably heard your father shouting his name after he'd been drinking? Someone none of you knew.' She watched his face glaze over. 'Hugh Doyle was beaten up by your father and Uncle Tom. In retaliation, the IRA came after your father big time. That was why he never wanted any of you involved with the organisation.'

The sound of his long inhale of breath was satisfying. She quickly kept going, mentioning how his aunt Nora stepped up to the plate when she realised that Dick had no intention of rearing that child.

'You probably all think your mother's ramblings about a Susan is nonsense. But it's not. There is no trace of Susan after your Aunt Nora died. By then, she'd have been just over a year old. A child who had to be gotten rid of quickly with no questions asked. Fostering would have left a trail. Adoption would have been the only solution. There were so many illegal adoptions back then.' She paused. 'What happened to her was a kept secret but Nora's older children would have remembered her, would probably have mentioned it to one of you, would have known she hadn't died like Eamon. If she had then where was her grave?'

With steel in his eyes, he said, 'Have you spoken to my mother?'

God was she enjoying this.

'It's a free country. I have visited that Nursing Home plenty of times. And your mother is a kindly lady who likes to talk.'

He squeezed his hand tightly into a fist. 'You are so stupid, you know that? After this, you can kiss goodbye to your career.'

She didn't flinch.

'That sister of yours whom you never got to know is now lying in a morgue.' She leaned forward in the chair. 'A solid bar of some kind punctured her womb in two places. She was alive when she entered the water.'

He bit his lip.

She kept going.

'I can understand why you didn't consider she was related to you up to this. But from what I've just told you and recalling what you'd have heard down through the years you must now consider it as a serious probability. You knew of the control your father had over your mother. She'd have been afraid to glance sideways at another man. She hadn't cheated on your father, but I doubt even with the accuracy of DNA he'd ever have been convinced otherwise.'

Martin glowered at her. 'You have no proof. You're working on pure speculation, nothing more. It's all hearsay. Nothing for anyone to take seriously and you know it.'

She hesitated. He had a point. All her gathered information might be a pie in the sky. What if she was mistaken, if she had got it wrong? But no, she didn't believe she was wrong.

'I can prove it. If I'm right, how do you think the papers will react to the truth? Imagine the headlines. *After denying her existence, another of Martin Rodgers siblings turns up mysteriously murdered.* You'd no longer be seen as the protective family man by those close to you, those you depend on.' She waited a moment before adding, 'Martin, I've no interest in making this public. That is up to you but if you don't pull your article for the Sunday paper then we can compare the victim's DNA against that of your mother's. That will be the ultimate proof. If you don't agree to it then it's possible your refusal could end up leaked to the media. That might leave those you deal with asking, *what's he afraid of?*'

He narrowed his eyes. 'You don't scare me. Now get out, before I throw you out.'

She stood up. 'She was your sister. The possible suspects are two foreigners who arrived here from Britain and may have booked into a hostel near Christchurch three weeks back. Last week they pawned rings that may have belonged to her at some pawnbroker's on Thomas Street.' Feeling those eyes boring through her, she bowed her head. 'If they are responsible for this, they are only the lackeys. We need to link them to those who gave the order to have her drowned.' She lifted a pen from his desk and wrote her mobile number on the notepad. 'I'm in Carrabhain these days.'

Madeline was coming from an open plan kitchen as she left the study. 'I'll show you to the door.' She walked ahead of her. 'I heard through the grapevine that Dan has found love again.' She opened the door wide. 'I always did feel he was too good for you. Do let him know I said hello.' Her smile was more of a sneer and Cathy noticed how her mascara was too heavily applied.

Cathy simply nodded by way of goodbye.

Once in the car, she felt her body relax.

Wednesday - 17th June

2.55pm

The previous Friday Cathy had contacted her neighbour in Dublin. Martina had a key to the house and had agreed to forward any post that arrived. Not surprising then to find a white envelope on the mat readdressed in Martina's handwriting. As expected, it was from Assistant Commissioner Keegan.

... Your behaviour on the day in question was unsatisfactory. However, after closely reviewing your years of service and your contribution to the force, it has been agreed that on this occasion no action will be taken against you. You are free to return to work as of Monday 23rd June.

She stood still for a minute to relish that sense of relief running through her. Then she thought of how her boss would be utterly disappointed with the decision. That cheered her up even more. She let out a whoop of joy in the hall. When she arrived in the kitchen, Truman looked at her suspiciously. She grinned back at him and then went to wrap her arms around him.

Cathy's colleagues would view the outcome as a win for her. Her boss would be so aware of that. He had believed from the start that the committee would see things his way, that his behaviour was without reproach. She was the one who deserved a reprimand, a warning. According to Philip, he had gone so far as to have her desk cleared and her belongings boxed away, sitting in storage labelled: *To be collected by DI Spragg.*

The letter was slipped back into the envelope. She chuckled to herself on thinking that Jeff Finnegan too was another disappointed camper. He'd have enjoyed the satisfaction of knowing he had gained from her misfortune. Oh yes, he would. She texted Philip. He replied that he'd guessed the outcome as the recent polite demeanour of Detective Superintendent Gavin had vanished in place of his former sharp acidy self.

On viewing the kitchen, she could see how much it needed a thorough cleaning. It was her usual routine to do the bare minimum while she was there, the odd scant rub of a cloth and the floor swept. But when it was time for her to leave, the house had to be left spotless, with the smell of lemon-scented detergent in the air and everything back in its place. It made returning more welcoming. Although she had a week's holiday booked for the following week, she would cancel it in favour of a week in late August if it were available; but even that wouldn't be long flying around.

Lucy phoned. No, she wasn't interested in discussing the weather or what she got up to while she was in Vienna but instead went to great lengths in venting her anger over how her DNA report had been viewed.

'There it was waiting for me when I got back. An urgent request to contact Superintendent Clarke. And was he not eager to rhyme off how Ken Rodgers' father, Dick, was a known womaniser and that being the case could I be certain that Ken Rodgers was the victim's full brother?' Was she fuming or what! 'That fact did cause me a certain concern. But she is as close as a full sister as I've ever come across. They should have been happy with that. It's not my job to find their suspects. You'd swear the messy way they questioned Martin Rodgers was down to me.'

Cathy felt partly to blame for Lucy's distressed state knowing her friend had been right all along with her findings. Yet she couldn't tell her that, not now, not ever.

Lucy's rant continued, 'I did a good job. Yet I'm the one viewed as being over-imaginative.'

Cathy replied, 'Lucy if it makes you feel any better, can I say that I would have kissed your feet if I'd been running the investigation and you had brought me that evidence. Both your feet and each of your toes if it came to that.'

Lucy laughed. She calmed even further when told of Cathy's reinstatement. They agreed to catch up when Cathy got back to town.

When the call finished, she reviewed all information to date. Apart from Jeff's third appeal for information on the suspects which included a not too clear photo of them both at the pawnbrokers, there had been little progress on the case. A further inquiry by the sergeant as to the whereabouts of Susan from Fr. Cleary had yielded nothing. According to what he'd got from Cummins, Jeff refused to consider the victim as a fully-fledged sister of Martin Rodgers. It was a no-go, dead-in-the-water lead not to be ever discussed again. Dick Rodgers was a known womaniser; the victim's mother could be anyone. Cathy hadn't confided with the sergeant that the victim was Martin Rodger's fully-fledged sister who had likely ended up adopted. It didn't feel right not to confide with him over what she knew but she'd keep her side of the bargain with Martin Rodgers. Unfortunately, there was nowhere to go from there. Nowhere. Adoption agencies were a closed shop when it came to disclosing the whereabouts of a child they helped place in a new home. What was disappointing was that the priest had no knowledge of where Tom and

Nora's two older children now lived in the States, they might have given them something.

Truman would be more of a nuisance while she worked on cleaning the place out. He had made for the door twice already as if wanting some outdoor exercise. She phoned Molly and yes, Adam would be happy to look after him for a couple of hours.

She welcomed the *ping* sound from her computer. Someone to share her good news. It was after three in the afternoon, after eleven with Sinead in Australia. What faced her was a spotty faced tired daughter. Cathy sounded like a happy kid as she announced the good news of her reinstatement. Sinead was pleased but not the *get out the band and release a stack load of balloons* kind of response Cathy had expected.

'My feet are sore,' Sinead moaned as she moved forward and back, massaging the foot on her lap. 'Today I worked two shifts, even though it was my day off but they were short staffed and we need the money.' Her face had broken out in a rash of spots. That always happened when she was stressed.

'Is Malcolm there with you?' Cathy asked.

Sinead continued to knead her foot. 'No, he's over at his friend's place but he'll be back soon.'

Watching her daughter, it was obvious something wasn't right. It was after eleven, why wasn't he there? 'Sinead, are you OK?'

Her daughter attempted to smile. 'Yeah, I'm just tired, that's all. I was thinking of you today Mam. I miss you.'

'I miss you too, love,' she almost cried.

She listened as Sinead went on about how Malcolm was finding it difficult at work as his commission was based on his sales. There were few sales of surf gear at this time of year. That left them with no spare cash for socialising. Cathy knew not to voice her opinion but to keep her mouth shut and just listen. Sinead was pleased to hear that Truman was on the mend. There was no mention of Jennifer as if knowing not to or perhaps her older sister hadn't confided in her yet over their quarrel.

The call left Cathy feeling uneasy. It sounded as if the honeymoon spell of Sinead's relationship with Malcolm was over. Something hard to come to terms with if you're still in love with the man and far from home.

Her mobile rang as she was heading to her bedroom after taking a shower.

It was the sergeant.

'I just got an odd phone call. The man asked to speak to you. When I told him you weren't stationed here, he replied, *tell her to check out the two foreigners admitted to St James's Hospital on Sunday night.* I asked for his name but he hung up. It was a withheld number and can't be traced.'

She tightened the towel around her. 'That was the message?' She checked the time. 'I don't understand why he phoned the station looking for me or how he had my name even.' At the sound of the doorbell, she asked the sergeant to hold as she opened the window and shouted down to Adam that the key was under the flower pot by the door. Pulling shut the window was the moment she made the connection. Martin Rodgers would never have contacted her directly, that wasn't his style. He would never want anything traced back to him. She had mentioned to him she was in Carrabhain. He had assumed she was working the case from the station. She abruptly finished the call with the sergeant. After dressing she phoned Philip. Yes, he knew of the two men admitted to St James's Hospital.

'They were found in a field near the accommodation centre for asylum seekers in Meath. One of them almost bled to death. He was operated on later that night. They had no identification. Those at the centre are too scared to say anything but according to the manager, neither men are regulars. Their car has a British registration. We're keeping it under wraps until we know a bit more.' Raising his voice, he asked, 'How did you get to hear about them?'

She pulled on her sandals. 'Sorry, don't have time to explain just now.'

'Yeah just as well. Gavin is heading in here with that bullhead of his. What a changed man.' He chuckled.

'See you Monday.' She ran down the stairs.

Adam had found Truman's lead and was heading out the door. She asked if he'd return Truman at around six o'clock. Yeah, that time suited him as he had football training at seven.

////////

4.35pm

No, she didn't have an appointment. But she repeated her name and asked for the Superintendent to be assured that it was important she talk to him.

A minute later the officer returned and sheepishly said, 'Sorry but he's busy for the rest of the day.'

Back in her car, there was nothing for it but to wait. A squad car pulled up. The rear door opened. A young man stood out shrugging his shoulders and shouting to be left alone. A guard directing him towards the station's entrance as Jeff arrived out walking with haste towards his car. She slumped right down to avoid being spotted.

When the Superintendent eventually appeared, she jumped out.

'Sir, could I have a word?'

Annoyed he said, 'Look, if things have gone pear-shaped for you at the bureau, I'm sorry but there isn't a position for you here.'

Surprised by his assumptions she stepped back from him.

'Sir, I have been reinstated. That's not why I'm here'

'I'm glad to hear it.' With a trace of suspicion, he asked, 'So, what's so important that you felt the need to ambush me here in the car park?'

She would have preferred if he were calmer.

'Sir, I've had a tip-off from a source I cannot name but it seems Jeff's suspects were admitted to St James's Hospital on Sunday night last.'

Apart from the sergeant, no one else in the force could learn of her visit to Martin Rodgers at his home. Nor would she mention to anyone the reason behind Martin's decision to pull the article from the Sunday paper as she had requested. His search for the suspects was further proof that he believed the victim was his sister. And that would remain their secret.

'Everyone is out to blame the mess-up with Martin Rodgers on the victim's DNA profile.' She took her time. 'The problem was in not securing enough information on her before facing Martin Rodgers. He had a so-called cousin Susan but there's no trace of her after Nora Rodgers died.' She needed to sew the seed of a connection, nothing more.

He looked smartly at her.

'So, you think she might be his cousin.'

Don't lie to him, her inner voice shouted.

'Well, they are closely related, no getting away from that.' She gave him an inquiring look as if to say *work it out for yourself.*

He stood by his car, briefcase in one hand, keys in the other. She noticed him glance in the opposite direction to her, as if not wanting her to guess that he too had questioned Jeff's handling of the case. The force was a close-knit organisation. It would surprise her if he hadn't learned of Jeff's exact whereabouts at the time Cummins and the sergeant were with Rodgers. And that would have galled him.

She mentioned the condition of the two men admitted to St James's Hospital and suggested they be questioned as soon as possible.

'How did you get this information?' He was now looking at her as if he wasn't fully sure whether to believe her or not. No, it was a more concerning expression, as if dreading her response.

'I can't tell you that.' She stuck her hands in her pockets.

'What are their names?' he asked a little less gruff than earlier.

'I don't know that either but they're in bad shape. One of them has already been operated on.'

He opened the car door. 'Leave it with me. I'll have it checked out.' Walking toward her car she considered how Martin Rodgers had fished out the culprits from a vast network totally rooted in crime. The force had failed to find these men after numerous pleas to the public for information. It was now up to Jeff to close the case. She was in no doubt that Martin Rodgers would follow with interest how the suspects would be dealt with. She imagined the rough time they would experience in prison. That same criminal network that tracked them down was just as powerful within the prison system as they were on the outside.

///////

6.30pm

It was five o'clock that morning when he and Gerard had gone jogging. Matt preferred the freshness of the morning air and the quiet roads to the busyness in the evenings. They had completed their run five seconds quicker than the previous week. The Athlone Triathlon was coming up at the end of July. They weren't fully fit but would make up their minds in the next week on whether or not to give it a go.

There had been a letter from the bank waiting for him when he had arrived home from work yesterday. Although it was addressed to both of them, Jackie hadn't bothered to open it. Due to a shortfall in their account, they had missed a mortgage payment. They rowed. He over Jackie's constant spending on improving the house. There had to be a stop to her painting every room, planting flower beds, buying unnecessary equipment such as the power hose or the loungers and chairs for the patio area or the coffee maker or the toys for the twins or paying anyone for babysitting. Then Jackie shouted at him that if he played his part with the twins, she wouldn't need to pay a babysitter. She then mentioned the running gear he had splashed out on the previous month and the heaps of books and magazines he'd bought on psychopaths, sociopaths and the like. And on and on it went.

From her facial expression, he knew it had scared her to hear how they could lose the house. And that was a strong possibility if they continued spending as they were. Of course, if she returned to work there wouldn't be a problem. He wouldn't say that to her. She had to come to that conclusion herself. When things calmed down between them, they had agreed to watch all future outgoings.

Garda Deegan answered the phone as Matt was about to head home. After uttering the words *Hold on,* he stretched the phone towards Matt.

'It's Detective Finnegan.' said Deegan.

Matt held the phone to his ear.

'Bracken, there are two men in Dublin's St James's Hospital that need to be interviewed. We should head up there straight away.'

Shit. Jackie had arranged a night out with friends from the bank. He had agreed to babysit. 'Sorry, I've made plans for tonight.'

His mind raced. According to what Cummins had last told him the manager of the hostel couldn't be sure if those from the pawnbrokers were the same men who had occupied a room at the hostel, his sight wasn't the best, neither was the photo of the men. McFadden had come up empty-handed with his check of all British vehicles entering the country. They had nothing, which was why Cummins had since been sent to Galway to help investigate an assault on a tourist. Matt thought of McFadden. He wasn't capable of accurately taking statements from these men.

But one thing Matt knew for sure, these were the same men referred to earlier in that phone call for DI Spragg.

'Are you refusing me?' The detective sounded angry. Surprise, surprise.

'As I said, I'm busy.'

'Big mistake if detective work is what you're hoping for,' he growled.

Matt wondered who had actually tipped off DI Spragg. Was it possible she had a snout that close to Martin Rodgers?

'You'll be sorry for this,' were the last words from the detective.

Matt handed the phone back to Deegan. 'See you tomorrow.'

Jackie was in their bedroom when he arrived home. Once out of his uniform, he bathed the twins and had them back in their carrier chairs.

'If anything happens, you'll phone me.' She sounded anxious when she appeared in the kitchen.

'Nothing is going to happen and you look great.'

She kissed the twins and gave him a peck on the cheek before leaving. The twins bounced away in their chairs, glancing up at the microwave as his dinner circled around inside. When his phone rang, he assumed it was Gerard who was planning on lengthening their running route. He'd promised to phone to discuss what he'd come up with and to arrange the following day's running session.

'Bracken, meet me here at six in the morning.' The detective hesitated before adding. 'See you then.'

Taking his dinner from the microwave, he felt pleased. He had stood his ground, but more importantly, he was now back in the loop. He so wanted to hear what these men had to say for themselves.

It wasn't surprising when Aiden stretched his hand towards Matt for some of his dinner. That kid would eat anything while Ella was a fussy eater. She watched as he fed Aiden a spoonful of mashed potatoes and raised her hand wanting the same. Matt half-filled a second spoon that Ella examined before sticking her fingers in it. Matt got up to find a cloth. When he returned, she had plastered the potato in her hair.

The two of them glanced at him as if waiting for his reaction. It made him laugh. And they laughed at him and then at each other.

Thursday - 18th June

8.05am

The traffic began to build up as they passed Lucan. Detective Finnegan had switched on the radio as soon as he'd sat into the car. There had been little or no conversation between them since. Once they arrived at the hospital, Matt made for the underground car park. As there was a queue, Detective Finnegan thought nothing of jumping out and heading towards the hospital's main entrance. Once parked, Matt took the stairs that opened up onto the main corridor. The detective was almost out of sight but Matt was quick to catch up with him. On the second floor, Finnegan nodded at the guard by a door. Inside were two men, battered and with bloated faces. One of them had a bandage covering his forehead, right eye and ear. His arm was in a sling. The other, breathing through his open mouth had teeth missing, nose heavily taped, possibly broken with strips of adhesive plaster along one arm. He had likely been cut with a knife. His leg was in traction. A tray of what remained of their liquidised breakfast sat in front of them.

'Well, well and what have we got here?' asked the detective. 'What are your names?' His voice was similar to that of a school principal. With no response forthcoming, he shouted the question a second time.

The men seemed dazed, not fully conscious. But then the largest of them made a noise that could have been a response, but not totally audible.

The detective approached him. 'Now look here, I want answers from you. What are your names?'

The larger man with his arm in a sling focused on the detective. 'Butrus Shala.' His mouth was dry. He ran his tongue along his bloated upper lip.

The smaller man with his leg in traction whispered, 'Urbonas Hoxha.'

The detective looked at them and then at Matt.

The men began whispering to themselves in a foreign language.

'They probably don't have much English.'

'They've English alright. This is a ploy to pretend not to understand, they probably think this charade prevents us from questioning them.'

If these men were the same men who had pawned those rings, then according to what the pawnbroker had mentioned, they were Libyan.

'Yeah, but we don't understand what they're saying to each other. We need a translator for that,' Matt suggested. 'Give me a minute.'

He left the room to phone a colleague, Joe O'Connor, stationed close by in Kilmainham. After supplying him with the contact details of a translator Joe said, 'If they're not Libyan come back to me.'

Matt contacted the translator. She had no problem translating over the phone. However, if she were expected to present herself at the hospital, it would be late afternoon before she could be there.

The detective had no intention of hanging about the hospital for most of the day and was happy for her to translate over the phone. The men were first asked if their fingerprints could be taken. When they nodded in agreement Matt carefully carried out the procedure although Butrus Shala's bandaged arm extended down over his hand so only one hand was fingerprinted. They were next asked for their address. The larger man was slow to respond. They had lived in Brighton for the last ten years and had family there. When questioned further he refused to state what they were doing in Ireland nor would he specify how they had come by their injuries.

They both lay staring at the ceiling. It seemed an effort for them to focus on who was asking the questions or who was even in the room.

'Tell them we have a sighting of them pawning two rings belonging to a woman who was found drowned.' The detective had no proof yet that the rings belonged to the victim. But these men weren't being interrogated, weren't yet suspects and the conversation wasn't being recorded.

No response from either of them.

After the detective stressed the importance of their co-operation, the slighter man, Urbonas Hoxha could be heard slurring words in anger. The barrage that continued between them was translated. Urbonas was blaming Butrus for involving him with the woman. He had been assured it was a simple job. But that was a lie. They'd been beaten up and were lucky to be alive. Butrus raised his voice in telling Urbonas to shut up and stay quiet.

It was then the door opened. In walked a tall bald man with an air of authority about him. 'What the hell are you two doing here?' He quietly closed the door behind him.

'Questioning these two,' replied Finnegan.

Completely at ease, the man glanced towards Matt and in a sharp voice asked, 'And who are you?'

After Matt gave his name and rank the man introduced himself as Detective Philip Long from the bureau.

'Why didn't you notify me that you were interested in these two?'

Finnegan replied, 'We are working on a tip-off. From what they've just relayed it seems they've been involved in something to do with a woman.'

Detective Long looked bewildered. 'You had a guard placed on the door for the night. If you'd notified us, you would have been told that in their condition they were going nowhere, they were safe.'

Detective Finnegan nodded. 'But whoever gave us our tip-off knew exactly where we'd find them so, perhaps not as safe as you thought.'

The obvious tension between both men was broken by the voice of the translator stating that she could only spare another five minutes on the call and asked if there were any other questions to be put to the men.

Detective Finnegan wasn't yet finished. 'Make it clear they understand what I've already mentioned regarding their co-operation. Ask them for the woman's name and the name of who they're working for.'

There was some discussion between the men before Butrus spoke in broken English. 'She was evil of the worst kind.'

'How do you know that?' asked Finnegan.

Butrus kept his mouth shut.

'What was her name?' pleaded Matt.

Urbonas replied, 'We do not ask.'

Moving closer to the bed Matt asked, 'Why did you drown her where you did?'

Urbonas, with eyes, still focused on the ceiling, whispered, 'It had to be there. We were told it had to be there.'

The next minute the door was opened by a nurse pushing a trolley of medication, followed by a senior nurse who focused on Detective Long. 'What is the meaning of this?

You are in a hospital, not a football field. There are too many of you in here.' She then stood between the beds. 'I think you've exhausted these men.' With a challenging look from one to the other of the detectives who now stood closer to the door, she asked, 'Did you get permission from their doctor to question them or do you think you can just walk in here and do as you like?'

That didn't require a response.

'Well then,' she continued. 'I suggest you leave. Tomorrow they may be up to speaking with you but not without permission from their doctor.' She busied herself with Butrus while Detective Long questioned her on their condition. 'They are now stable and making progress.' She glanced towards Butrus. 'He lost a lot of blood from injuries he received to one of his testicles. He could have died.'

After thanking the translator, Matt quietly turned to Urbonas.

'Why did you wound her shoulder?'

He lay with eyes shut. 'She tried to escape us. First, we warn her, second time we cut her as we said we would do.'

The senior nurse glared at Matt. 'Now that's enough.'

They all left the room together. Along the corridor, Detective Long suggested for Detective Superintendent Gavin to phone Superintendent Clark.

'You heard what they told us, they are our suspects.' Detective Finnegan sounded pleased with himself. 'And if they are, then they're our responsibility.'

On the return journey, Finnegan was more talkative. He asked Matt if he had a family and spoke of his daughter who had completed her first year in college. Matt felt relaxed enough to ask if he imagined the men were confused over their instructions as to where to drown her or was it possible, they had ended up in the wrong location?

Finnegan seemed pleased to be asked for his opinion.

'Maybe the woman lived in the village at one stage. She might still have family there. Then again it might be someone she had married. But no, I think she is connected to or associated with the place in some way.'

There should have been a sense of satisfaction that they had found those responsible for her drowning. But who had they drowned? That was now the question before they could even consider who had wanted her drowned?

///////

1.55pm

After washing the hall floor, Cathy opened the front door for it to dry quicker. Truman was again with Adam at his place. She'd already cleaned out every cupboard in the kitchen. The fridge had been emptied, trays and shelves removed and washed in warm sudsy water. The cooker was gleaming. Now on to the bathroom. She preferred to work on her own with her favourite music loudly playing in the background. Noticing the sergeant approaching she switched off the CD player and signalled for him to come in around to the back of the house.

He came through the patio door as she filled the kettle.

'We've spoken to those men in St James's hospital.' His wide-earnest eyes met hers. 'That call I took yesterday. That was the tip-off on where to find them?'

Her hands were raised in front of her, palms facing him.

'Don't ask me who tipped me off. It's something I can't tell you. Let's just leave it at that.'

Telling him it was Martin Rodgers would only lead him to ask, *But why?* He'd not be happy until he knew everything. She couldn't tell him everything.

Her attention turned from him to the wet cloth she had placed on the worktop. She picked it up and washed it out. Her hands had been in water most of the morning and she should have worn gloves for she hated that feeling of detergent on her wrinkled fingers.

With a look of disappointment, he explained what they'd got from the suspects. They'd been caught on CCTV footage on Thursday 21st May boarding the ferry at Holyhead. The passport presented on the victim's behalf turned out to be fake. Once they had boarded the ferry, they could be seen either side of her making their way to the café area. She was unsteady on her feet, doped, hadn't a clue what was happening to her.

'Forensics are checking their car found at the asylum centre for fingerprints. Traces of blood on the back seat might be hers. It seemed that after drowning her, they returned to Dublin and booked into the hostel on Saturday night and returned to the UK by ferry early Sunday morning. They re-entered the country via Rosslare and after collecting the rings from the hostel manager, they pawned them straight away.'

It all fitted nicely together. 'But had no one checked CCTV to see if she'd entered the country by ferry? She'd have been easily recognisable.'

He nodded. 'That was down to McFadden.' A slight grin spread across his face. 'Just let's say he's no longer part of the investigating team nor will he ever be part of one again.' Then with a look of bewilderment, he explained how the victim was clearly on view on the footage of CCTV taken on the ferry which they had obtained. Not just that but the vehicle had not been picked up entering and exiting the country three weeks back and returning last week. 'I don't know what he was up to.' When she remained silent, he added, 'Detective Finnegan is of the belief the victim is connected to this village.'

The sergeant looked doubtful. 'She might have left when she was a child. Maybe it's her parents or her husband with the connection.' He gave himself a minute to think about it. 'That's the thing. If she or her family left here some years back then how are we to know who she is? And if she still has family here, surely, they would be concerned over not hearing from her? We've no way of knowing how long she's out of the country.'

Cathy's head filled with faces of women she remembered from the village. She had come to know them through Molly but they now lived in England. Faces she barely recognised when they returned. There was Betty Harte's sister who settled in Liverpool, Nancy Brennan's sister in Newcastle, Harry Lennon's cousin in Birmingham and not forgetting Tess's daughter Catherine, in London, although she couldn't remember her at all.

'I'm due back at the bureau on Monday.' She instinctively leaned forward on the chair with her cloth in hand to rub out a mark on the table. There was still so much that needed to be done around the house.

After he left, she stripped everything from Truman's basket for washing. Taking the mop to the floor there was nothing to fill her head apart from what they had discussed. She quickly came to the conclusion that if the victim's drowning had been carried out at the correct location then she had a serious link to the village. Not just that, but if the suspects were not concerned over where to drown her, she'd have ended up in the first river or canal they had come across. She again ran through the women she knew from the village who lived in England taking into account what she remembered of the victim's photo and age. Still, nothing came to mind. When she added to that the vital fact that should have been first up in her mind that the victim was Martin Rodger's sister Susan, she stood with the mop in her hand and froze. No, she thought, it couldn't be. Her inner voice shouted at her. *What is wrong with you? It's been staring you in the face all along.* That one fact that separated their victim from other women in the village was that she had been adopted. Catherine Fowley had been adopted.

Cathy attempted to settle her thoughts. Last year when Tess had invited her in for tea Cathy had lifted that framed photo of Catherine off the top of the television. The attractive blonde-haired woman in her forties living the high life in London, that had been the impression she had been left with.

In the bathroom, she took a light scrubber soaked in Jiff to clean down the walls. No, she wouldn't be happy until she had either proved or disproved her suspicions.

The washing machine was loaded and more than enough detergent poured into the dousing ball. Firmly closing it shut, she switched it on. There was a mild breeze. The walk would do her good, keep her calm. She rang Molly to say she was on her way to the village. Instead of Adam returning with Truman she'd pick him up on her way back. She tried to think if she had ever crossed paths with Catherine Fowley on all those trips down to stay with her father during the holidays. According to her calculations, Catherine would have been four to six years her junior. No better one than Molly to fill her in on Catherine Fowley.

There was no sign of Patrick's car when she reached the village.

Tess's face beamed when she found Cathy at her door.

'Well, this is a surprise.'

Cathy stepped in. 'Just thought I'd call to see Patrick and Melissa.'

Tess led her down to the kitchen. 'They've gone to Cork for the day.' She placed the kettle on the range. 'Now you're here we'll have a cup of tea.'

Cathy sat in the same chair she'd sat in the only other time she'd been to the house. On top of the television was a framed photo, not the one she hoped to find but one of Patrick with his family. Tess talked about the house being too small for all of them but that she was enjoying having them stay. Thankfully, there was a childlike glint in her eyes when she spoke of the prospects of visiting Vancouver for a holiday.

Casually Cathy said, 'No sign of Catherine coming to visit?'

Tess drew back slightly from the table. 'She's not back yet from her holidays. She'll phone me when she gets back. Maybe then she'll come.' She lifted the milk jug from the fridge.

The doorbell went.

'I wonder who that could be? Here all day on my own without a call from anyone and then two within five minutes.' She left the kitchen. 'Pour yourself a cup of tea.'

Once Tess could be heard in conversation, Cathy made for the television stand and pulled open the lower drawer. Under a pile of Christmas cards, she found what she was looking for. The victim was smiling at her with hair lifted by the breeze and her eyes hidden behind those large sunglasses. Cathy studied her sallow-skinned husband leaning towards her with his arm around her waist holding her tight. A picture of total contentment.

With the sound of silence, she returned the photo to the drawer before closing it shut. She barely made it to the chair as Tess returned.

'That was Ciara Allen, looking for Heather. I think they have planned to go somewhere tonight.' She noticed both cups still empty. 'And you didn't pour yourself any tea?' She lifted the teapot and poured for them both.

Cathy faked a smile as Tess described how Heather was good at sports, the total opposite of Brandon. He was only an average student who preferred computer games. Tess appeared happy with life. Cathy grimaced, aware of how the rug was about to be pulled from under her. Even if there was something odd about their relationship, Tess would still be heartbroken to learn the details of her daughter's death.

'Are you alright?' Tess asked when she caught Cathy staring.

'Yeah, no I'm fine,' she replied. She went on to mention how the magazine, *The Astronomy Updates* had featured a full article written by Pat Lynch. But of course, Mrs. Lynch had already informed Tess of how he had taken first prize in the competition. She had also dropped her in a copy of the magazine with his featured article.

Tess sounded pleased as she said, 'He's a changed man these days. Seems to be more confident in himself. To be honest, I couldn't understand anything of what he'd written about, but if the best of them in that field appreciate his pictures, then good for him.'

Tess frowned when Cathy moved from the table.

'But you didn't finish your tea or even take a biscuit.'

'I need to watch my weight, Tess. And I've some shopping to do before I collect Truman from Molly's.'

Tess also stood. 'I'll tell Patrick and Melissa you called.'

With Tess remaining by her front door Cathy couldn't just cross the street to slip into the station. Instead, she headed for the supermarket where she picked up some milk and dog food. The street was quiet when she emerged. Like a thief in the night, she advanced carefully to the station.

Garda Deegan was at his desk and seemed surprised to see her.

'Can I help you, Ma'am?'

She couldn't stop herself fidgeting with the carton of milk.

'Ah, I was just looking for the sergeant. Nothing important.'

The sergeant arrived in from the rear corridor holding a file. He too seemed surprised to find her there.

She rolled the tin of dog food between both hands while the carton of milk was now tightly held under her arm. 'Could I have a word with you in private?'

Deegan stood up and left through the same door the sergeant had come through.

'I'm sorry about this.' She beckoned the sergeant towards her for she couldn't be sure if Deegan might still hear what she was about to say. 'I know the identity of the victim,' she whispered. It was the second time she'd made that statement. But even first time around she'd been right.

'It's Tess's daughter Catherine. I've just seen her photo. It's her, no doubt about it. She was married and lived in London but I don't know her married name or what part of London she lived in.'

With a look of bewilderment, he placed the file he was holding on the counter.

She ran her hand across her forehead. 'I suppose I could come straight out and ask Patrick about her but that might seem suspicious seeing as I never knew her or was even interested in her in any way up to now.'

After a short silence, the sergeant said, 'At the party, Gerard asked Patrick about Catherine. He mentioned that she's married to an Egyptian. Her married name is Muscanna, Catherine Muscanna. They live in Richmond.'

'Yes,' she quietly yelped. That gave them their starting point.

To be doubly sure she asked him to check if Catherine Muscanna was a customer at the DL Gasur store in Richmond and if she'd bought the items worn by the victim. Cathy had once been to Richmond with Dan and the girls when they visited Kew Gardens. It had some fine houses along the river. She imagined such a store would do well there.

Deegan returned.

As she left, she mouthed soundlessly to the sergeant, *Call out when you have something.*

Friday - 19th June

1.35pm

She didn't get much of a night's sleep. It was seven when she rose. In the kitchen, as she was having breakfast, she dropped a half carton of yogurt on the spotless floor. When she had pressed the lever with her foot to open the bin it had turned over and emptied its contents over that same floor. Nothing for it but to scrub the floor, then the bin. After that, she had headed upstairs to continue the house clean-up.

She was glad of a break from the monotonous chores when the sergeant arrived.

He seemed excited; his eyes fired up.

'Catherine Muscanna was a regular customer of the DL Gasur store in Richmond and had bought every item worn by the victim. She was considered a cautious buyer who waited for the sales unless something totally took her fancy. The assistant gave me the name of a lingerie store on that same street who stock the Marine Mabson range of underwear. I contacted them and yes, she had purchased the items worn by the victim there also.'

Just as she had suspected.

The sergeant had also phoned Cummins for an update. He'd been called back to assist Detective Finnegan now that they had their suspects and McFadden had returned to uniform.

'The blood on the backseat is a match to the victim's.

It was also Butrus Shala's fingerprints on the rings. On hearing that, the second suspect, Urbonas Hoxha was all talk. He blamed everything on Butrus. She was handed over to them at Holyhead, heavily doped. They boarded the ferry but when it came time to return to their car, she attempted to make a run for it. She wasn't fully conscious and with everyone rushing, anxious to disembark, no one took any notice of her. When they pulled in for something to eat at a service station on the motorway, she broke free and rushed up to a man telling him she had been kidnapped. But he happened to be a foreigner, didn't understand what she was saying. Back in the car, it was Butrus Shala who cut her shoulder. He threatened to cut open her face if she tried anything like that again. But according to Cummins, neither of them have a notion of naming those they're working for.' The sergeant paused, but it was clear he had more to tell.

'Both suspects are adamant she is responsible for some deplorable crime but they won't elaborate further. Cummins isn't sure if they actually know themselves what she's suspected of doing. For now, the heat is off the case. They have those responsible for drowning her. That's enough for Superintendent Clarke.'

It sounded to her that everything had been meticulously planned. By involving both jurisdictions it made it difficult for either to investigate it thoroughly. The Irish authorities had those who drowned her, but no idea who they were working for. The British authorities were without any suspects or any wrongdoing by anyone. Convenient.

'So, the suspects only returned to sell the rings? If they had stayed put in Brighton they'd never have been tracked down.' She could hear that satisfaction in her voice.

The sergeant nodded. 'Not with the haphazard way

McFadden checked through the CCTV as well as the list of vehicles that had re-entered the country from Britain.'

'Yes, but they arrived back through Rosslare, not Dublin.' She knew how much McFadden irritated him.

'But how come he never picked her out from all that CCTV footage.' He tossed his head with agitation. But then grinned when he found her grinning. She was out to rise him. Back to his notebook. 'Butrus Shala has a cousin living at that centre in Meath whose daughter was getting married so they decided to stay for the celebrations. They refuse to discuss anything to do with their injuries.'

'How were they to be paid?' she asked.

'Each of them received £5,000 for the job, half up front and the rest was pushed through their letterbox on the day they originally returned home.'

'Her life was worth £10,000.' She glanced across at him. 'Did you hear back from Andy Scott,' she asked.

He shook his head, 'Just an email stating there was no report of a woman missing that matched our victim.'

She leaned back in the chair. 'So, no one has reported her missing.' She thought of that photo of Catherine and her husband with his arm around her. To Cathy, both of them seemed content with each other. How wrong she'd been.

'What was it that made you think it was Tess's daughter, Catherine,' he asked.

She knew that question was coming. She focused on the table.

'If she was Susan Rodgers and had disappeared after her mother died then I guessed she would have been adopted. The only one I knew around here who'd been adopted was Tess's daughter, Catherine.'

He seemed satisfied with her clarification of only half the truth. She felt uncomfortable not telling him everything, but that was how it had to be.

'Detective Finnegan should be informed of all this.' He was watching for her reaction.

'I disagree.' She noticed his instant frown.

Her paws were all over the case. That was what worried her. She was the one who had made the connection yet how could she explain herself without admitting she had studied the victim's pathology report which included her photo. Even if she did admit to that, how would she explain that she believed Lucy's theory if she shouldn't have known about it? Nor could she explain what had occurred to have triggered the shot in the dark memory of that photo on top of Tess's TV. She would never convince others as easily as she'd convinced the sergeant. But then again she wasn't too sure if she had convinced him. She reminded him that he would also be in deep shit for handing her the pathologist's report in the first place. His chance of a transfer gone forever.

She paced the floor.

'We need to figure out a way of having her identified without disclosing our involvement.' Even as she uttered the words it sounded an impossibility. A troubled glance from the sergeant confirmed it.

After some minutes of soul-searching, the sergeant said, 'We can't do this on our own. We need Patrick on board.'

She had arrived at the same conclusion. It was their only option. It wasn't the time to acknowledge that their scheming on this was totally improper. She was known for being straighter than straight in doing things by the book. If the truth were to come out then she'd end up demoted. That was the risk she was taking.

'You don't think he could be involved in this?' asked the sergeant.

The thought had more than once crossed her mind. 'I don't know. He doesn't seem capable of organising something so well planned. On the other hand, he was in London that week she was abducted.'

They tussled some more over what Patrick should be told. Both accepted that if he had anything to do with his sister's murder then they were about to head into the mouth of madness.

Eventually, she picked up her mobile and punched in the number rhymed off by the sergeant. When Tess answered she was on for a chat. Cathy could hear herself sound abrupt in cutting her short and asking to speak to Patrick. He came on the line all cheerful explaining how they had decided to take it easy for the day and how sorry they were to have missed her the previous afternoon when she'd called. He went quiet when Cathy asked if he would call out to her.

'It won't take long. Just something I need to discuss with you privately.'

Sounding concerned he asked, 'What is it?'

'Please Patrick, when you get here, I'll tell you all.'

After the call finished, the sergeant, with a mug of tea in hand opened the patio door and made himself comfortable out on the swing chair. Cathy filled the washing machines with towels and bed linen. There was the warm smell of laundry from the clothes she lifted from the dryer and brought upstairs. Returning to the kitchen, a tin of food was emptied for Truman. The rinsed tin was dropped into the recycling bin. And then the doorbell went.

It wasn't just Patrick at the door but also Melissa.

'What's this about?' Patrick asked as they followed her into the kitchen. His expression darkened when Matt arrived in through the sliding door.

'Let's all just take a seat.' Cathy pulled a chair from under the table.

Patrick seemed ever so uncomfortable as he did the same; unlike Melissa, he had caught the seriousness of the situation.

Melissa dropped into the chair next to Patrick.

'I hope you don't mind me tagging along. Patrick and I have no secrets.' A twitch of a smile. She was finding it all so intriguing.

The sergeant took the chair next to Cathy.

'Well,' said Melissa crossing one leg over the other and allowing her foot to swing. 'What is it you want to tell him?'

The sergeant opened the file and placed a photo in front of Patrick. 'This is the woman found drowned in Doonaleigh.'

Melissa's foot stopped swinging. 'Don't tell me you think Patrick returned to the village to drown some unknown woman.' Her eyes were wild in her head. 'I don't think so.'

Simultaneously Patrick leaned back stiffly in his chair as if afraid of what the photo held. It took him some seconds to recognise her. Then his eyes narrowed, his body fell forward and his hand shot up to support his forehead.

When Melissa casually turned to Patrick as if expecting him to back up her argument, it clicked that something was seriously wrong.

'Honey are you OK, what is it?' She scanned the photo straight on. Like a magnet, she seemed drawn into that pale dull image of Catherine. Her breath caught when she inhaled. 'Oh my God,' she cried staring at her dead sister-in-law.

There was a moment of complete silence.

Cathy watched as Melissa held Patrick's hand. She searched Melissa's expression for a flicker of doubt or even suspicion that Patrick might be responsible for this. But all she sensed was sympathy. Something other than that could have been there, well hidden, but if so, it was impossible to find.

Patrick sat as if he'd seen a ghost, emotions shut down, total blankness. Common behaviour from someone guilty, someone who knew to guard their emotions against betraying them.

Cathy spoke quietly. 'The suspects are in custody. But this was a job they were paid to do. They won't say who paid them.'

That stirred Patrick from his blankness.

'Where is her husband?'

Cathy returned Patrick's gaze. 'We don't know.'

He looked away.

'The last time we spoke Catherine mentioned that Elijah was heading to Cairo for a holiday.'

'Was she not going with him?' asked the sergeant.

Patrick shook his head. 'She told me he was going on his own.'

'But Tess believed she went with him.' Cathy sounded confused.

'Catherine could change her mind at the toss of a hat,' replied Patrick.

Elijah was now certainly assuming the position of the prime suspect.

'What can you tell us about your sister?' asked the sergeant.

Melissa stretched her arm across Patrick's shoulder for support.

'Not much. Catherine went to university in London and graduated with a science degree. She married Elijah Muscanna who operates a chain of opticians around

London.' His hand dropped to the table. 'They travel a lot to Egypt. That's all I know.'

'Did you meet her when you were in London?' Cathy asked.

He made a sound when he inhaled.

'Three months back I contacted her. We hadn't been in touch in over twenty years. She sounded glad to hear from me and agreed for us to meet up when I arrived in London. I had the impression she didn't want me to turn up at her place. But when I got to London and phoned her, she sounded different. She mentioned how she was busy as Elijah was heading to Cairo the following day. She took my number and promised to phone me on Thursday after Elijah had left. When I got no call, I phoned every day for a week. On the following Wednesday, a woman answered. She was the housekeeper and told me that the Muscannas had left for Cairo the previous week. She refused to say when they were due back. Melissa phoned the following Wednesday, the housekeeper again answered and again she said they were in Cairo.' He bit his bottom lip. 'I was furious. I presumed she had lied to me. That she had left with Elijah like she was laughing at the idea of us resolving things.'

'What day was it when you contacted her in London?' asked the sergeant.

Patrick struggled to remember.

Melissa was more forthcoming. 'We arrived in London on Monday, May 18th. Patrick contacted her on Tuesday, May 19th.'

The sergeant wrote it down.

'How did the two of you get on growing up?' asked Cathy.

Patrick cupped his hand together. 'We didn't get on as kids. She liked things her way, enjoyed being the centre of attention and could wrap my father around her little finger. On the other hand, Tess sided with me. That became a problem for Catherine after our father died.' Melissa covered his hands with hers before he added, 'But if I can do anything to find out what happened to her, I will, I must. There is no one else to look out for her.'

No arguing with that. Unfortunately, time wasn't a luxury they could afford themselves, decisions needed to be made. The more evidence the British Police had to work with the more successful they would be in finding those responsible.

'You have to understand, within the force here it's just myself and the sergeant who know her true identity.' Cathy wondered how long it would take Jeff to make the connection. She doubted he ever would. 'The suspects did mention she was involved in something evil; we don't know what that was exactly or if it's the truth. It might just have been something they were told to make the job easier to carry out.' She'd spoken those last words without thinking. They sounded heartless.

Patrick glanced at Melissa.

'This will devastate Tess.' He lowered his head.

It was Melissa who eyeballed her. 'You recognised her from that photo you saw of her last year in Tess's, didn't you?'

Cathy nodded thinking how it wasn't her only lead and that she should have made the connection sooner than she did.

A mobile phone went off. The sergeant moved out onto the deck. When he returned, he explained he was needed at the station. Cathy walked him to the door.

When she arrived back into the kitchen the pair were whispering to themselves before Patrick asked, 'Would it be possible for you both to keep this to yourselves for a week?' He glanced up at her. 'More than half my life we were estranged. I'd like to find out what I can before Tess needs to be told.' With a pleading expression, he added, 'I'd really appreciate it. In the end, does it matter when the truth comes out?'

It was the response Cathy had hoped for. 'You'll need to head to London. When you have discovered what you can you will have to report her missing. I'll give you the name of someone whom I'm sure will help you out.' With Andy Scott involved, they might get somewhere fast. Jeff hadn't the resources to uncover the truth in another jurisdiction. But Andy had.

Cathy asked the question that so puzzled her.

'Why didn't Catherine return to visit Tess? I mean London is only a short flight away. They keep in touch with postcards and the odd phone call but that's it.' Cathy played with the teaspoon she was holding. 'It struck me last year when Tess's photo fronted the local paper on receiving that award for the money she had found. There she was surrounded by locals but no Catherine to share in her glory.'

Patrick lifted his chin off his chest. 'Nor me.'

'Yes, that's true.'

Patrick studied her. 'Every family has its secrets, even ours. The reason she doesn't return here has nothing to do with her ending up drowned. It was a serious family row that ripped us apart but I've no intention of divulging any more than that.' He glanced at Melissa who squeezed his hand.

If Cathy were more involved with the case she'd have wanted to know more. But it wasn't her case. Even if it was and he refused to talk about it, there was nothing she could do to make him talk. She had to be thankful that without much persuasion Patrick was heading to London.

Melissa was adamant she would accompany him.

With a look of concern, Melissa then turned to Cathy.

'I know this is a lot to ask but we'll be useless there on our own.' She paused. 'Is it possible you could come with us?' Raising her voice, she added, 'We'll pay for everything, but we need to do this as quickly as possible. I mean, it will only be the start of it when Catherine is reported missing. And if that housekeeper was there on a Wednesday, then that's when we need to be at the Muscanna residence.'

Cathy was taken aback by her request. She was due back to work on Monday fresh and clear-headed after her long spell of suspension. There was a backlog of work waiting for her attention. But nothing overly interesting according to Philip. On the other hand, she had forgotten to cancel her week's holiday. Her boss would know not to challenge her on the matter when it had already been sanctioned, even if she had left it so late to bring it to his attention. She had felt pulled into this case at every turn. Why not stay with it to the next level? What were they likely to achieve on their own? They hadn't a clue what to look for. And when Patrick went to report her missing, he might be tempted to blather everything about her exact location and end up as suspect number one. She imagined that neither of them had grasped just how delicately this matter had to be handled. For her, the notion of returning to London stirred up something inside. She so loved that city. Perhaps it wasn't yet the right time to return to that straight and narrow road of correct procedure. Perhaps playing the part of a private detective would hold a touch of adventure. Yeah, she'd be up for that.

'We should head over on Tuesday,' she said. 'But I'll pay

my own way.' She wouldn't leave herself open to having a possible suspect pay for her trip.

'Thank you.' Melissa sounded appreciative.

When they left, she sat down to plan things through in her head. In his condition, it would be unfair to expect Truman to settle in a kennel. He'd prefer to stay with Adam. She'd arrange that. But first things first, she found her computer and emailed her boss to apologise in not notifying him sooner of her week's holiday. Then she found her mobile and scrolled down through her list of contacts until she reached his number. She hadn't spoken to him since her time in London and had ignored his many calls since. He could easily hang up if he were miffed over her treatment of him, but she had a good reason for ignoring him. He would know that. She pressed the call button and listened to it ring.

'This sure is a surprise.' She could hear the smile in his voice.

'How are you?' She sounded business-like.

'I'm good,' again, that lightness of voice. 'I heard from that sergeant friend of yours. Unfortunately, I was no help to him this time around.' He was easy to listen to.

She mustn't allow her mind to wander.

'I'll be in London next week. I might need your help.'

Another pause that she knew he had to fill. 'You don't need to ask. If I can I will.' And then he added, 'It will be my pleasure.'

Their relationship was well behind her. She needed to remain focused.

'Thank you.'

'When are you arriving? Where are you staying?' he asked.

'Ah, no plans made yet but I will let you know as soon as we've something confirmed.'

'We? Who is coming with you?'

'Patrick Fowley from the village here. He's concerned over his sister who lives in Richmond. He hasn't heard from her in a while.'

'But has he contacted her family and friends here?'

She didn't want to go through it all with him just then. She still needed to decide what he had to be told and what to keep secret.

'I'll explain all when I see you.'

'I'm in court next week, but I'll meet up with you when you arrive. Send me a text with the details.'

'Will do and again, thanks.'

What a pity he found it so easy to lie, not just to her but to his wife.

Tuesday - 23rd June

9.45am

It was *go go go* until she reached the Aircoach stop. When the coach arrived, she again checked that she had her ticket, drivers' licence, and sterling. Just as well she didn't need a passport for the trip as she couldn't find it. Once settled on the coach she relaxed. She was on her way, time to calm down.

It didn't matter that the traffic was busy. She always gave herself plenty of time when she was taking a flight. She disliked flying long distance, but London she could handle. It was a trip she was used to from her childhood. That look of excitement on her mother's face as they boarded their flight for their holiday to her cousin for two weeks, was a memory not to be forgotten.

Arriving at the airport she secured her boarding card and went straight through security. She hadn't had time for breakfast. With an hour to spare and the gate number registered on her brain, she decided on a croissant and coffee. After that, she made for the shopping area. There she found Melissa with Patrick buying chocolates. For Patrick, with the jury still out on his involvement in his sister's murder, this trip would be no bag of laughs in either case.

Melissa explained how she had enrolled Brandon and Heather on a week's horse-riding course they had been interested in.

'Patrick's excuse to Tess for this trip was that he had to check out machinery in Liverpool. Heather was quick to ask how come the machinery wasn't available at home. Then Brandon posed the question of whether or not the machine would need a serious overhaul to enable it to work off our system of electricity. Another time they'd hardly take in what you were telling them.' Her mouth tightened.

Cathy left them to it and headed towards the departure gate where she found a seat. She was too used to living on her own. This trip would be challenging if they overly invaded her space.

The sun shone through the extensive width of glass. She pulled her book from her bag but with the soothing heat on her face, she didn't feel like reading and just sat with her eyes closed. When her mobile rang, the glare of the sun prevented her from recognising the number ID.

'Mam, where are you?' asked an anxious voice.

'Sinead, I'm at the airport heading to London, what's wrong?'

'Oh Mam,' she cried. 'It's all over between Malcolm and me. We had an awful row and now he's left. He's been cheating on me. Can you believe it after all I've done for him?'

'I'm so sorry.' Her sense of pity came through in her words.

Sinead's voice continued to break. 'I don't know what I'm going to do without him, he was everything to me.' Obvious pain in her voice.

Cathy stood up and headed towards the window away from everyone while dragging her bag behind her.

Sinead was sobbing now.

'I thought I knew him. I really did. We were talking about getting married next year. And now I don't know if

I want to stay here on my own.'

How much Cathy would give to have her daughter home! But no matter where Sinead ended up, she still had to deal with this breakup. There was no point running from it. If she came home there had to be no regrets at leaving Australia. Up to that point, she had loved living there.

'Now listen to me.' Cathy softened her tone. 'You told me yourself there are plenty of Irish out there. Now is the time to get to know them better. You will be heading home for good in September, that's not too far off.' Sinead was like Dan, sociable, easy in company. It wasn't a problem for her to make friends. 'If it upsets you to see Malcolm with this new girlfriend of his, then move away from that area, show him he has no control over you.'

When the crying continued, Cathy felt her eyes closing as she formed a mental picture of her daughter standing in front of her. 'Sinead, imagine I'm hugging you this minute, hugging you tight, telling you how much we all love you and only want the best for you.'

'I know.' Sinead sobbed.

Cathy could now feel the anger rising in her.

'If he thinks it's OK to treat you like this now, then how do you think things would have worked out further down the track? You're a giver Sinead, you just have to make sure that the one you're giving to deserves you. Malcolm doesn't.'

More sniffling.

''That's just a crap logical response. It doesn't help me in the least,' Sinead bawled.

Jeez, she couldn't help but put her foot rightly in it.

Then came the sound of a ringing mobile.

'There is a call coming through, it might be him. Will you skype me when you can?' Sinead sounded anxious.

'Early tomorrow morning and we can talk for longer.' Cathy felt that dragging sinking feeling in her stomach. She returned to her seat. Who was she to give such logical advice? What would her daughters think of her affair with Andy and he married with a family? She knew how to talk the talk over what made sense yet when strong emotions were added to the mix, what made sense went scampering out the window. You so wanted to hold on, knowing how hard it would be to walk away. If you were left with a sense of satisfaction in doing the right thing, in walking away that would be something. But all that swamped you was that dragging feeling of loss.

'You look lonely here on your own,' said Melissa as she sat down next to her.

////////

1.50pm

Accommodation in London was expensive at the best of times but worse during the summer months. Melissa had taken charge of booking their accommodation. Taking into account there were three of them, she had booked rooms in a hotel in Greenford. It took an hour to get there by bus from the airport. That wouldn't have been a problem but they got off at the wrong stop and had a ten-minute walk back to the hotel. The heat had Cathy's feet burning from the leather of her new sandals, on top of that her stomach felt queasy and Sinead was occupying her mind. Not a great start.

Arriving at her hotel room, she threw down her bag, flung off her sandals, stripped off her clothes and for twenty minutes stood under a tepid shower. Feeling the spray of water on her face she wondered if she was soft in the head for accompanying them here to London. The sergeant almost had a hissy fit when she told him of her plan. She had ignored his claim that she was being reckless. Perhaps he was right. The sooner they discovered all they could, the better.

Once out of the shower she found her iPad and googled a map of the London Underground. They weren't on a direct line to Richmond. Even with changing trains, it would be at least an hour's journey to get there. The image of them arriving at the residence like worn out tourists would be a big mistake especially if their intention was to win over the housekeeper who might need some serious convincing to allow them inside.

Over a cup of tea at Molly's when leaving Truman off with Adam she had casually inquired about Catherine Fowley.

'Oh, she was herself,' replied Molly. 'Do you not remember her walking up to communion in that cream skirt open almost at her waist over matching leggings?' She began to smile. 'Now she was ahead of herself when it came to fashion and she knew it. The first one I ever saw wearing leggings. Only they were like cream long johns me grandfather used to wear. She had a matching vest and lace-up brown boots. Do you not remember her? You'd swear she was strolling along the catwalk.'

Cathy remembered. An attractive girl, not tall but she walked with a sense of elegance as if she was about to stand on her toes and glide forward like a ballerina. And yet her clothes, her sometimes stoical stance cried *rebel*.

'For her sixteenth birthday, she got her hair braided like Bo Derek's. Do you not remember?'

Yeah, that too she vaguely remembered.

'Did she pal around with Nancy from the supermarket?' asked Cathy.

Molly had nodded. 'The two of them were as thick as thieves back then. I think they still keep in touch. Catherine had a way with the fellas. Once she threw her eyes their way, that was it.' A frown hardened her expression. 'I had been going out with Damien Kusher for six months. He was my first love but he broke it off to take up with Catherine. And then she tried to tell me she had no idea we'd been seeing each other like she was upset to have hurt my feelings.' She had then rolled her eyes.

Cathy imagined that Catherine's previous short-comings would be forever forgiven once Molly learned the details of her demise.

'But then she met James Hurley,' Molly had sounded satisfied over that. 'I think it was the fact no one liked him that made her mad to have him. She had him for a while. There she'd be sitting in that makeshift sports car of his and he screeching around the roads at speed. That fella was dangerous. We all knew it. She had to be so careful Tess never found out she was seeing him. Tess had warned her against him. But,' her eyes opened wide, 'Catherine took it badly when he dumped her for Nora Aldridge. Then Patrick left home and the next thing she was off to London.'

As often happened when a topic of interest was discussed, Molly wasn't yet ready to let go of those memories. 'For the first couple of years, she came back for Christmas. It was the least she could do when Tess was paying for her over there. When she was in school, she told anyone that was interested that she was adopted. I think she imagined she was someone of importance. She didn't care about hurting Tess's feelings. Maybe Catherine went in search of her real parents. That's what they're all doing these days. That could be why she turned up her nose at Tess.'

And then the topic rested.

It was after six when Cathy had a call from Andy. He was downstairs. She sprayed herself with perfume before heading down to meet him. *Remember, this is work,* she told herself. She made for the bar. On noticing him she had to admit it didn't take much to smarten him up. A dark grey tailored suit for his court appearance did the trick. His hair was greying at the edges and those intensely blue eyes of his were as solid as ever.

'It's good to see you again,' he said as she drew near to him.

'The same here,' she replied as he lightly kissed her cheek.

A bit too familiar but she'd ignore it she told herself.

He ordered a gin and tonic for them both before they headed for the empty table in the corner. She was conscious of the way he watched her while she explained Patrick's search for his sister. She finished off by adding that Patrick was Tess Fowley's son.

He looked surprised. 'Tess who found that sterling in the church?'

'The very one.'

It had been agreed between Patrick, Melissa and herself that Andy wasn't to be told the crucial facts until after they had first checked out the Muscanna residence. It was why she could understand his puzzlement on her arriving in London on so little.

'I'll check out her husband Elijah and see what I come up with but if no one here suspects anything sinister in Catherine remaining in Cairo then I can't see what concerns Patrick on not hearing from her.'

She sipped her drink.

'Answers would be more forthcoming if those who knew her didn't think they were being dragged into something unpleasant.'

He looked at her sharply. 'So, you think she's in some kind of danger?'

'Yeah, I do.' Her head remained bowed. 'I could be wrong.'

Fortunately, Patrick and Melissa arrived just then, introductions were gone through with Patrick adding how much he appreciated Andy's help.

Andy moved closer to Cathy.

'I can't guarantee you anything.' He almost sounded embarrassed. 'I need to make that clear straight off.'

Patrick rhymed off the same details they had agreed on.

Melissa relaxed back into the sofa and with those wide-earnest eyes of hers, she said, 'Tess never met Elijah. Catherine phoned to tell her she was married. She never came home after that.'

More than ever Andy remained unconvinced of any wrongdoing by anyone after their partially factual details had been gone through. They weren't lying just being frugal with the truth, that's what her logic self told her.

Sitting opposite Andy, Melissa went on to ask him about his job while Cathy's mind wandered back to the Catherine walking down the aisle at Mass in Carrabhain. Then there was the Catherine on that yacht leaning against her smiling husband. If she'd been her daughter, that confidence of hers was something she'd have admired. But did that confidence blind her to what was real, to the possibility of over-reaching herself? If she had remained with her true family and had heeded Martin's advice, she'd have been savvier in knowing who to trust and who to discount.

They headed to a restaurant Melissa had booked. The place was bright and the food good. Melissa inquired from Andy if he were married. Separated was his answer. The same answer he'd given Cathy when she'd first met him. An answer she had been quick to believe.

Melissa asked him about his children.

'The eldest, Vicky, has just sat her GCSEs and the youngest, Nina, wants to be an actress.'

Melissa was a talker. She was interested to know more about the British educational system. Andy seemed happy to converse with her. Patrick, like Cathy was content to sit back and just listen.

Wednesday - 24th June

7.25am

The hotel was next to the A40 Western Avenue. It wasn't the traffic that woke her but her concern for Sinead. Once out of bed she opened the window. That humming noise, so different from what she was used to, energised her.

After a shower, she skyped Sinead. Repeatedly she was told how much Malcolm had meant to her. Cathy responded that she understood. Even when Sinead dropped the bombshell that the €1,000 she had received as a present from both her and Dan for Christmas was used as a deposit on their apartment. All Cathy could do was listen while asking herself why Sinead believed that by paying their bills Malcolm would appreciate her all the more. Where had she and Dan gone wrong with their daughters? Neither of them seemed interested in supporting themselves independently. Needing someone to share in life's experiences was their goal, at all cost. But then Cathy checked herself, she at Sinead's age was married. So, who was she to talk!

'Mam, I loved him.' Sinead appeared so vulnerable.

'I know you did. It's not going to be easy but eventually, you'll forget him, even if that seems impossible to you now.'

Sinead blankly viewed the screen. 'I don't know if I will.' She then went over it all again, how she had been blind to the number of times Malcolm was spending with his friend Alex who happened to share the apartment with Lauren, Malcolm's new girlfriend.

'Is she Australian?' Cathy asked.

'Yeah, why?'

'No, just wondering, that's all.' She had found Malcolm to be charming, but how quickly he could disregard Sinead without a second thought. There had to be a reason, for Cathy didn't honestly believe he loved this Lauren any more than he had loved Sinead. But when he'd been to visit at Christmas, more than once he'd mentioned how he loved Australia. Similar to Sinead, he didn't have a profession the Aussie's desperately needed. Now Lauren just might be his ticket to his future. When Sinead was well and truly over him, she'd tell her that. Or maybe she'll figure it out for herself.

Over breakfast, she pulled out a map of London and spread it across the table to pinpoint their destination, Petersham Road in Richmond. From her mobile, she searched for the nearest car hire firm. It was a fifteen-minute walk from the hotel. She checked the time. If she left straight away, she'd be there when it opened at nine. After folding up the map, she dropped it into her bag. As she left the dining room, she bumped into the others.

'I'm hiring a car and will pick you up from the front of the hotel at half-past-nine. Don't keep me waiting.'

Patrick stepped in front of her as she went to pass.

'There is something I have to tell you.'

Cathy caught Melissa lowering her head to focus on the floor.

Patrick sounded hesitant. 'I did go to Catherine's residence on that Thursday. I had found her address when I was back in Carrabhain at Christmas. I wanted us to sort things out once and for all.'

Cathy felt herself stepping back. This man was either climbing closer to the position of the prime suspect or was stupid enough not to have been honest with her from the start.

He ignored her reaction.

'There was a gardener at the house when I arrived. He's married to the housekeeper. It was he who told me there was no one home, that the Muscannas had both left the previous day for Cairo. He laughed when I explained that I was Catherine's brother, he said Catherine was an only child and her parents were dead. That was what his wife had told him.' He shook his head. 'I did phone every day after that until the housekeeper answered. And she too confirmed that they had left the previous week.'

This was all wrong. She stood staring from one to the other of them in disbelief. Did they think she was that easily fooled? Her feet needed to take control and walk her upstairs to pack her bag and head home leaving them here to fend for themselves. But there was such massive deceit in all this. The housekeeper and gardener convinced she was in Cairo. No one with a clue she was dead. If her husband, Elijah, had wanted her murdered, hats off to how well he'd planned it. And what if it had only dawned on Patrick that he was a suspect? What if he was afraid of being accused of something he knew nothing about? And would he have returned to London knowing he could so easily be trapped?

She sucked in her lower lip as she grasped the mega difficulty they were facing. How were they to gain entrance if the housekeeper had no reason to believe Patrick was Catherine's brother?

'You wait until now before telling me this?' She couldn't quite believe it.

Patrick closed in on her. 'I swear I had nothing to do with what happened to Catherine. I swear it on Tess's life. Please help me out here.'

The idea of returning home with nothing further on the case would bring her no satisfaction. But if what she discovered convinced her in the slightest that Patrick was involved in this then she'd arrest him herself. No qualms about it.

But how they were meant to continue with their original plan was anyone's guess. Just keep going she told herself as she walked away from them. Crossing the street at the pedestrian crossing she asked herself why Catherine would have lied about having a brother or that both her parents were dead. Unless of course, that family argument had affected her deeply and she was out to erase the past.

At the car rental, it didn't take long to run through the paperwork. Twice she was told the car had an up-to-date sat nav. Anyone who knew her would tell you she wasn't the most careful of drivers and driving in the wrong direction on a one-way-street wasn't beyond her. Not forgetting, for the three of them, this would all be new territory.

Approaching the hotel, she noticed Patrick and Melissa, waiting. Patrick in his well-worn shorts and colourful shirt clashing with his greying ginger hair. Melissa is gladiator sandals, full skirt to the ankles and a money belt across her stomach loudly screamed *tourist*. Neither of them conducive to Cathy's plan which meant she would have to work alone.

Once in the car, Melissa took charge of the sat nav. Catherine's address was entered as their destination. Cathy took a left turn onto the motorway heading for the city. She made it to Hangers Lane which was buzzing as she breezed through onto the North Circular Road and beyond that, they skimmed the lush landscape of Kew.

Reaching the streets of Richmond, she noticed how the

boutiques had little or nothing on display in the windows. In contrast, a charity shop had plenty. An idea suddenly struck her. She pulled into the next available car parking space. After feeding the meter she asked Patrick and Melissa to follow her. In the charity shop, she picked out navy pants, a tailored jacket and a light blue shirt for him. A brown linen suit with matching shoes for her.

'You are no good to me dressed as you are,' she said, holding up both hangers.

They glanced down at their attire before taking what she handed them.

They arrived out from the changing rooms transformed. The items were paid for. Their own clothes bagged and handed to them.

On Petersham Road, Cathy pulled up across the road from the residence. Surprisingly the gate was open. It was a large two-story house with curtained windows, steps to the front door and a eucalyptus tree shading most of the front garden. A black Mercedes was parked in front. A Volkswagen golf to the side. The previous night she had checked prices of property in the area. A two-bedroom apartment was going for £999,950. A house of that size could cost anything up to €4,000,000.

There was no sign of any activity. She imagined the property was solidly alarmed. Within minutes of parking there a cream mini pulled into the driveway behind the Mercedes. A woman in her sixties with a pixie hairstyle got out. She headed up the steps before rummaging in her bag for a key. There was the sound of the alarm when she let herself in suggesting there had been no one there.

They watched the woman's outline through the dappled glass of the front door as she hung her bag on what Cathy presumed was a coat stand. Then she walked out of sight.

'It doesn't make sense that she comes to work in a house with no one living in it and there's nothing to be done,' said Melissa, voicing Cathy's own thoughts.

'But we can't be sure if Elijah has returned from Cairo,' replied Cathy chiding herself that they should have arrived earlier on the off chance he had already left for work.

Two dog walkers passed. In front of them, a woman dragged a bin out onto the path. The neighbourhood was quiet which was why she almost jumped when her phone rang.

It was Dan. 'I just had a call from Sinead............' He spoke as if he was entitled to her full attention.

'Yeah well, that's what happens when a relationship doesn't work out.'

'And what is going on between you and Jennifer? She won't say much but it's left her really upset.'

She rolled her eyes. 'Dan I can't....'

He cut her off without a thought. 'I can understand your dislike of Neil.'

'Dan, listen to me.' He again tried to talk over her but she didn't have time for his ranting. She loudly shouted, 'LISTEN TO ME.' That silenced him. 'I can't talk right now. I'll phone you when I can.'

They slouched down when a Mercedes pulled up behind the mini. The crisp suited man with a sallow complexion headed up the steps. He rang the doorbell which ruled him out as being Elijah. The door was barely opened by the housekeeper. They spoke, he with outstretched arms talking at an ever so quick pace. Cathy buzzed down the window. They weren't close enough to hear what he was saying as his words were spoken with a dense pronunciation that was hard to grasp. But the housekeeper's voice carried. She sounded feisty, *I'm not interested in what you have to*

say….. there is no reason for you to come into the house……..
but why doesn't Elijah tell me this himself?

With her mobile, Cathy snapped a shot of the Mercedes' registration then the man himself as he turned and headed down the steps after the door had been shut. They remained slouched until they heard the car pull out and drive away.

After a deep inhale Cathy yanked the keys from the ignition.

'OK, now both of you follow me. Think of yourselves as my assistants. Let me do the talking. Don't touch anything.' Her face pulled tight, stern, solid, no-nonsense here. 'Don't open your mouth.'

They looked like a pair of scared chickens. Though Cathy might have had the appearance of being in control, the pounding sound of her heart beating contradicted that. Pulling herself out of the car she felt thankful she wasn't going it alone. With her head bowed, she walked steadily forward clasping her ID in her hand. The others followed behind.

When the door opened the woman appeared relieved to find them there. She asked, 'Can I help you?'

Cathy raised her ID in an ever so quick gesture covering part of it with her hand. 'Good morning, I am DI Spragg; we got a call of a disturbance at this address during the night and were asked to investigate. Are you Catherine Muscanna?' Sounding efficient came naturally to her.

The woman looked bewildered. 'No, no. I'm afraid she's not here at the moment. But the alarm was on when I arrived in earlier. I'll check it again if you like.' She spritely rushed along the hallway with its white and black tiled floor and sounded ever so reassuring when she returned. 'No, the alarm never went off last night. It must be another residence in the neighbourhood.'

Cathy frowned. 'No, this was the address we were given. I wonder would it be possible for you to contact either Catherine or Elijah Muscanna to confirm if they had a disturbance during the night or was it just a false alarm?' She pretended to read from the notebook she was holding.

The woman held up her hand, 'They're on holidays and I've no way of contacting them,' came her reply.

Cathy nodded. 'When are they due back?'

Her forehead creased. 'I'm not sure exactly.'

'So, when previously to your knowledge did anyone enter this house before today?'

'I was here last Wednesday. My husband was here on Thursday, but he didn't enter the house.'

Cathy nodded. 'So, you wouldn't know if anything is missing? I mean it's not out of the question that someone with the alarm code had entered these premises in the last week without your knowledge. If items were stolen, do you think your employers might be annoyed when their insurance company questions the fact that when we called you were adamant nothing had been taken?' She slapped shut her notebook. 'It makes no difference to me one way or the other.' She half-turned as if she had better things to do.

The woman stepped forward. 'I see what you mean.'

'And your name?' asked Cathy as she again faced her.

'Mary Simpson, I'm the housekeeper.'

'If you would allow us a quick inspection of the residence, with your assistance, of course, that's all it will take,' Cathy spoke as if in a hurry.

Mary watched her for a moment then took in Patrick and Melissa before moving aside and allowing them to enter. They made for the first room on the right with the housekeeper in tow.

'How long have you worked here?' Cathy asked scanning the unusually decorated room with its high ceiling and a baby grand piano to the side. Walls painted a definite green with an oriental rug stretched across the floor. Scandinavian style chairs scattered around the room. In the centre was an old comfortable looking leather sofa piled high with cushions. Alcoves painted a light orange either side of an original massive granite fireplace like you'd see in one of those Jane Austin dramas.

'Fifteen years now,' replied the housekeeper.

Cathy was drawn to the framed photo of the smiling couple sitting on top of the baby piano. Elijah with his arm around Catherine's shoulder as she snuggled into his chest. 'Are these your employers?'

The housekeeper nodded. 'Yes, that's them.' The warmth in her voice suggested the woman was fond of them.

When Patrick approached, he went to lift the frame. Cathy shook her head and he moved away. They left to check the room opposite. It was furnished in a way more in tune with the building itself. Rich wood flooring, a large sleek dining room table, unusual leaf-shaped chandeliers. On the walls were a selection of abstract bright pictures of all shapes in heavy boxed frames. The chairs around the table were all upholstered in a heavy pink velvet fabric.

Back in the hallway, they moved to the next room on the right. Cathy stood back for Mary to open the door.

Mary remained where she stood.

'That is Mr. Muscanna's office; he's the only one with a key.'

Cathy couldn't risk insisting that the door should be opened. She suspected the housekeeper was slightly uneasy over her decision to allow them to enter the residence. It wasn't the time to sound forceful.

Instead, she asked, 'What business is Mr. Muscanna involved in?'

'He has a chain of optician stores around London.'

'And Mrs. Muscanna?'

'Oh, she's the Chairwoman of the Aid for Children Foundation.'

Cathy made for the stairs and felt the smoothness of the wooden banister. And then she got the full view of the framed picture on the wall opposite the landing. A large painting of a cow happily eating grass. Cathy couldn't help but smile.

'That reminds her of her homeplace in Ireland,' the housekeeper remarked on noticing Cathy's reaction.

The main bedroom had a masculine richness to it, muted colours of damask curtains, heavy satin wallpaper, silk cushions and throws in matching fabric. An array of lamps on every surface. All of it blending against the dark polished furniture. A row of pictures on the wall she presumed was of Elijah's family, all in heavy gold frames with what Cathy suspected was Egyptian writing along the bottom. The windowsill had a simple birthday card of a couple walking along a beach holding hands, dated two months back. The inscription inside read: *Catherine, I'll love you always, Elijah.* Not something you would write to a wife you intended to have murdered but it could be a ploy to have everyone thinking exactly as she was thinking.

Three other bedrooms were smaller but of the same ilk. From the back window was a view of a courtyard. The last room, according to the housekeeper, was Catherine's office but the key was downstairs.

Feeling more in control Cathy said, 'It would be best to check it out seeing as the window backs out onto that courtyard.' She sounded indifferent but her logical voice was there too. Enough to persuade the housekeeper to rush off and fetch the key.

Melissa looked baffled. 'This house is full of positive energy. Not what I expected.'

Cathy nodded. There was nothing dull anywhere, pieces happily blended into a mix and match mode. The furnishing worked perfectly. It would have cost some money to put together.

Melissa whispered, 'I can't believe he'd have wanted her murdered.'

The housekeeper returned to open the door. They entered. Cathy scanned the room. The first thing to catch her eye was a small framed photo on the top shelf of a book stand by the far wall. It wasn't prominently positioned but at the same time, she was drawn to the photo that had been taken over twenty years back. There was Tess at her front door next to a man Cathy presumed was her husband. Patrick in bellbottom jeans and a green tank top, his hair wild as a bush and he leaning against the windowsill. Catherine in that skirt and leggings that Molly clearly remembered, her arm around her father.

'They were her parents. They're both dead now,' said the housekeeper.

Cathy offhandedly asked, 'Is the boy her brother?'

'No. He was just a neighbour.'

Patrick studied the photo as Cathy made for the desk. When the housekeeper excused herself to open a window in the main bedroom, Cathy took the edge of her shirt to pull open the top drawer. Sitting on top of a pile of papers was a passport she quickly slipped into her pocket. On the side wall were three abstract paintings by a New York artist, Maggie Williams. They were drab and held little or no content. Next to them was a framed piece on the artist's working techniques. It included a photo of the woman in her late fifties. The best of the paintings, but even that was dull, was of a door opening into a room where the side wall stood lit from the sun shining through an obvious window.

When the housekeeper returned, Cathy asked, 'When exactly did the Muscannas leave?'

A noticeable touch of caution in Mary's voice when she replied, 'Wednesday 20th May. Catherine told me not to bother coming that day. She said she'd be gone for at least two weeks but that Elijah was staying longer. She often changes her mind if she's enjoying herself. They hate anyone to disturb them once they're there.'

'So, they're gone almost a month at this stage.' Cathy frowned. 'And you have no idea when to expect them back?'

The housekeeper scratched her arm. 'No, not yet.'

'Has Mr. Muscanna any business partners here in London?'

'Yes, Ali Defel and Andrew Palmer.'

After Cathy wrote down their names, she noticed the housekeeper's look of concern. She eyed Melissa and Patrick to leave the room. When they did, she moved closer to the woman all confidential like as if ready to hear what was about to fall from the grapevine.

'Is there something the matter?' she sounded ever so considerate.

'Ali Defel was here this morning just before you called.' Mary Simpson needed to talk. Now that she had come to believe they were actually the police, who better to open up to than to them? 'It's the second time he's come asking for Elijah Muscanna's computer. Like he thinks that will wash with me.'

'Do you know of anyone else with a key to this residence?'

She shook her head. 'No. My husband sometimes has my key when he comes of a Thursday to look after the garden and empty the bins. But the last time he emptied the bins was the Thursday after the Muscannas left.' Cathy waited for her to continue. 'Most times when there's a change of plan, I'll find a postcard waiting for me here on the mat telling me when to expect them home. But there's been no postcard so far.'

'I'm sure you'll hear something soon.' It was a typical everyday response from an officer whose aim was to appease an individual's concerns.

Before leaving the room, Cathy closely examined that photo on the shelf. There was a mixture of joy, youthfulness, and devilment in both Catherine's eyes and expression. She thought of that saying of how *the eyes are the windows to the soul.*

Heading down the stairs Cathy asked, 'How long have your employers known this Ali Defel?'

Mary was more relaxed in herself now that they were about to leave. 'He is a friend of Mr. Muscanna from childhood. They both attended university together in Oxford. But Mrs. Muscanna isn't that fond of him. She thinks he's just riding on her husband's coattails.'

At the door, Cathy asked and was given Mary's mobile number in case there was a need to contact her for further information.

Before turning to leave Cathy had one last question.

'Was there anything out of the ordinary about the place after they had left?'

Mary moved closer to Cathy as if there was an understanding between them. 'They must have left in a hurry. They both forgot their mobiles.' She rolled her eyes. 'The bedroom and living room were in a right mess. Things were thrown around the place. But I tidied everything away. That's my job.'

Cathy headed down the steps imagining the woman vigorously wiping clean all fingerprints and every scrap of evidence vital to forensics.

///////

5.40pm

Cathy had spent the afternoon in her room. Although it had been child's play to gain entrance to the residence, her mistakes were obvious to her now. Stating her actual name for starters was a big no-no. Parking so close to the residence was another. If the housekeeper had been suspicious and had sussed the car registration, that would lead right back to her. Fingers crossed she hadn't.

Again, she checked Catherine's passport that had been stamped every time she travelled to Cairo. The last occasion was in March. The information she'd gained from their morning's work was that the Muscannas had enjoyed a lavish lifestyle. If Elijah Muscanna was Muslim, he was sufficiently westernised to allow Catherine the freedom she enjoyed. Two months back he had written her a loving inscription in a birthday card. The couple had planned to leave for Cairo on Wednesday 20th May, a day the housekeeper wasn't required. The following week when the housekeeper had turned up for work, she'd found the place messed up and both their mobiles left behind. She was now expecting a postcard stating the date of their return.

Driving back from Richmond, Melissa had sounded her usual frank self. She couldn't imagine Elijah would have wanted to harm Catherine. Her opinion had so annoyed Patrick who insisted that Elijah had to be the guilty one. Cathy strained more towards Patrick's way of thinking even if she kept her opinion to herself. As the couple argued, it had been Catherine's last moments in her fine house that had filled Cathy's head. What thoughts must have run through her mind? From what she knew of her, Catherine seemed to have been a capable, self-assured woman. On realising she was no longer in control of her life; total fear must have gripped her tighter than she'd have ever imagined possible.

If only she could contact Philip to ask if he'd check whether Interpol had anything on Elijah Muscanna. But she couldn't. He'd phoned her on Monday all annoyed that she hadn't returned to work. It had left his plan of a short break to Kerry with his wife up in the air. And if she were on holidays, then why would she want him to check up on anyone?

When she arrived down to the bar, she was glad to find Andy there seated next to Melissa while Patrick was about to order a round of drinks.

Andy's day in court had gone well. Their suspect was found guilty of the murder of a teenage girl coming from school. He was handed an eighteen-year sentence. Melissa questioned him on the man's age, if he had an addiction of any kind, what was his background and if he had shown any remorse for his actions.

'No,' replied Andy. 'He never wavered from the belief that she was asking for it, even though he was a complete stranger to her. According to him, things were fine between them until it got more heated and then she suddenly changed her mind and began screaming.'

'A good result then,' said Cathy knowing the lengthy process involved when a suspect pleaded not guilty. And you were dreading that sliver of a possibility of something cropping up to benefit the suspect's case.

Their drinks arrived.

'Yeah, glad it's over.' And with his drink in hand, he sat back and casually asked. 'So, tell me, how did you fill your day?'

The question was directed from one to the other of them but then all eyes were on Cathy. It was time for the truth, no more beating around the bush.

'Andy, we haven't been fully honest with you.' She lowered her eyes towards the table. 'Patrick didn't report his sister as missing.' She took a deep breath. 'The woman found drowned in Carrabhain, the one Sergeant Bracken had contacted you about was Patrick's sister Catherine Muscanna.'

He sat like a programmed zombie staring at her. Eventually, he spoke. 'Then what the hell are you doing here and why didn't you tell me this from the start?'

Her head leaned against her right shoulder. 'You weren't any help and you in court. We just wanted to check out where she lived, see if we could pick up anything as to why she was murdered. The suspects are in custody. But they won't say who paid to have her drowned.' She watched herself being assessed by two sharp mistrustful eyes.

'And what. You thought you could do a better job than us?'

Patrick moved forward in his chair. 'It's my fault,' he sounded so apologetic. 'I asked for her help.'

Andy rolled the glass around in his hand, tossing the whiskey from side to side. 'So, let's start again, and this time tell me everything,' he demanded.

She told him everything she knew about Catherine apart from her connection to Martin Rodgers. When she placed Catherine's passport in front of him, she mentioned the couple's planned trip to Cairo and how the housekeeper believed they were both there on holidays. She went on to mention Ali Defel and Andrew Palmer as Elijah's business partners and how the housekeeper had refused to allow Ali Defel to enter the residence to search for Elijah's computer.

'Mary Simpson is the kind of woman you'd want on your side.' Her ill-judged attempt of humour was lost on Andy.

And as he looked away, she wondered if he were about to stand up and walk out. She tried to imagine if the shoe was on the other foot how would she have reacted. Yes, she understood how he was feeling.

Thankfully, he remained seated. But his attention was on Patrick. 'If her husband is responsible for this, why did he have her taken all the way to Carrabhain?' A second's pause. 'Why not dump her body here in the Thames or even finish her off in Cairo where her death wouldn't be a problem to anyone?' His words sounded like a nasty attack.

Cathy kept her mouth shut as an upset Melissa wrapped her arm around Patrick's. An awkward silence followed. Cathy didn't want a row. She turned her attention to the man at the far end of the bar, on his own with two pints of Guinness in front of him.

She couldn't help but notice Melissa nudge Patrick before they both stood with Melissa saying, 'I think we need some fresh air.'

After they left, she and Andy continued to sit for some time in silence.

'There is something else you need to know,' she said on noticing his hands clasped together and him rubbing one thumb hard against the other. 'Catherine and Patrick hadn't spoken in years due to a serious family fall-out, and he was here in London the week she was abducted.'

'Jesus', he said and moved right in next to her. 'Have you any idea what you've got yourself into here?'

She remained calm.

His voice glittered with anger. 'You arrived here with Patrick aware of the situation and thought nothing of entering a residence under false pretences. And now, for some reason, you think I should be in on this?' He pulled back from her.

Never before her involvement with this case would she have been viewed as someone reckless. Yet she had been reckless more than once. But even acknowledging the mistakes she had made that morning there had been a thrill to it all. And up to then she had presumed Andy would have understood a little of that. She hadn't imagined him as being such a thoroughly honest law-abiding detective who did everything by the book.

'Is this how you operate?' That flash of anger in his expression left her feeling she was back in school being blamed for misbehaving.

The blame game wouldn't solve anything.

'Look, perhaps I shouldn't have got involved in this but I did. I made the connection as to her identity from information I should not have been privy to. The only way to put things right is for you to solve this case.'

'Me?' he hissed.

'Yes, you.' She took a mouthful of whiskey. Now was not the time for him to behave like a sulky kid. 'When Patrick submits a Missing Person's Report, he'll mention you more than once as someone who helped solve our murder case from last year. He will also state how his mother, Tess, was caught up in that same case. Even if only to ensure that Patrick's concerns should be considered legit, you will be contacted.' He held a puzzled expression. 'And you decide to check it out. When you're at the Muscanna's residence you find her passport which you'll have planted. Then everything changes from there.'

Andy inhaled. 'We both know if Elijah is responsible for this and he's contacted then he'll remain in Cairo.'

'Then he's not to be contacted.' She lowered her voice on having got a bit carried away with herself. 'No one here knows his wife has been murdered but you. You just have to take charge of the case and run with it.' From her bag, she removed a slip of paper. 'This is the housekeeper's mobile number, Mary Simpson. When you speak to her and to Ali Defel make out you are just following up on a suspected burglary at the residence. If Ali was to learn that Patrick reported Catherine missing, he'd inform Elijah. They could be in this together. This way they'll not suspect anything.' When he took the note from her, she added, 'This has the possibility of a win-win for you, Andy. Of course, you can walk away, pretend you know nothing. It's up to you.'

He finished his drink and slapped the glass on the table. He wasn't making it easy for her.

'I'm sorry if I've given you cause to mistrust me. It wasn't my intention. Just so you know even those involved with the case at home apart from Sergeant Bracken haven't as yet figured out her identity.'

He shook his head. 'Patrick is a serious suspect in this.'

She could understand his sentiments.

'This is your case. You run it your way and if Patrick is guilty then prove it.'

When a waiter arrived, another two whiskeys were

ordered.

'You think Elijah is behind this? he asked.

'He's in Cairo. He hasn't reported her missing, so yes, I do.'

He excused himself when his phone rang.

She was left wondering if the call was from his wife. No, he wasn't so squeaky clean as he liked to portray.

Friday - 26th June

12.25pm

They had spent the previous day in Richmond where Melissa accompanied Patrick to the police station. Aware of the length of time it would take to complete a Missing Person's Report Cathy had driven to the Muscanna residence. There she sat for half-an-hour until she was convinced there was no one there, not even the gardener. She then drove back to Richmond. All the eating and drinking she'd enjoyed since arriving in London had left her feeling bloated. In need of exercise, she had taken a walk along the street. At the bridge, she noticed the well-established route along the river and decided to check it out. It surprised her to find a café beneath the bridge with generous space in front for anyone to sit and enjoy the view of the Thames. She had passed tourists lining up to take a boat trip down the river. Further on, she continued along the path through a meadow where cows grazed. It reminded her of home. She had arrived at a garden nursery and café where she sat and enjoyed some perfectly strong tea. She had found herself smiling on hearing an Irish accent from the couple at the next table.

It was eight the previous night when Andy had contacted her. Within hours of Patrick leaving the police station, Andy had put their plan in motion. When he had contacted the housekeeper, Mary Simpson, her first question to him was how had he gotten her number. Andy made out that she was named as a keyholder with the alarm company responsible for securing the residence. He felt sure she believed him.

He kept talking. 'Then she asked if I had anything to do with the detective who had called yesterday. You're lucky she couldn't remember your name. I explained there was a large number of us working in the department but that I'd check it out.'

Mary Simpson had agreed to meet him at the residence where he'd replaced Catherine's passport in the drawer. He allowed his colleague Ben to find it. Unlike Cathy, Andy had been permitted to enter Elijah's office. On checking Elijah's computer Andy found emails referring to the embezzlement of money by Andrew Palmer which was being checked out. From there he had contacted the bank. According to their records, Elijah had close to £400,000 in his personal bank account on the day he left for Cairo. There had been no withdrawals since then or any suspiciously large withdrawals or payments to anyone in the past six months. Nor was there anything unusual in their joint account that had a balance of close to £20,000. No money had been withdrawn since Elijah had left for Cairo. Andy suspected he had another bank account there.

Fortunately, they were short staffed in Richmond Station and as a result of Catherine's passport being discovered, Andy had been asked to investigate her whereabouts without being obvious until they knew more.

'Catherine's mobile had been found under a cushion in the living room while Elijah's was in the cabinet of their bathroom en-suite.'

'An odd place to leave a mobile,' Cathy had remarked.

The most damning evidence against Elijah was the strong smell of fish in the kitchen when Mary Simpson had arrived at the residence the following week. She'd found the remains of a tub of prawns in salad dressing hidden away in the cupboard. The label had been removed. Mary couldn't understand it as Catherine had an allergy to prawns.

'It's a low-key case for now. Mary Simpson insisted I was wasting time, nothing had been taken. She seemed pleased that I agreed with her.' Andy concluded.

If Catherine's murder had gone according to plan no one would ever have guessed she'd even been abducted. Elijah could return to London to settle his affairs making out she had decided to remain in Cairo.

When Melissa and Patrick joined her for breakfast, Cathy suggested that as it was their last day in London, they should make the most of it.

They took the underground into Oxford Street and agreed to meet up for lunch. Cathy went to check out Liberty's, a store she loved. No longer was there fabric flowing from one shelf to the next. Now it was flat rolls piled in perfect rows. On the first floor, she found a large selection of wool next to a stand of knitting patterns. Molly was part of a knitting club and as she was a difficult one to buy for, Cathy chose wool and a pattern for a colourful throw. On the top floor, she checked out the magnificent oriental rugs similar to what she'd seen in the Muscanna residence. She considered buying one that would suit perfectly in her living room until she checked the price which didn't include the cost of delivery to Dublin.

They met up for lunch in a nearby pub. Patrick appeared bored; apart from Liberty's Cathy had no interest in shopping. After lunch, it was decided they would do their own thing and meet up later in the hotel for dinner. There was the buzz of her mobile as she headed for the underground.

Andy again.

'Elijah and Catherine were booked on a flight to Cairo but neither of them showed up.'

'So, he's hiding out somewhere here in London.'

'No, he took a flight later that afternoon with a different airline. They confirmed he booked it that same morning at about ten minutes to twelve.'

She listened to him explain how Elijah's mobile had been checked. Most of his calls were to and from Ali Defel.

'My colleague Ben tried to contact Ali. He even phoned him from Elijah's mobile but he didn't answer. According to the receptionist at their head-office, he's not working today nor is he at his residence.'

She wondered if Ali had assisted Elijah with his plan. Who better to lend a hand than a loyal friend? Not forgetting what Mary Simpson had mentioned that Catherine wasn't keen on Ali.

'What about us having dinner this evening?' Andy asked. 'We can discuss it further. I'll book us a restaurant.'

She had returned out onto the street. Without thinking she went to cross and was almost knocked down by a cyclist shouting at her to watch where she was going.

Back on the path, she found her breath. 'That sounds good. Make it for four. It can be a farewell dinner. Our treat for all your help.'

He wouldn't be comfortable dining with Patrick and Melissa. And she was aware of that even if Patrick's involvement seemed to be weakening by the day.

'Look it will be fine,' she said in answer to his hesitation.

'I'll pick you up about seven.'

When the green man lit up, she was part of the wave of pedestrians to cross the street. She checked out the shop window before heading into John Lewis.

6.45pm

Cathy phoned Molly. Truman was doing fine, the apple and pear trees were being watered daily as was the gooseberry bush, the rabbit at the bottom of the garden was being fed lettuce and no, Molly hadn't seen the sergeant in the past week.

From her daily conversations with Sinead, it was fair to say she was still upset over Malcolm. The difference between Sinead and Jennifer was that Sinead talked about her problems. After every skype, Cathy felt Sinead had peeled off another layer of hurt. She and Malcolm had lived together for well over a year, it would take time to clear him from her system.

There was nothing from Jennifer. That didn't surprise her as her daughter would expect Cathy to make that initial call. Jennifer was good at playing the victim, reasoning things out with the help of Neil that she had done nothing wrong. That Cathy had been utterly beastly, yes that was a word she would use to describe her mother. Things between them were so strained she wondered if they needed counselling or was it too late for that? Jennifer had her good points, she was a great organiser, got things done with little or no fuss. It was just that she viewed life as a mountain to be climbed. As Cathy massaged in body lotion after her long bath, she recognised the similarities between herself and her daughter for neither did she know much about having real fun. The cruise trip on the Lemoy River had been Neil's idea. Jennifer would never have been imaginative enough to think it up on her own. Neither would she at Jennifer's age.

Lucy would be the one to advise her on how to heal the

mother-daughter rift. She'd discuss it with her when she got home.

Slipping into the dress she'd bought earlier she felt pleased when she viewed herself in the mirror. It made her stomach appear almost flattened. She'd treated herself to a manicure and pedicure at a beautician's she came across in the city. Without much persuasion, she had bought a lipstick that matched the soft-rose coloured nail varnish. About to walk from the room she pulled her mobile from her bag. *Jenn, I was upset you didn't think to call when you were down my way, even if it were just for lunch or a cup of coffee. I love you, Mam XXXX.* Then on to Sinead. *Love you lots, home tomorrow, remember you are stronger than you think, Mam XXXX.*

Both Melissa and Patrick did a double take when she entered the bar. Andy, she was told, was on the corridor taking a call. She could see him pace up and down, hand out in front of him as he spoke. Twice he shook his head. When he returned, he checked his watch. It was a twenty-minute drive to the restaurant and it was time they were leaving.

'You look great,' he whispered as he cupped her elbow and walked her out.

The restaurant was busy. As they waited to be seated Andy ordered a round of Martinis. Cathy was that hungry she ate both olives from her drink and his. On her second glass of wine over dinner, Melissa loosened up and teased Patrick over how her mother never forgot his birthday.

'Every year she requests the same song on the local radio station, Meatloaf's, *Two out of three ain't bad*. Every year.' She laughed across the table at Cathy and winked. 'She doesn't listen to it herself but likes to be told by friends that they heard it. I think it is her way of making him feel he's where he belongs.'

She then caught Patrick's hand and squeezed it. Such a tactile kind of woman. But she knew exactly what she was doing. Through each of her words, there was her strong and total support for her husband. Whatever story she had told her mother to do with Patrick's reluctance to return to Carrabhain, it had been believed. Every word of it. That too she wanted them to grasp. Another layer of support piled on top of that hidden secret.

Weak-smiling troubled Patrick sat like a duck out of water. She guessed he would prefer to be anywhere but there with herself Melissa and Andy, in that restaurant in London. She wanted to find him innocent, but she couldn't be sure if he was or if he had been upfront with Melissa over the family feud. After all, Melissa's opinion of Catherine had been based on what Patrick had told her.

Her attention returned to Andy who was reminiscing over his school days. He had been nicked once for stealing cigarettes. They all laughed at his portrayal of his God-fearing mother. It was good to hear him admit he wasn't so squeaky-clean after all. A couple of times she caught him watching her. Even though she wouldn't be bowled over by him, she did feel flattered.

It was after eleven when they returned to the hotel. Melissa and Patrick excused themselves. She and Andy found a corner booth and after ordering drinks, Andy opened up on details which he insisted were for her ears only.

'There were two texts from Elijah's mobile to a friend Mohamed in Cairo. It seems this Mohamed had agreed to collect Elijah from the airport. Our translator texted Mohamed under the pretence she needed to contact Elijah over a suspected break-in at the house. He hasn't replied. Elijah's computer and mobile were left in the house, so no emails, calls or texts from Elijah informing Mohamed of his change of plans or of his time of arrival on the re-scheduled flight. But there were four messages from Mohamad to Elijah at the time Elijah should have arrived on his original flight, inquiring as to where he was exactly.'

She considered it. 'Sounds like Elijah hadn't covered everything.' Then she asked the question that had bothered her all day. 'Is there any way Elijah and Ali Defel could be involved in a terrorist organisation?'

An adamant shake of the head from Andy. 'They're Egyptian. Neither of them ever warranted any kind of surveillance. According to intelligence, Elijah's father, Khafu, is a high ranking general in the army. If Elijah was responsible for his wife's death, it will be difficult to make a case against him without solid evidence of his involvement. As Catherine has not yet been confirmed as the woman drowned in Doonaleigh, we have no reason to notify Elijah of that yet. Thankfully.'

The waiter arrived with their drinks.

'And if his plan was to remain there, then surely he'd have transferred his money to an Egyptian bank by now.' She wanted to wrap up what didn't make sense, aware that once she left London in the morning her involvement in the case would end.

The waiter returned with Andy's change.

Andy leaned in closer to her.

'He must have disguised those prawns in some dish without her knowledge, knowing they would make her ill. He will find it hard to explain why he left without her or why he hasn't reported her missing.'

Yeah, she agreed with that.

'And why leave his mobile behind in the bathroom cabinet of all places? If he had a second mobile, he'd have notified his friend of his re-scheduled flight. But that didn't happen.'

Andy grinned. 'You know you're good at this.'

'Sometimes I think it's the only thing I'm good at.' She took another mouthful of wine.

'I wouldn't say that.' His grin stretched further out.

The cheeky git she thought even if she couldn't help but smile. But she was quick to return to the matter in hand.

'And why did Catherine tell Patrick she would call him on Thursday if she was booked on a flight to Cairo the previous day?'

He finally replied, 'Nursing a lifelong grudge could be a serious factor in this. Only Patrick's word that Catherine made that arrangement.' He played with the drinks mat. 'The thing is, Patrick can't return to Canada until he's eliminated from this inquiry. Extraditing him from there would be difficult.' He pulled his face close to hers. 'I'm doing my part in this. Now I need you to do yours. His passport can be returned to him when we're satisfied he'd nothing to do with it.'

The idea of expecting Patrick to do what was required wasn't going to be easy. But she nodded in agreement.

Andy finished his drink. 'Those suspects that are in custody, have they contacted anyone since their arrest?'

She shook her head. 'They had no mobiles on them when they were dumped at the hospital. No way of contacting anyone. I would imagine anyone who knows them is scared to admit it.'

'Good. The fewer who know about their situation, the better, for now.'

It was getting late.

'Thanks for tonight.' She stood to leave.

When he got to his feet, he caught her hand.

'It's been great having you around.'

She nodded. 'Yeah, it's been good to catch up.'

They moved out of the bar. As she approached the lift he leaned over and kissed her hard on the lips. 'Don't leave it as long to return.'

Watching him walk away she knew she was leaving behind far more than a working colleague. In the last few days, she'd felt more buzzed up than she had in ages. No matter how she had warned herself, she had so enjoyed working with him again.

Tuesday - 30th June

8.10am

Matt sat rubbing the lines across his forehead. This was getting more and more complicated by the minute. DI Spragg's long conversation with him yesterday hadn't helped his general unease. Apparently, she'd had a fierce argument with Patrick at the airport when he refused to surrender his passport. He became so irate and accused her of using him for her own benefit. Melissa had ended up bursting into tears.

It now made sense why Patrick had avoided him since he'd returned. And on recognising him on the street the previous day Melissa had crossed to the other side.

DI Spragg had sounded stressed out by it all.

'Molly mentioned a guy by the name of James Hurley, Catherine was serious about him at one stage, just wondering if you knew of him and if he still lives around the village?'

Matt's eyebrows had risen at the mention of his name.

'Know him; he's just out of prison for robbery and assault on an elderly woman. He left her deaf in one ear from a blow to the side of her head. He doesn't care about anyone, has about ten kids from three different women. According to Deegan two of his offspring were born a day apart in the same hospital. He now lives with some young one in Athlone.'

She had then suggested that he talk to Nancy from the supermarket in the hope she might open up over what she knew regarding that relationship.

'Remember Catherine had a termination some years back. It could be what caused that family row.'

It was down to a game of waiting was how she'd put it. She felt confident that with Andy on the case he would fill them in on every turn. She made it sound as if they were the best of friends. Some turnaround there!

The previous week he'd found Tess on the street complaining over the litter spilling out from the overly full bin by the entrance to the supermarket. She wasn't bothered that Nancy could hear her as could those in the supermarket at the time.

Matt had advised her to calm down.

She seemed agitated. 'I don't know what's wrong with me. What will I be like when they leave? They're what's keeping me going.'

He had sounded tactful when he replied, 'Tess, you're probably tired from looking after them even if you enjoy having them around. That's all it is.'

'I hope you're right.' She then had walked away.

And what had bugged Matt for the last week was that DI Spragg hadn't been fully up front with him on everything she knew or was thinking. But he was beginning to think it was just as well, perhaps he knew enough without crossing the line more than he already had.

12.55pm

Cathy was at the counter in the canteen listening to Philip describe at length the cottage he'd booked in Louisburgh for the following week. His tray held a dinner of lasagne and a bottle of water.

'No place like it. Our pick of beaches. The weather promises to be good. Stress-free enjoyment, just what we both need.'

She had chosen a chicken salad.

They found a table for two. She didn't want anyone joining them. A nod from Ken in the corner, happy now that he was retiring at the end of September. She was already beginning to miss him as she watched him raise a napkin to wipe off a dollop of salad dressing from his mouth.

She lifted her mobile off the table when it lit up.

'I need to take this.' She headed for the door. 'Hi,' she whispered as she walked out.

'We caught up with Ali Defel this morning. He had surprised his family and taken them away for a couple of days. According to him, Elijah has a second wife in Cairo. This planned trip coincided with his son Ahmed's birthday party and the birth of his second child due any day. Ali hasn't had any reason to phone Elijah since he left but he's expecting a call when the baby arrives. Our Elijah likes his privacy.'

Cathy couldn't imagine that feisty, determined Catherine having taken kindly to sharing her husband. Elijah was wealthy enough to support a second wife; surely Catherine had to have known that was a strong possibility. Surely she hadn't imagined he loved her enough not to have wanted children. The first wife was considered the matriarch among such wives but with Catherine childless, that position would have been seriously undermined. The message from Elijah on that birthday card might have been a way of alleviating her doubts. And when that didn't work or knowing that if they divorced, she'd be entitled to a generous share of his wealth, perhaps he imagined there was nothing for it but to have her removed.

'Elijah was planning on returning permanently to Cairo and Catherine was looking forward to joining him there according to Ali.'

Cathy inhaled a deep breath. Substitute her free lavish London lifestyle for a repressed Cairo way of living with its lack of gender equality and her her being totally dependent on Elijah. No, Catherine would never have been content with that.

Cathy's boss ignored her as he passed. 'What's Ali Defel's opinion of Catherine?' she asked softly, moving further down the corridor.

'Not much, apart from the fact that she keeps herself busy with her charity work. He was surprised to hear I was pursuing a possible break-in at the Muscanna residence. But I made it sound ever so casual.'

'Why was he looking for Elijah's computer?'

'It seems Elijah received an email from their solicitor with a recommendation on how best to deal with Andrew Palmer's embezzlement. He had promised to forward it to Ali but hadn't.' There was a sudden dip in his voice. 'We're checking all CCTV street footage leading to or heading from the Petersham Road on the day Elijah left for Cairo. We might just recognise someone close to Elijah who shouldn't have been there then. But nothing so far.' The line was breaking up. 'Look, I have to go.' And he was gone.

She returned to reality as Cummins approached. He had returned to the bureau and was assigned to work with her on a case involving a large drug haul that had arrived into the city two days previously. Full of gusto he informed her that three henchmen from a well-known drug cartel had arrived at the warehouse they had under surveillance.

They needed to get there pronto.

Thursday - 2nd July

9.15am

She came to a complete standstill on Morehampton Road. Yesterday, with solicitors in tow, those arrested on Tuesday for smuggling drugs into the country had been questioned. Not for the first time had they found themselves on the wrong side of the law. And they knew the drill, knew to keep their mouths shut even if the evidence against them was enough to convict them. Today she would start on preparing a file for the DPP. One thing about Cummins, you could trust him to properly detail the evidence in a case.

The traffic moved forward by the length of two cars. It wasn't just the traffic that bothered her. She and Dan had spoken, to be more accurate, she had listened to his annoyance over Sinead's intention to head to Canada for a year instead of returning home to start a university degree course.

His voice went up a few decibels.

'I never liked Malcolm, he was nothing if not charming. And how Sinead couldn't see through him is beyond me.'

She made no response. Even if they were singing from the same hymn sheet there was no point wasting energy discussing Malcolm further. He was no longer part of their lives. Supporting Sinead had to be their focus.

His voice then softened. 'You need to work things out with Jennifer. I know you think she is as hard as nails, but she's not. Just sort it out with her and move on. Cathy, life is too short.' He had made it sound so clear-cut.

She knew there was nothing to be gained by allowing an argument to fester into a monstrous pile of anger. That didn't mean she was just going to apologise, but there had to be a way to break the ice between them.

On top of all that she hadn't heard from Andy since Tuesday. There had to be some progress on the case since then. Perhaps he no longer felt the need to involve her as she'd hoped.

The previous afternoon she had spoken to Sergeant Bracken after he'd dropped into the supermarket and broached the subject with Nancy of Catherine Fowley's relationship with James Hurley. She had been quick to ask if Patrick had told him everything. When the sergeant responded with a nod Nancy admitted to feeling partly to blame for what had happened. Unfortunately, the sergeant should have probed a bit deeper, asked what she'd meant by that. Instead, he allowed her to talk about how, when Catherine had headed to London, she'd forgotten the episode with James Hurley. But then the previous year when Tess was in hospital Nancy went to see her thinking Tess was at death's door. She had wanted her to know the truth. But the truth had upset Tess and Nancy still wasn't sure if she'd been forgiven for not being upfront sooner.

It was obvious from the dismissive way Tess had treated Nancy at the party, that yes, Nancy was right in thinking she hadn't been forgiven. If Catherine had a termination, there was a strong possibility that it resulted from her relationship with James Hurley. An event that would have called for all that *hush hush don't tell anyone* kind of secrecy back then. Was it possible that Tess had been in the dark over Catherine's pregnancy? When she'd been told the truth last year by Nancy while she was in the hospital, it was then she became anxious in her search for Patrick. But why would Patrick have kept the truth from her?

Pulling into her usual car-parking space she turned off the engine and sat feeling totally flat, lethargic even. This couldn't continue, she needed to pull herself together and not be maudlin as she was. On taking a seriously deep breath, she grabbed her bag off the passengers seat, stepped out of the car and walked forward with as much determination as she could muster.

///////

4.59pm

Matt listened carefully.

'I've just attended a meeting in Dublin this afternoon. Some important information has come to light regarding our victim. Tomorrow morning at 9 o'clock be at my office and don't be late.' Superintendent Clarke sounded flustered as he rushed his words down the phone.

He was glad not to be standing in front of him.

'Yes, Sir.'

It was anyone's guess as to what was coming down the line. If Catherine's identity had been discovered, how did that come about? Surely, he'd have heard before then if Patrick had made a statement to blow things up in their faces? If he was out to destroy them both then he'd gone about it the right way. Agreeing with DI Spragg that Catherine's identity should be withheld might have been a serious mistake, informing Patrick of the true facts might have been another. Jesus, where was it all going to end?

He wondered if DI Spragg knew something he didn't. So much for Andy keeping them up-to-date on his progress. If only he was close enough to Finnegan to inquire as to what was new to the case. But the thought of hearing Finnegan almost smirk down the phone on possibly knowing that Matt was in the shit was enough to prevent him from making that call. He'd just have to be patient. Then he thought of Tess and of her reaction when told it was Catherine who'd been drowned, not a stone's throw from where she'd been reared. A task he was dreading having to undertake.

Leave your worries at the door, he told himself as he pulled up outside the house. It was what his father used to say. He had a shower when he arrived in. Back in the kitchen, he decided to start on dinner, it would take his mind off things. He lifted out the frying pan, placed it on the cooker, poured on enough olive oil and found the lamb chunks in the fridge. Jackie was on the floor playing with the twins. She mentioned that her sister Aine had booked a house in West Cork for the following week.

'It now turns out that Seamus can't join her owing to some major work commitment.' She badly attempted to mimic Seamus's broad cultured voice. 'Anyway, Aine wants Mam and myself to join her. It's a four bedroomed house, all fully paid for so it won't cost me anything.'

Jackie wasn't the safest of drivers, West Cork was a fair distance and once off the main road, it could be tricky manoeuvring around those narrow byroads. But that aside, they couldn't afford a holiday. This would do her good and the twins wouldn't be such a handful with a bucket load of support from a doting Gran and aunt.

'Why don't I drive you down on Saturday? Aine's jeep has plenty of space for all of you during the week.' He enjoyed driving. The scenery would be an added bonus.

'That's your way of telling me you don't trust my driving.' She grinned up at him.

And of course, she was right.

////////

8.06pm

Even Truman was up for another round of the park. There were the usual high-pitched squeals from kids in the playground. Pockets of teenagers nestled among the high rocks by the tennis courts. All the soccer pitches in use with supporters along the edge shouting encouragement. At the far end of the park, she stopped to admire the view across the city. A couple of cranes signalled the return of some serious construction. Sometimes you had to appreciate what you had and she was fortunate to have this on her doorstep.

That afternoon she had scanned through what she could find on Egypt's political history. A revolution in 2011 had the Supreme Council of the Armed Forces taking control after the president was removed. The following year Mohamed Morsi was sworn in as president. He promoted Abdel Tettah-et-Sisi as Minister of Defence and ultimately Commander-in-Chief of the Egyptian Armed Forces. But the president's push for unlimited power by freely legislating without answering to anyone led quickly to protests around the country calling for his resignation. Abdel Tettah-et-Sisi was involved with the military coup that removed Morsi from office. In 2014 Sisi was sworn in as president. His government had given the army unchecked powers.

After reading it through Cathy was under no illusion of the powerful position held by Elijah's father, Khafu, in Egypt. She was aware of how political favours worked between nations. You scratch my back and I'll scratch yours and it will remain our secret. If Egypt and Britain were involved in such games and if Elijah was responsible for Catherine's drowning, then it was unlikely he would pay for his crime.

Once home she took a call from the sergeant. A call she'd been expecting.

'You're not the only one summonsed and no question of changing the time with me having to travel down from Dublin.' She cut herself a slice of soda bread. 'Whatever he's about to tell us is anyone's guess.'

It had been late afternoon when Superintendent Clarke contacted her. He had already passed it by her boss and advised her not to be late. He'd no intention of discussing the matter further until then.

'We don't know if Jeff is to be present, but I'm sure he will. Cummins hasn't been notified of anything or he'd have told me.' She opened the fridge and checked through the second shelf until she found the tub of pesto.

There was the sound of a baby crying in the background as he asked, 'Would Andy know anything about this?'

'I don't know.' She had attempted to contact him that afternoon but her call just rang out. He hadn't thought it worth his while to call her back.

'Right, well, I'll see you in the morning then.' He sounded relieved that it wasn't just him with no clue of what was going on.

'See you then.'

She had the most to lose. It had been her plan, her push to convince the sergeant to keep quiet on what he knew. What if she ended up charged with entering the Muscanna's residence under false pretences? Even Melissa and Patrick were in the clear. Again, that too had been her plan.

Hopefully, she wasn't about to be found out and end up having to pay the pied piper.

friday - 3rd july

Friday - 3rd July

An accident on the motorway had traffic backed up for three kilometres. As she nudged along the hard shoulder, she noticed the fragments of a blown-out tyre and then the two-car pile-up by the centre road barrier. In off the motorway was an ambulance with paramedics dealing with a man lying on a stretcher. Next up, were two teenagers being questioned by gardai. A garda stepped in front of her and raised his hand. She stopped. Rolling down her window she heard a driver on her right loudly asking, *Who the hell do ya think ya are?* She noticed the garda nod. However, on producing her ID, he was quick to clear the way and wave her through.

Totally flustered and ten minutes late when she arrived at the station, she was glad to find Sergeant Bracken waiting for her in the public office. After she quickly freshened up, they were both escorted to the Superintendent's office.

She beckoned the sergeant to go ahead of her. On noticing Jeff all buttoned up in the corner she pulled her shoulders back and stepped forward. But when she entered, she suddenly felt her knees about to go from under her when she recognised who it was sitting opposite the Superintendent.

'DI Spragg, I understand you already know DI Andy Scott.' The Superintendent sounded ever so chummy.

Andy's eyes narrowed as he flaunted a smile. 'It's good to see you again, DI Spragg.' His tight grip of her hand told her she could stop worrying. But by God did he have some explaining to do!

The Superintendent sounded anxious to get started.

'DI Scott here believes there may be a connection between our victim and the disappearance of a woman from London. This missing woman was a Catherine Muscanna, originally from Carrabhain. She was the daughter of Tess Fowley.' He turned to Cathy. 'I believe it was Tess Fowley who found that stolen money last year which helped close off your investigation at the time. I presume you and the sergeant here are well acquainted with her.'

She and the sergeant nodded.

The Superintendent continued. 'We will first need to confirm DI Scott's theory. Catherine Muscanna's dental records have been forwarded to the forensic team. They should have something for us later today.' He sat back in his chair. 'If it is her, it's hard to believe her mother wasn't concerned on not hearing from her in almost a month yet her brother saw it fit to head to London and report her missing?'

Cathy was almost afraid to breathe.

It was Andy who replied, 'According to the housekeeper, Catherine Muscanna had implied that her parents were dead. Not the strongest of family ties by all account. And of course her link with Carrabhain cannot be overlooked seeing as it was where she was drowned.'

The superintendent turned to the sergeant. 'Were you aware that Patrick Fowley had gone to London to report her missing?'

His eyebrows rose. 'I knew he was heading to London to check up on her before he planned to return to Canada.'

Cathy bunched up her mouth to smother a smile at how believable he sounded. But any trace of that smile vanished when she sensed the Superintendent's eyes on her. He was no one's fool; it wouldn't surprise her if he knew of her plan to return to work only to notify her boss at the last minute of her week's holiday. A week that coincided with Patrick's trip to London. Conscious that she and Jeff were anything but close, it would be best if Jeff was left thinking that she knew less about the case than she did. She had been the one to tip him off on the whereabouts of the suspects. But the Superintendent also had to consider that if she had been to London, she had possibly met Andy Scott which was why he found himself assigned to the case. It would only lead to further complications if he were to dwell on it too deeply now that the London Metropolitan Police were involved.

His focus turned to Andy. 'From this station, Detective Finnegan and Sergeant Bracken here will be on hand if you need them for anything.'

Jeff nodded towards Andy.

'Now we get to the hub of the situation. DI Scott here is in charge of this ongoing investigation.' The Superintendent gestured towards Andy. 'You take it from here.'

Andy glanced around at his assembled audience.

'There is a strong possibility that Catherine's husband, Elijah Muscanna, is responsible for his wife's disappearance.' His voice exuded authority. 'However, last week his father, Khafu, contacted the British Embassy to report his son missing. We have Elijah on CCTV boarding a flight to Cairo. He appears to be alone but his father believes he was abducted on that flight. He also believes that Elijah's wife, Catherine, was behind such an abduction.'

'What?' Cathy blurted out.

But a glance from Andy told her to shut it. His eyes were then quick to settle on Jeff in the corner. 'Until we know for sure that what we've been told is the truth and if your victim is Catherine Muscanna then we need to keep a lid on this in the hope of smoking out whoever is responsible.' His attention returned to the Superintendent. 'Khafu insisted there be no media coverage over his son's disappearance. We have agreed to that but we have also decided to keep from Elijah's family that Catherine had been reported missing.' He then focused on her. 'At least until we are sure that Elijah is in the clear with regard to his wife's disappearance.'

The information was so far from what she'd expected. If Elijah were in hiding and supported by his father then the investigation was going nowhere.

Andy held up his hand when she went to ask a question.

'Elijah's father is not someone to be ignored. He's highly ranked in the Egyptian Army. It seems his youngest son was kidnapped last year. He successfully negotiated with his abductors and expects to do the same again. We can't say for sure if his father is out to protect Elijah or if Elijah was actually abducted.'

'And what about Catherine?' Cathy asked without thinking. She was too keenly aware of the facts he hadn't mentioned such as the empty tub of prawns hidden in the cupboard. Elijah's wife in Cairo expecting their second child, or his plan to return and live permanently in Cairo. Vital facts he wasn't prepared to reveal.

Andy took on a stubborn look. 'We'll do everything to get to the bottom of this. But her identity must remain classified until we know more.'

Jeff mentioned how the suspects in custody believed Catherine was an evil woman.

Andy nodded. 'I checked them out. They have been involved in small time burglaries but nothing as serious as murder.'

'Torture and murder was way out of their league. I mean they just didn't murder her they also tortured her,' remarked the sergeant.

Andy eyed him closely. 'Yeah, you're right.'

The sergeant's glance in her direction was met with blankness.

'Did neighbours notice anything suspicious about the Muscannas?' asked Jeff.

'They were a couple who kept to themselves, were happily married for twenty years and had no children.'

'If Catherine Muscanna is our victim then we have her identity and those responsible for her drowning.' The satisfaction in the Superintendent's voice was unmissable. For him, the prospects of the case being nicely packaged for the DPP was a perfect result.

Andy nodded. 'It was a stroke of genius to come by such an accurate tip-off of their whereabouts as quickly as you did.'

Cathy felt herself stiffen in the chair.

'Yes, we were fortunate there.' The Superintendent fiddled with his pen but never looked up. He thankfully didn't intend to add anything more.

Then Jeff put the question that she herself was about to ask.

'What has DI Spragg to do with this case?'

The Superintendent capped his pen. 'Ah yes, well, DI Scott has previously worked with DI Spragg. And with Reeves out of work for the next few weeks, someone needs to hold the fort here. If the victim is Catherine Muscanna, liaison departments in both jurisdictions have agreed to allow DI Spragg to work alongside DI Scott on this for a week.' He took in Jeff. 'You will need to finalise the case for the DPP.' He then turned to Cathy. 'Your job is to find anything that links our victim to our suspects. You will share your findings with Detective Finnegan and DI Scott's team.'

'But she has nothing to do with this investigation.' Jeff sounded so adamant as if driven by a sense of fair justice on the correct procedure to be adhered to rather than accepting that he was being sidelined. After all, he was in charge of the investigation, the one who should have made such a decision or at least have been privy to it before then.

The Superintendent again lifted his pen off the desk. 'You're needed here.' And with no response required to that, he added, 'I think that's everything covered for now.'

As Cathy stood, she heard the Superintendent explain to Andy how one of the suspects had a steel plate inserted in his leg while the other was lucky not to have lost his sight. She glanced back at Andy from the doorway. There he sat like the cat that got the cream.

As she and the sergeant arrived at the car park, he asked, 'How do you think Elijah's father will react when he discovers that Catherine is dead?'

She clicked open her car door.

'He might already be aware of it if his son murdered her. It might be their defence mechanism. You know, get in there first with British intelligence to make a case for Elijah's so-called abduction by focusing on them as being in some way responsible. God knows how long he'll remain hidden away.'

She sat into her car and drove from the car park.

10.45am

When Matt dropped into the driver's seat, he smiled at the thought of how lucky he'd been. Not only was he safe from any internal investigation but he was back in the loop, for now. His name would be attributed to the investigation. That was another step forward. Before starting his shift at the station, he decided he'd head home first and share a coffee with Jackie.

She was in the kitchen organising clothes while the twins busied themselves in the playpen.

'This is a surprise,' she said when he came up and hugged her.

He listened to her suggestion that they leave early the following morning for Cork. She had it all worked out, the twins were usually fine up to about noon. If they arrived at the cottage by then she would put them down for a nap and that would give her and Matt time to empty the car and sit around to enjoy lunch.

Yeah, that sounded like a plan. He nodded as he switched on the kettle.

Ella began to cry, which had them turning in time to watch Aiden step shakily across the playpen. His first step. Jackie grabbed her mobile and began recording. 'Come on, do it again Aiden,' she said when he dropped onto his backside.

Encouraged by them both, Aiden pulled himself up and glanced up at them before taking another two steps. Then he flopped down again on his backside as if he'd had enough.

As Ella continued to cry Matt picked her up. Her fingernails scratched the flesh of his neck but it didn't take from how he was feeling. That was one happy moment.

Another surprise awaited him at the station where he found Andy Scott by the counter in conversation with Deegan. Andy explained how he was anxious to view the precise location where the victim had been found.

Once out on the street, Andy pulled on Matt as he made for the squad car. 'I'd also like to talk to Patrick, not question him as such, just an informal chat. Could you arrange it?'

'Wait here a minute.' Matt crossed the street.

Thankfully it was Patrick who answered the door. He focused on DI Scott across the street as Matt made his request.

'I don't see why I should talk to him.' He sounded gruff and went to close over the door.

Matt raised his hand to stop him. 'He's here to help. What's the problem in talking to him for even five minutes?'

Patrick studied him for a minute.

'I won't talk to him here. Tell him to be at the bridge in Croon in twenty minutes.'

Matt nodded, that gave him enough time to head to Doonaleigh for a quick inspection of the marina.

Twenty minutes later Matt pulled up by the bridge. Croon seemed lifeless. Patrick was by the first picnic table along the river walk. With a bag of lettuce in hand, he was feeding a family of four swans. Noticing them approach he threw what remained in the bag far enough out for the swans to turn and glide out to fetch it.

The three of them neatly sat around the table.

'Thanks for agreeing to talk to me,' said Andy.

No further pleasantries were forthcoming, no sense of friendliness, no smiles, no *great to see you again* or *how are things?* They could just as easily have been strangers who'd never met before.

'What do you want?' Patrick's accusing tone was full on.

Matt wondered if Patrick had guessed it had been Andy who had asked that Patrick hand over his passport. Yeah, if he were a betting man, he'd bet on it.

'Talk us through your recent contact with Catherine?' Andy asked.

A sharp inhale of breath. 'I'll not repeat what I've already told you.'

Matt felt Andy should have eased slowly into a chat and made Patrick feel more comfortable before sounding so direct.

'Elijah? Have you ever spoken to him?' There he was, straight in again.

Patrick looked out from those hooded eyes of his watching the swan gliding back towards the river bank.

'I've spoken to him a couple of times.'

Patrick's words had sent a ding through the air that hit the high note. Matt couldn't decide if he should be writing it all down. But reckoned if he produced his notebook Patrick was sure to get up and walk away. After all, it was only an informal chat.

'Why didn't you mention that before now?' asked Andy.

'You never asked,' replied Patrick.

'Who contacted who first?' asked Matt.

Patrick focused on the swans bunched together in front of them hoping there was more food to feed on.

'He contacted me after I'd initially spoken to Catherine. It was he who encouraged me to visit London first before coming here. He even suggested that the end of May would be the best time to see London.'

Matt couldn't understand why Patrick was being so furtive with the truth. 'Why are you so sure that Elijah is responsible for Catherine's murder?'

Patrick glanced at him as if he were dealing with a moron. The recent children's party and past pleasantries forgotten about, Matt too was now viewed as a stranger.

'It was he who suggested I come to London in late May. He planned for me to be there, to be his fall guy if things went wrong.'

All calls to and from Elijah's mobile, landline and business number would be scrutinised. Patrick's mobile number was on file from the information he provided on the Missing Person's Report. Those calls to Patrick would be picked up. The three of them sitting there knew that. Perhaps that was why Patrick had decided to come clean.

'Did Catherine know you had spoken to Elijah?' asked Matt.

He watched Patrick think, no split-second decisions here, *will I or won't I* was being weighed up until his response was settled on.

'Yeah, she knew,' replied Patrick.

Andy tapped his fingers off the table.

'What caused the family row years back?'

Patrick was slow to answer. 'If you want to know that then you better ask Tess. And if Tess is questioned then we'll go public on identifying Catherine as your drowned victim.' He folded his arms. 'I haven't yet figured out why her identity hasn't been revealed but I don't think it's something you want.'

With that, he pulled himself up, grabbed the empty bag and walked away from them.

6.30pm

She had to pull in onto the hard shoulder when Andy had phoned her half an hour after she'd left the meeting. She listened to his apology on not returning her call, his offer of dinner was another means of saying sorry. Happy that this case would have her following him to London had more than calmed her down. She hadn't felt like recommending a restaurant. The last thing she needed was to have to rush home to make herself presentable for a dinner date. Not forgetting he'd already seen her in the only decent dress to her name.

'So, you're not keen in meeting up this evening. I'm heading back in the morning.' He had sounded disappointed.

She owed him big time. And spending the evening with him to hear the unscripted version of what he knew on the case would be interesting.

'Why don't you come to my place for dinner?' In her own surroundings, she'd feel more comfortable.

When that had been agreed on, she had given him her address.

She had left work early for her hairdresser appointment. Then it was on to Supervalu for a dinner dish and the bakery next door for dessert. Arriving home, she took a quick shower and changed into her best jeans and silk camisole top. She hadn't weighed herself but the jeans were a good fit.

When Andy arrived with a bottle of expensive wine, Truman barked before leaning in against her leg. He held a look of suspicion when Andy went to rub him down.

In the kitchen, she checked on the chicken dish and remembered to place the garlic bread in the oven while

Andy filled her in on his afternoon with the sergeant and his *chat* with Patrick.

Confounded by the news she said, 'How could Patrick have forgotten to mention his contact with Elijah?'

Andy stood with an inquiring expression.

'We have a contact in the Vancouver police. According to him after Patrick had been granted citizenship, his girlfriend at the time contacted them three times claiming he assaulted her. But she later dropped those claims.'

It alarmed her that Patrick had previous for assault. But she'd like to read the case notes for herself. It wasn't that she didn't believe Andy. But the response he got from the police officer could have been down to the questions he'd been asked and how they'd been asked.

She found the corkscrew for the bottle Andy was holding. And Truman continued to watch him from his basket.

With a glass of wine in hand, Andy walked around, checking the place over. He complimented her on the garden which fortunately had the benefit of her dahlias blooming earlier than expected. Her favourite ink blue salvias mixed in with her light and dark coloured agapanthus couldn't have looked more impressive. He viewed the large painting on the wall in the living room. It was of a box with a jumbled-up number of eyes, ears and noses. The trick was to guess how many there were of each. It pleased her that no one had yet guessed correctly.

'What more have you discovered on Elijah?' she asked when all dishes had been placed on the table and they took their seats.

'He met Catherine in his final year at Oxford and decided to remain in London. He was into stocks and shares even while he was in college. He set up his business with the money he'd made. His parents were unhappy when he married Catherine. Elijah drew away from them at that stage.' He helped himself to a generous serving of chicken.

'Our Ambassador there happens to be a friend of Khafu Muscanna. It seems there was a family reconciliation some years back. His father arranged his second marriage.'

There was an obvious heathery scent of rosemary from the chicken.

'They felt Catherine had too much control over Elijah. When his second wife provided a son, Elijah gave Catherine an ultimatum. Either his second wife came and lived with them in London or they all settled in Cairo. Catherine never wanted to live there which is why they believe she is behind whatever happened to him.'

She watched him sip his wine.

'Do you believe that Elijah was abducted?'

He was quick to answer. 'Those at the Embassy believe it. The family is deeply upset. His second son was born on Tuesday.' He sat forward. 'Not something he'd have wanted to miss.'

She agreed.

He re-filled both glasses.

'I had a call from Nigel Green of Scotland Yard late on Tuesday. He sounded overly interested in this, wants a daily up-to-date report on our progress. It's my guess he knows more than he's prepared to say. That lot is always cloak and dagger in secrecy. It was also he who insisted that if it's confirmed that Catherine Muscanna is your victim that it remains confidential until Elijah's whereabouts are established. The last thing he wants are rumours bubbling up around the place. He's determined that we are seen to be making every effort to bring those responsible to justice. I think he's afraid that if Elijah was abducted on that flight and his wife abducted in London this could explode into something impossible to control when it's eventually picked up by the media.'

When she asked why he hadn't returned her call from the previous day he replied, 'Once you're asked to a meeting with an official from Scotland Yard you suddenly get paranoid. I couldn't be sure if calls to and from my mobile were being tracked. Nor could I risk them knowing we were in contact especially when I had recommended your assistance on this.' He smirked. 'And the idea of surprising you was too good an opportunity to miss.'

She could feel herself smile.

'OK so now explain to me why I'm heading to London? This excuse of wanting to find out more about Catherine Muscanna is a bit of a whitewash.' She arched her eyebrows. 'For our part, we know her identity and have our murderers, end of. Nothing more required.'

He took her in with a look of satisfaction. 'OK, the truth is that Scotland Yard together with the London Met wants total control of this. Concealing her identity is paramount.' He stopped eating. With elbows on the table, he raised both hands and clasped them together. 'Remember that drug bust from six months back.' She nodded. 'A major part of the intelligence on that came from us. This is what we want in return.'

'But why?' she asked.

'Elijah's father is a powerful man. We can't afford to damage relationships between both countries over this. That could easily happen.'

The asparagus had a crunch to it which was the way she liked it and the garlic bread for once wasn't burnt.

'This is really good,' he said taking a second helping of chicken. 'By the way, I loved your place in Carrabhain although it wasn't what I'd expected.'

She grinned. 'What, you imagined *chickens in around the door and pigs in the yard* kind of house?'

'No,' he looked affronted. 'But it was more modern than I expected.' After a moment he added, 'maybe I was expecting *chickens in around the door.*'

She was glad that the dinner had passed muster. After he finished his sticky toffee pudding, they moved to the living room and made themselves comfortable on the sofa.

She couldn't easily shift the case from her mind. Suddenly struck by a thought she asked, 'When the housekeeper arrived on that Wednesday after they'd left, was the house alarmed?'

'No. Mary Simpson guessed they'd left in a hurry and before you ask, no that had never happened before. And no again, never before had she been asked to stay away on a day they had planned to leave.'

She considered this. 'If on the one hand Elijah was responsible for the abduction of Catherine and something went wrong which was why he changed his travel arrangements, leaving the place in a mess wouldn't have bothered him knowing Mary would arrive the following week to put things right. But leaving without alarming the house wasn't something he'd have done, especially when he had left his mobile and computer behind. He was a practical man by all accounts. Practical men make sure to alarm their valuable property.' She watched Andy watching her. 'Now let's assume that Catherine was ill in bed from eating those prawns when Elijah left. Then how did her kidnappers enter the house? There was no evidence of a break-in. Just imagine Catherine making for the window on hearing the doorbell. She sees strangers on the doorstep. Do you honestly think she'd have dragged herself down the stairs to inquire as to what they wanted?'

He nodded. 'And if they had arrived while Elijah was there or he had given them a key he'd have insisted they alarm the house before they left.' He made a face. 'But perhaps he wasn't thinking straight if he was about to have his wife disposed of.'

She watched him.

'Will you do something for me?'

He squinted, unsure of what was coming next. 'What?'

She drew in a careful breath. 'If I'm heading to London to work with you on this, it would really help if Sergeant Bracken accompanied me.' She raised a hand when he sat up ready to object. 'I know he doesn't have much experience as a detective but he's someone I can depend on.' She left her glass on the table and fully turned to him. 'Think about it for a minute. When you and I worked together before on a case it just wasn't me, there were two others from my team. We worked well because we didn't depend on each other.'

'Is that what you're afraid of, having to depend on me?'

She shook her head. He wasn't getting her meaning. 'You are in charge of this case and I'm the outsider. Your team is already fully involved. Do you expect them to take time to show me the ropes when this investigation isn't your ordinary run of the mill case?' She came closer to him. 'Let's make this productive for all involved.'

'I don't think Superintendent Clarke will agree to this.' He sounded certain.

'Oh, I think he will.' She knew it wouldn't take much of a push for it to happen. 'You can be pretty persuasive when you want to be.'

'OK,' he grinned. 'I'll see what I can do.'

On noticing the extended rack of CDs against the wall he rose to check them out. After a minute he opened the CD player and replaced the CD she'd probably listened to a month ago with the one he'd chosen. She was surprised to hear that voice of Ed Sheeran singing *Thinking out loud*. It was one of Sinead's favourites.

'Will you dance?' he asked stretching his hand towards her.

'No way,' she cried in a laugh.

'Oh, come on, just live a little.'

This is crazy she told herself as she stood to take his hand.

His arm went around her. The music happily carried her along. Her head dropped against his shoulder and he pulled her closer. When the music eventually stopped, she stood feeling his breath on her cheek.

But the moment was abruptly shattered by the sound of the doorbell. Truman loudly barked and moved out along the hallway only to return to encourage her forward as he excitably slid along the tiled floor.

'It's only me,' came a familiar voice.

Cathy opened the door.

'I was out visiting Aoife. I tried your mobile but as usual, it's switched off.' She stepped in from the porch. 'When I saw your car, I decided I'd call in for a minute.' Cathy was handed a jar. 'Aoife gave it to me. It's supposed to be the best but I'm really not one for chutney.' She screwed up her face. 'By the way who's that second car in the driveway? I hate parking on the road.'

In the kitchen, Andy seemed at home refilling both glasses. Lucy stood with her mouth open as Cathy introduced him.

'How about a glass of wine?' he asked her.

'No thanks,' replied a gobsmacked Lucy. 'I'm driving.'

Saturday - 4ᵗʰ July

11.30am

It wasn't easy to drink another large glass of water. She imagined her bladder would burst from all it was holding.

It was before ten that morning when she answered Andy's third call in his attempt to contact her. His boss had left him a message. The dental records of Catherine Muscanna matched those of the victim. He suggested for Andy to talk with the suspects before returning to London. Authorities had sanctioned it. Andy believed it would be beneficial for her to accompany him.

They had enjoyed too much wine the previous night leaving Lucy the job of driving Andy back to his hotel. His car was parked in her driveway. He had agreed to take a taxi to her place and they would travel together to the hospital.

When the doorbell went, she left without even setting the alarm.

They argued in the driveway over who would drive. To prevent such nonsense continuing she sat into her car, pulled on her seatbelt and revved up. Andy eventually sat into the passenger seat.

Driving through Ranelagh she realised that Lucy knew of Catherine's identity the previous night when she'd called. But like the rest of them, it was top secret information.

On arriving at the hospital, they easily found the private room with a guard stationed at the door.

Both men watched them enter. She introduced herself

and then Andy. It concerned her that a translator might be required. She should have covered that possibility before turning up but she guessed it would be next to impossible to find an available translator on a Saturday afternoon.

She glanced from one to the other of these murderers surprised at how vulnerable they appeared. Not a couple likely to instill fear in anyone. She could identify them from what the sergeant had told her. The larger one was Butrus Shala, his right eye bandaged, his arm in a sling. While the other with his leg in traction was Urbonas Hoxha.

Andy looked up after studying their charts.

'We have identified the woman you drowned.'

No response from either of them.

'After you serve your time here for murder you will then be returned to the UK to serve time for abduction.'

'No, no,' cried Butrus. 'We live in UK, do time in UK prison. She very evil woman.' He pulled himself around and lowered his feet to the ground.

Then Urbonas nodded at Butrus.

'We do time in UK prison.' His breathing sounded heavy.

As the men perfectly understood what had been said, the fog began to clear from across Cathy's brain. These men had fully believed they'd be heading back to the UK. Realising that wasn't going to happen had naturally scared them. They feared what treatment might await them in our prisons.

Cathy stood in front of Butrus's bed. 'It doesn't work like that. You do the crime here, you do the time here.' She sounded more determined than she felt. 'Those who beat you up might have done so on discovering what you did to that woman. That made them angry.' She ignored Andy's puzzled glance towards her. 'If we were to report that you were remorseful. That you fully-cooperated with us on what you know about the woman, it would help your case. I could also recommend that you are isolated in prison from anyone likely to harm you.'

She could make out from their reaction that they understood her.

Urbonas cowered further in the bed, the blanket raised up to his chin. If it were possible, he'd happily disappear. He spoke to Butrus in their language. That was followed by a lengthy response.

When the men were silent Andy said, 'She wasn't an evil woman. She worked to support children from immigrant families living in the UK.' Noticing the look of suspicion from both men he added. 'It's the truth.'

Butrus sat with a look of total confusion.

'He tell me she and husband live rich life from money made from boats full of migrants crossing to Italy.'

'That's not true. Now, who told you that?' asked Andy.

Cathy couldn't catch what he said but Andy did.

'Nathan Warral,' Andy answered her look of inquiry. 'A man who doesn't do murder himself but knows who to get to do it at the right price.'

Butrus's shoulders dropped further as he repeated himself, 'He contact me. He tell me she was evil, that she make money from boats full of migrants who then drown in the sea.'

'How did he contact you?' she asked.

'I have second mobile at my home. He contact me through that. That is all I know.' He stood up and slowly walked towards the bathroom.

'No, wait.' She reached for his arm. 'Why did you torture

her?' She looked into his eyes. Her hand felt like ripping his arm out of its socket in retaliation of his treatment of Catherine.

His eyes filled up before he glanced at his feet.

'My sister, she fifteen, she and me flee Libya and take a boat to Italy. Men in charge of boat torture her in front of me. She bleed to death. He,' a quick glance towards Urbonas. 'His mother and father drown in boat.' His lips quivered. 'Revenge. That was why.' He pulled away from her.

She took a deep breath thinking how he possibly would have been a decent man if he hadn't witnessed what he had.

Butrus walked into the bathroom and slammed the door shut.

They had all they were going to get and left.

Monday - 6th July

4.50pm

He thought he was hearing things when he got that call from Superintendent Clarke. Earlier he had worked with Detective Finnegan in preparing the file for the DPP, it was interesting to learn the exact procedure in compiling such a file. The suspects had named Nathan Warral as the man who had paid them for drowning their victim. But according to Detective Finnegan, he was just the middle-man in it all.

Matt replayed the Superintendent's words around in his head.

'I've agreed that you can work on the case with DI Spragg in London for the week. All arrangements have been made. This will be no holiday. You will be working early mornings and late into the evenings. And remember, keep it to yourself, this is just between us for now. Don't go mentioning it to anyone, especially Detective Finnegan. Make out you are taking holidays and leave it at that.'

'Thank you, Sir,' was all he had managed.

He'd arrived back from Cork the previous evening to a house that felt as empty as a grave without Jackie and the kids. He never imagined that such an unexpected trip to London would land in his lap at such an opportune time. And to be involved in such a high-profile case involving the London Met with Andy Scott in charge was something he'd have dreamt of. Of course, he knew the decision to include him on this investigation wasn't just down to the

Superintendent. DI Spragg must have had a say in it. She could have picked anyone to accompany her. And she'd picked him.

He told Deegan he'd decided to join Jackie and the kids for the week. Deegan was happy to take responsibility for the station. It wouldn't be a problem for him. And he'd texted Detective Finnegan with the same line but hadn't received a response.

He noticed Patrick crossing the street. There was now an obvious heaviness in his stance and a roundness in the shoulders. He was thinner than when he'd arrived at the start of his holiday. There had been no sign of Melissa or the kids all week. Matt didn't know if they had left for somewhere.

The sooner they had the truth on what happened to Catherine the better for all of them. When Matt got to London, his job would be to prove whether Patrick was innocent or guilty.

He headed home to pack for his early morning start.

//////

4.07pm

Cathy had left work early. It was such a warm summer's day that patients and visitors sat out around the grounds of the hospital. Inside she bought a bottle of sparkling water from the shop before checking the hospital's directory. From there she continued along the corridor to the lift.

The previous Friday after Lucy's initial shock of finding

Andy at the house, they'd sat and chatted for hours. Although Cathy and Andy had been drinking, she remembered with some clarity about how Andy had described his difficulty in being the tough guy with his kids.

'Vicky and a mate were arrested for disturbance of the peace after leaving a night club stoned out of their minds.' He had shaken his head. 'Still in school and underaged, both sets of parents lied to.' He made it sound baffling. 'If you met them you would think butter wouldn't melt in their mouth.'

When Lucy asked how he'd handled her he replied, 'I had to accept that she couldn't be trusted. Now she never knows where I might pop up. I call to her school whenever I pass that way, just to check in on her, make sure she's actually there. Even when she's at her friends, I'd personally call with an excuse I need to talk to her.' His smile widened. 'The thing is she knows exactly what I'm up to. It embarrasses the hell out of her. Embarrassment hits a kid better than anything.'

When the lift opened on the second floor she stepped out to head as directed. About to pass a ward, she stopped when she recognised Jennifer by a bed. She was dealing with a patient who kept nodding. It was hard to tell if the patient was taking anything in or if her nodding was her mechanism of blanking what she didn't want to hear. The nodding stopped as Jennifer wrote up her case notes. Without even a smile she walked away and made for the door.

A look of shock took hold on finding Cathy in front of her. She wrapped her arms around the chart she was holding.

'What are you doing here?'

Cathy remembered Lucy's advice. *Imagine yourself as an*

actress, playing a part in a film.

With a lightness of voice, she replied, 'Well, I can't seem to get hold of you on the phone. Nothing for it then but to come in person.' She smiled.

Jennifer stared at her.

'Are you serious!'

'Well, why else would I be here?' She then checked her mobile for the time. 'Any chance of us having a coffee and a chat? Surely you're due a break at some stage.'

Jennifer did a quick glance around her.

'I can't just leave to accommodate you.' Her voice, hard as nails.

'Why not?' Cathy sounded disappointed.

Coming closer, Jennifer replied, 'Because I am working, that's why.'

Cathy sighed before she said, 'Fine, but I just wanted to make sure things are OK between us.'

A ward orderly glanced at them as she passed with a trolley load of cups, saucers, plates of biscuits, teapots, and coffee thermal canisters.

Cathy smothered a smile when Jennifer sounded suspicious in asking, 'Are you drunk?'

With her mouth hanging open she took a second to reply, 'Drunk! Me! Of course not. Is it that difficult to believe I want to know things are fine between us?' She lifted her eyebrows and held her eyes open wide.

A doctor came through a set of doors at the end of the corridor and was heading towards them.

'You better leave,' snapped Jennifer.

'So, we're OK then? asked Cathy.

As if not sure how to respond but aware of the doctor almost on top of her, Jennifer replied, 'Yeah, we're OK. Now go.'

'Here, I got you this.' She pulled the bottle of water from her bag. 'As you say yourself it's important to stay hydrated. I remembered you prefer sparking to natural water.'

The bottle was snatched from her hand.

Attempting to hug her daughter would be a step too far. As if imagining that was a possibility Jennifer was quick to join the doctor and head down the corridor away from her.

It wasn't like all had been forgiven but at least she'd broken the ice. She made for the lift imagining that Jennifer was perhaps wondering if her mother was showing the first signs of Alzheimer's.

Tuesday - 7th July

10.03am

Since the Superintendent had agreed to allow Sergeant Bracken to accompany her, their stay in London had been reduced to four days instead of five. On the flight to London, Cathy had explained to the sergeant how they would need to remain in the background on this as it was Andy's investigation. Attempting to include detectives from other jurisdictions onto an investigation was never easy. The one thing they had to avoid was being considered a nuisance. The sergeant, in turn, had wanted to know everything she knew about the Muscannas from her previous trip to London. She *forwarded* him the photos she'd taken of Ali Defel at the Muscanna residence, which he carefully studied, she also explained about the housekeeper, Mary Simpson.

Arriving into the open plan office, the place pulsed from that familiar energy of phones ringing, copying machines hissing, water dispenser gurgling as well as that tapping away on computers.

Andy introduced her to the team as a senior detective and Sergeant Bracken as an assistant, both on loan for just a week. Interesting how he emphasised that word *just*.

The team consisted of Ben, a man in his forties, tall and thin, badly in need of a haircut who continually chewed gum. Mark was in his thirties with a snub nose and flushed faced. He seemed absorbed by whatever he was viewing on his computer screen but acknowledged them with a wave of his hand. Eric was in his forties, impeccably dressed and bald as an egg, which suited him perfectly. In her thirties was Rebecca, her short skirt emphasised her long legs and obvious hips while her smile was borderline pleasant.

'They are familiar with Catherine Muscanna's family, the Fowley's of Carrabhain. We are fortunate to have them on board,' Andy concluded.

A nod from Ben as he cleared a desk which was next to an empty one by the window. She and the sergeant settled in.

Rebecca dropped three large files in front of Cathy. 'Something for you both to be getting on with.' She then joined Andy in his office.

The vertical blinds shook and swayed when she solidly closed over Andy's door. The two interacted in a very business-like manner and for some reason, Cathy imagined the conversation had to do with their arrival. She might have been paranoid but she would make sure never to ask Rebecca for any assistance.

Cathy began to scan through the files that related to Catherine Muscanna. She took a minute to assess how best they could make headway efficiently before handing the sergeant the top file which included details from Catherine's credit card statements plus receipts for the last month.

'Start by mapping back on her movements from Tuesday 19th May from the attached receipts.'

She pulled the second file towards her and read the glowing report of her employer from the housekeeper, Mary Simpson. Behind it was a note from Ben. He had Mary checked out. She had no previous conviction of any kind; however, her husband had twice been charged with theft. Scanning Catherine's visa card statements going back six months she found the largest payout was for £3,000. How easy it made things when the invoice covering that amount was attached to the statement.

It was a payment for paintings. Cathy recognised the name of the artist, Maggie Williams. Odd that Catherine, known to be frugal would have paid that amount for amateurish work. Hand-written on the bottom of the invoice was, *Catherine, I so appreciate your continual support, Maggie.* Cathy googled the artist. The woman exhibited her work a few times a year in New York. Her paintings could be bought online but none of them costing anything like the amount Catherine had paid out for her pieces. The fact those paintings hung in Catherine's office was significant enough for Cathy to decide to check it out further.

Eric was arguing with someone on the phone, Ben appeared engrossed in a conversation with Rebecca and Mark was heading out the door. As she hadn't a clue how to work the phone system, she grabbed her mobile from her bag and dialled the number from the invoice. It went to voice mail. She gave her name and asked Maggie if she would call her when she got a chance.

////////

12.35pm

When Andy returned and entered his office Matt noticed the case board facing him on the other side of the open door. Not so much a case board but a wall of glass covered with information. He went to check it out. Photos ran along the top. First up was of Catherine from the autopsy report, all relevant details underneath. Next was Elijah, nothing there that Matt hadn't already known. But he hadn't known that Ali Defel had only returned to London in 2010 or that Andrew Palmer had admitted to drug and gambling addictions.

Then, Patrick Fowley, the photo had been taken by Andy on Friday.

Refuses to explain why he and Catherine were estranged for so long.

At the residence on Thursday 21st May, the day Catherine was handed over to the suspects at Holyhead. (Only his word that Catherine had suggested they meet up that day).

HAS FORM FOR ASSAULT. (Assaulted previous girlfriend).

NEVER MENTIONED HIS COMMUNICATION WITH ELIJAH.

SURRENDERED HIS PASSPORT.

Matt smiled on thinking how DI Spragg had forgotten to mention how Patrick had refused to surrender his passport.

Last up was a photo of a Nathan Warral.

Known associate of Butrus Shala.

The link between suspects and those wanting her murdered. Nowhere to be found.

At lunchtime, he and DI Spragg headed down to the river which was only a short distance from the station. The sun shone and the place was buzzing with those out to enjoy the day that was in it. They were lucky to find space on a bench where they sat to enjoy their lunch. He mentioned the information regarding Patrick from the case board as DI Spragg pulled clingfilm from around her chicken sandwich.

'Until there is an obvious clear-cut connection to his involvement in this then they can write what they like about him.' Her voice of reason. 'Let's pray nothing to do with his passport is up for discussion.'

He watched the busy traffic crossing the bridge as he tucked into his egg and avocado bap unsure of what was annoying him.

After finishing her first mouthful of sandwich, she said, 'What I'd be interested in knowing is whether Patrick's assault on a previous girlfriend was actually that.' She drank some water. 'Just keep your eyes peeled, see if you come across who exactly spoke to the Vancouver police officer.'

He nodded.

All the team, apart from Andy were at their desks when they returned.

Matt checked through Catherine's neatly folded receipts that Ben had found in her handbag. Starting early that Tuesday morning, Catherine had been to the beautician and from there to a hair salon where she'd been charged £220 for a colour and cut. Three hours later she'd dropped into *Moonglow* where she bought an Americano and an apple.

Andy returned somewhat subdued. Rebecca followed him into his office. The blinds were open wide enough for Matt to notice him pace the floor from the window to his desk all the time talking and tossing his head while Rebecca stood with arms folded. When he eventually calmed, he nodded in agreement with whatever she had said.

They arrived out together.

Standing in the centre of the office, Andy had their full attention.

'Our Embassy in Cairo are expecting confirmation that a

decomposed body found on a beach near Alexandria is that of Elijah Muscanna.' There was an underlying frustration in his voice.

This information was the last thing any of them would have expected to hear. And once it registered with Matt, he knew it had turned the case totally on its head.

Eric smacked his forehead and flung his pen across his desk. 'No shit Sherlock.'

No prize for guessing who'd been working on the prime lead of Elijah being responsible for Catherine's murder.

The silence that followed was broken by DI Spragg.

'Are they sure it isn't some kind of cover-up?'

Andy shook his head. 'They're preparing for some serious fall-out over this.' He swiped his hand out in front of him. 'Elijah's father has again contacted our Ambassador to express his frustration over our lack of progress in finding those responsible. We will be notified as soon as the body has been officially identified. As the family prepares for a time of mourning there is to be no media coverage on this whatsoever.' He punched his fist into the palm of his other hand. 'If someone from here was involved in Elijah's abduction we need to identify them, soon.'

Rebecca with that straight stance of hers remained by his side.

'Let's reflect on what we have so far.' She sounded defiant.

Mark had been checking Elijah's business affairs and swung further around in his chair to face everyone.

'Andrew Palmer's embezzlement came to light six weeks back. His mother has agreed to pay off the amount he stole on condition no charge is brought against him and he's allowed to remain on as a partner.' A sharp glance towards Andy. 'Andrew's wife walked out on him and without a job, his mother feels he'll have difficulty holding it together. He doesn't have an alibi for the days in question, said he was home alone, two days later he was admitted to rehab.'

With a pen, Rebecca added those details to the glass board.

Matt studied the photo of Andrew Palmer. He had a soft face, a weak chin, and sad eyes. Nothing aggressive or calculating about him but he'd been clever enough to embezzle money over such a long period of time without it being noticed. To feed a drug and gambling addiction wasn't cheap. If his involvement came at a good enough price, he might have caved in. And then realising the implications of what he had done might be the reason he'd hidden away in rehab.

Rebecca continued. 'Ali Defel was at work on both days and at home with his family in the evenings, his mobile's GPS confirms this. Neither cars belonging to Ali Defel or Andrew Palmer were picked up from CCTV cameras in the Richmond area in the week of her abduction.'

Ben was dealing with all mobile communications for those associated with the case. 'The mobile found at Butrus Shala's home should arrive here today. I've checked out three months of calls to and from both Catherine and Elijah Muscanna's mobiles. There's nothing unusual apart from one thing.' He held that moment of anticipation with satisfaction before adding, 'There is no record of Elijah ever contacting Patrick Fowley.'

Matt couldn't understand it.

Rebecca underlined the information under Patrick's photo.

'Why admit to having spoken to him if he hadn't?' DI Spragg snapped.

No one responded.

Rebecca then added her share to the pot. 'According to the taxi company, the driver, Derek, had been assigned to the Muscannas. Elijah had phoned twice on Wednesday 20th May.' She moved across to a display that graphed the time frame of Elijah's movements. 'First, at eight that morning to cancel the ten o'clock booking.' She marked it in. 'Just before noon he again called to request for Derek to collect him at three o'clock.' Also marked in.

'According to Derek, the couple always seemed pleasant and easy with each other. That day Elijah mentioned that Catherine had been ill but she would join him later in the week. What's interesting is that they were halfway to the airport when Elijah became seriously annoyed when he couldn't find his mobile. None of his family knew of his change of plan, no one was organised to collect him at the airport. There wasn't time to return to the residence. Derek offered him his mobile but Elijah didn't know anyone's number offhand. Derek then phoned the Muscanna residence but Catherine didn't answer. They assumed she was resting. Derek suggested to Elijah that when he arrived in Cairo he could take a taxi home and surprise them. I've had Derek checked out. He's in his early sixties and has no previous convictions of any kind. I think we can rule him out as being anyway involved with what happened to Elijah.'

It didn't stack up for Ben.

'If someone had abducted Elijah from here, how would they have known the flight he'd be on or that he wouldn't have his mobile on him?'

That left all of them staring at the board.

Eric, sitting with hands crossed behind his head asked, 'Did Catherine contact anyone on that Wednesday or Thursday?'

Ben shook his head. 'No calls to or from her mobile on either day.'

Andy ran his hand up the side of his jaw. 'Someone close to Elijah and Catherine was involved in this for it to work. Ali Defel and Andrew Palmer were the closest to him.'

Rebecca stepped back to view the board after adding Elijah's time of arrival at the airport, four o'clock. 'Ali Defel has an alibi. Patrick Fowley doesn't. Not only that but he's constantly tripping himself up when he's questioned. Not forgetting, Carrabhain was where she was drowned.' Her pronunciation of Carrabhain sounded twisted.

'On that Wednesday there are photos of him with his family at the Tower of London, outside the house of Parliament and having dinner at a restaurant.' Matt pointed out.

Rebecca stood with pen poised. 'But where was he on Wednesday night? He knew to admit he was at the residence on Thursday, but what if he'd been there on Wednesday night also?' She stared from Matt to DI Spragg with a look that said, *need I say more!*

But DI Spragg matched her stare.

'Yes, but on Thursday he arrived when Catherine had already left. I'm sure with all the CCTV coverage you have of that morning you pinpointed exactly when Patrick arrived at Richmond Station. I presume it was long after Catherine had been driven to Holyhead to make that ferry crossing. And I am sure that there is no sighting of him anywhere near Richmond Station on that Wednesday night or you would have found it by now.' If the noose were to be tightened around Patrick's neck, she wouldn't be the one doing it.

Andy had heard enough.

'OK,' he was playing referee. 'Let's run down what needs

to be done.' He threw an inquiring glance towards Eric.

'I have ten minutes with Andrew Palmer today and after that, I'm meeting Ali Defel.'

'We also need to question Catherine's friends, see what they might give us,' said Andy.

'Leave that to me,' replied Mark.

DI Spragg raised her head.

'Are we still holding back on Catherine being murdered? If so, then what excuse is there to contact her friends?'

Andy shook his head. 'We remain tight-lipped on her murder. No one especially Ali Defel or Andrew Palmer are to be informed of that just yet.' He glanced at Mark. 'To her friends use the cover that her brother reported her missing and we're just making inquiries. To Ali Defel and Andrew Palmer, you are just inquiring over the break-in at the house and the embezzlement of money. Ali no doubt will have been informed of the situation by Elijah's father and he will imagine that it's why we need to talk to him seeing as he is his closest friend.'

Mark nodded.

DI Spragg was straight in, 'Sergeant Bracken has partly retraced Catherine's steps via her credit card statements. Perhaps he should work with Mark.' She smiled towards Mark before adding, 'And if it's OK I'll tag along with Eric.' She then threw him a friendly smile.

Rebecca turned to Andy with eyes of steel and no hint of a smile. She was waiting for his response. He was in charge, but it was their case and DI Spragg had overstepped her brief. She was an outsider as was Matt.

'OK.' Andy again played referee. He ignored Rebecca whose head jerked in the opposite direction to him. 'Right then, I'll leave you to it.'

That ended the briefing.

2.57pm

It was a thirty-minute drive to the clinic. Eric wasn't the talkative type but he did mention how he and his wife enjoyed their once only visit to Dublin.

The clinic was part of a Georgian terrace of houses with an impressive frontage that included a balcony on the first floor. The steps dipped in the middle from wear and the front door was painted black.

Inside the place had a sense of an institution about it and was seriously in need of a makeover. On the walls were soft encouraging posters on the importance of inner peace and the acceptance of who you are. They were shown to a yellow-walled room with four chairs around a table. Cathy was surprised when Andrew Palmer arrived in with eyes clearer than she would have expected.

'Thank you for seeing us.' Eric managed the introductions.

Speaking frankly Andrew said, 'I hope you know the money I took from the business will be repaid.' He made it sound as if it were significant for him to get that off his chest.

'What did you use the money for?' asked Eric.

'Drugs and gambling. But gambling was my worst addiction. The more money I lost the more convinced I was that I could just as easily win it back.' Then with a bow of the head, he added, 'But of course it never happened.'

Cathy imagined him as a kind of a truth robot, nothing but the truth had to be told. Any lies and his progress would be delayed and he'd be pulled right back into his world of lies and illusions.

'We are also investigating a break-in at the Muscanna residence and were wondering if you socialised with Elijah

Muscanna or if you had visited them at their home?' asked Eric.

Andrew knitted his fingers together, released them and did it again. 'We have worked together for twenty years; in that time, I've been to his home about four times.' His chin rose. 'We don't socialise if that's what you are asking but he and Ali are close friends.'

'That doesn't bother you?' asked Cathy

Andrew turned fully towards her. 'Why should it?'

'Two partners against another can cause friction in a business.'

There was a fraction of a pause.

'No, there was no friction between us,' he replied but Cathy imagined the truth robot had stalled.

'And the business. If you don't repay what you owe, will it survive?' she asked.

Andrew had made such a good start but again he was stalling, not so easy to admit the consequences of what he'd caused.

'Yes, of course, it would have pulled through.' An obvious catch in his voice.

Cathy imagined that Andrew had hidden behind lies for God knows how long. It was difficult for him to be honest, easier to lie.

The room was on the ground floor with a window close enough to the path that those passing were no more than an arm's length away.

'And if you don't return to the business what's your plan?' asked Eric.

Andrew again became that truth robot. No fear with this question, not the first time he'd have pondered on his future. 'I'd prefer to continue in the business but if not then I'll help run my mother's Nursing Home in Devon.'

He had an out if his position at the company was over. She wondered if the reason his mother was willing to pay off his debts had more to do with her dread of having him work for her and nothing to do with his wife leaving him. To Cathy it seemed that Andrew Palmer for all his faults wanted to move on, to leave his past behind, not an easy task if you were to be haunted by your involvement in a murder. But then she might be reading him all wrong.

'And Catherine Muscanna, did you come across her much?' asked Eric.

Andrew screwed up his face. 'Why ask me about her?'

'Just wondering, that's all,' In an absent-minded fashion, Eric wrote something in his notebook.

Andrew shook his head. 'I manage a number of the outlets and am usually needed at one or the other of them. Elijah would do the same. Our paths would seldom cross apart from our weekly management meetings. The Christmas party is when I would come across Catherine. She is always pleasant. They make a great couple.'

'How would you describe your relationship with Elijah?' Cathy asked.

His eyes flickered. He was preparing his answer. 'He's a fair man, hopefully, with support from him and Ali, we can get beyond this.'

He then checked his watch.

'I have a group therapy session in five minutes.' There was satisfaction in his voice.

He looked pleased as they all stood. He had passed the test, survived their ten-minute chat.

3.55pm

Ali Defel, in an expensive dark suit, was at his desk when they entered his office. He stood and gestured for them to take a seat and went on to explain how he'd been in touch with Elijah's father and was aware of the situation.

'I've been asked to behave as I normally would. Otherwise, I wouldn't be here.' He sounded weighed down as he fidgeted with his pen. 'It is so tragic, so unbelievable.' Then lifting his head, he said, 'All we can do is hope and pray that the decomposed body is not that of Elijah.'

It felt right to give him a minute.

Cathy had googled the company before leaving the station. The outlets were simply fitted out and not as bright or sophisticated as other opticians but when you compared prices, this company provided the cheapest product.

'What about Catherine, where has she disappeared to, I wonder?' Elijah asked with that underlining anger in his voice.

Eric replied, 'We have nothing to suggest she was in any way involved with Elijah's abduction.'

Not what Ali wanted to hear it seemed.

His eyes flashed. 'But it has to be her. What other reason would she have for disappearing? Elijah's father won't rest until she is tracked down and made pay for what she had done.' His jaw hardening.

'But it's possible she too has been abducted,' said Cathy and immediately sensed Eric stiffen in the chair.

Beneath those dark brows of his, Ali regarded her.

'Why would anyone abduct *her?*'

She slowly replied, 'She is Elijah's wife. Perhaps it's an attack on all of Elijah's family. And if she were here on her own, she was a sitting duck.'

He again considered her.

'I refuse to believe that unless she turns up dead.'

She watched him think as Eric asked after the current financial state of the company.

'I'm not sure what will happen now. I mean, with no Elijah and this embezzlement by Andrew Palmer,' he shook his head. 'I cannot understand why Elijah hadn't noticed sooner how money was going missing. And for Andrew to betray him like that.' He sounded like he was talking to himself.

'What share of the business is yours? She attempted to sound casual.

He stared at her with such intensity that Cathy imagined those eyes boring through her skull to view her thoughts. He considered whether to answer. But she imagined the reason he did was that he knew she'd easily find the answer for herself.

'15%. Elijah is the main shareholder with 45% and the remaining 40% is Andrew Palmer's.'

'Have you any idea who would have wanted to abduct Elijah?' Eric was picking his words, not mentioning murder, not necessary just yet. And as an afterthought he added, 'Apart from Catherine that is.'

'No, I have no clue.' He threw his pen on the desk and leaned back in his leather chair.

A sense of heaviness emanated from him.

'I am sorry I can't help you further. Tomorrow evening I fly to Cairo to be with Elijah's family.'

Eric thanked him for his time and they both left.

8.45pm

When Matt arrived at his room, he ate his takeaway spiced chicken wings and tacos. He then drank half the bottle of water, all in an enjoyable silence. He had figured out what was annoying him. Similar to how the team was anxious to prove that those responsible for Elijah's abduction weren't British, he hoped Catherine's abduction had nothing to do with Patrick. If it had then the effect on the village but in particular on Tess, would be devastating.

When he had finished, he wiped his hands and jammed the takeaway wrappings in the bin. Then he pulled his phone from his trouser pocket.

'Hi,' he said when she answered.

'I thought I'd have heard from you before now.'

'I'm not long finished work.'

'Are you enjoying it there.'

He moved to open the window.

'Enjoy isn't the word I'd use but it's different. It's warmer here than at home. Richmond is a more reserved part of London. You'd like it.'

'Those you're working with, are they snotty-nosed know-it-all's?'

He grinned. 'Not really. Ben is the friendliest. He gave me a lesson on how and what you can get from mobile servers. That was an interesting discussion. How are the kids?'

Even with the window open, the curtain remained static, the room still stuffy. He walked to near the door and switched on the air-conditioning.

'They're fine. Ella is walking now. She's even steadier on her feet than Aiden.' She sounded proud of that. 'And he's teething and is so contrary.'

'That's no fun.'

'No. But the weather's been good. We've got to the beach every morning, so that makes up for it.'

He found the remote and lowered the volume before switching it on. David Attenborough in a forest zooming in on a small lizard-like creature leaping at speed from one tree to another.

Jackie sighed. 'I had a text from Nancy. Patrick and Melissa are heading home earlier than planned. I had hoped we could have had them for dinner some evening but at least I'll get to see them before they leave.'

Matt kept his voice casual. 'When are they leaving?'

'They have an early flight Monday morning.'

And then came the sound of a baby crying and the voice of Jackie's mother in the background saying she would handle him.

There was silence and then Jackie whispered, 'Do you miss me?'

Matt felt himself grin. 'That goes without saying.'

'No,' she teased, 'A wife likes to hear she's missed.'

'You are so missed Jackie, my wife, my lovely.'

There was fun in her voice when she said, 'I better go.'

'OK, talk to you tomorrow.'

He felt tired. A thumping of a headache was coming on.

Patrick had rightly guessed that the powers to be in London didn't want the details of Catherine's demise known. If push came to shove, he'd reveal it. If he were arrested then Melissa would do the revealing.

He had been surprised and pleased when Ben admitted he wasn't convinced that Patrick was behind his sister's abduction.

'Motive, that is what you have to ask yourself. What was his motive?'

Ben then rubbished the idea of the family rift.

'You get that in every family. He went years without doing anything about it and then elaborately plans to have her murdered at a time when he's on holidays here.' He rolled his eyes. 'I mean, why wouldn't he have planned it so he was in Vancouver when the deed was done?'

Matt breathed in a lungful of cooler air as he headed for a shower. After that, he'd take a walk along the river or up into the park. He hadn't yet made up his mind.

///////

8.55pm

Cathy found Andy downing a whiskey at the bar.

'It's been confirmed. The body is that of Elijah Muscanna.' He ordered one for her.

'What I didn't disclose this afternoon was that according to Nigel Green, fifteen months ago a man by the name of Omar Bakari made a complaint to Scotland Yard against Elijah. He claimed that Elijah was involved in human trafficking. Omar Bakari believed there would be no justice for Elijah in Egypt with his father's senior position in the army. He stressed how it would be inhuman for the British Government to freely harbour a mass murderer. He even mentioned the notion of complaining to the European Court of Human Rights if nothing was done about it.'

When her drink arrived, Andy insisted on paying for it.

'Omar produced a photo of Elijah in conversation with a man named Ahmad, known to front such an operation. It wasn't a case for Scotland Yard.'

She remembered how those same facts had been mentioned to the suspects, by Nathan Warral.

'Do you believe this Omar Bakari's story?' she asked.

He shrugged. 'Intelligence checked it out. Elijah attended the same school as Ahmad. That was their only connection. Remember, for almost fifteen years Elijah had never returned to Cairo. Ahmad, who coincidently died of an overdose wasn't much of a businessman, everything he made from human trafficking could be traced. None of it ended up in Elijah's or anyone else's bank account.'

That sounded convincing to her.

'But how can you walk in off the street and expect to have the ear of a senior official of Scotland Yard on a complaint about someone living here?'

Andy glanced at his glass of whiskey. 'I was told it was someone with authority in the Egyptian Army who vouched for Omar. They won't say who exactly, not that that matters but they're keeping quiet about it.'

She sipped her drink. 'So, let's get this straight.' She raised the first finger of her right hand. 'Nigel Green was aware that Elijah's brother had been abducted in Egypt last year, so Elijah's safety here should have been a priority.' She raised the second finger of her hand. 'If Omar Bakari was working for someone out to damage Khafu's position in the army then that same person could have vouched for Omar with Scotland Yard and Nigel Green knows the identity of that person.' Her third finger went up. 'Now Elijah has been murdered. If Omar Bakari had anything to do with it and spills the beans on his meeting with Nigel Green,' her eyebrows rose, 'Then Khafu will demand answers as to why such a meeting hadn't been reported to him. If it had, his son's death might have been prevented.' She paused a moment and noticed the tiredness in Andy's expression. 'Or was there some kind of collusion from one of Khafu's enemies? Some plot to force Khafu's resignation in favour of someone who might encourage the president to consider a more democratic outlook for the country? We know of the recent unrest in that country and how the President rules with the iron hand of the army. Perhaps your government intelligence concerned themselves too closely with the inner politics of that country. A country whose strategic position makes them a necessary ally to all the great powers.'

He made no response but gave her a look that said, *back off.*

After a long silence, he said, 'One thing I did prise from Nigel was a mobile number given by Omar Bakari as a means of contacting him. That might give us something.'

Cathy was starving. After finishing their drinks, they headed to the nearby restaurant. The sergeant had declined her offer of dinner.

Wednesday - 8ᵗʰ July

8.45am

Cathy smiled to herself as she and the sergeant walked to work. She'd spoken to Sinead that morning. Although her daughter remained subdued at least she'd decided to return home in September and not travel to Canada. She had sounded her old self when she mentioned Cathy's trip to the hospital to face Jennifer.

'I'd love to have been a fly on the wall when she recognised you.' She had laughed. 'Why did you do it?'

'Something had to be done. Both of us can be so stubborn.'

'When she complained to Dad, he told her to lighten up, he doesn't want to hear another word about it.'

With no sympathy from anyone, apart from Neil that was, Jennifer would have to put their recent argument behind her.

They arrived at the office just as Rebecca was explaining to the others how her neighbours were Muslims.

There she stood with a closed fist resting on her hip. 'Family members and close friends can view the corpse. Once dead, the body is washed, wrapped in clean sheets and buried before sunset within the next 24 hours.'

Mark who seemed to be half-listening arched his neck forward. 'That's how come Dodi Fayed was rushed off to be buried after that crash in Paris.'

Rebecca nodded. 'So, for Elijah's body to be left to decompose and it smothered in the sand for all to see, to Muslims that would be considered blasphemous.'

267

Another attack on his father's position was Ben's take on it.

'It's a pity there wasn't a funeral.' Cathy was by then at her desk. 'Funerals can be so revealing.'

Nods of agreement ended the topic.

As Andy was meeting his boss, Rebecca took charge of the briefing.

Ben mentioned the mobile found at the home of Butrus Shala.

'It was activated last April. I'm checking through it.'

Eric confirmed their meetings with Andrew Palmer and Ali Defel.

'They both sounded up-front. Nothing to make you suspect they were lying.' He glanced towards Cathy who nodded in agreement.

Over breakfast that morning with the sergeant Cathy had learned that after devising a list of Catherine's friends from her mobile contacts, Mark had handed the sergeant half the list with the words, 'You work on those.'

Cathy watched the slouching Mark. He was a loner who preferred to do his own thing. He had no interest in male bonding or the notion of teamwork, he just wanted the job done.

Mark began to read from his notebook.

'Catherine's friends never knew she had a brother. Those who had met her on Tuesday said she was looking forward to her trip to Cairo.'

With a sense of tenacity in his voice, the sergeant added, 'I got the same response from those I contacted. But a Laura Allwood let slip how Catherine seemed worried in herself about two years back but then she eventually pulled out of it.'

Rebecca didn't write it up.

'That was when Elijah married his second wife.'

Then Rebecca marked off a square of space on the board. Before writing anything, she turned and explained the complaint made by Omar Bakari to Scotland Yard. 'It appears that Omar Bakari arrived in London to muddy Elijah's name with authorities here. It turned out there was no truth to his allegations. While he was here, he stayed in a Kensington hotel and activated this mobile number.' She made it sound as if she'd secured the information all on her own as she wrote the number on the board.

The idea of stripping everything from that number had Ben smiling.

Rebecca had more to say.

'I've also checked through all the CCTV footage from when Elijah Muscanna arrived at Heathrow and boarded his flight. Nothing out of the ordinary there.' She smiled. 'However, the footage we've received from Cairo airport shows Elijah stepping off the plane and being escorted by two men to a waiting car. Now, Mark, I want you to check if anything from that footage can give us the car's registration.'

Mark nodded.

'If Elijah was abducted it happened in Cairo, not here.' There was a glow of satisfaction in Rebecca's smile.

Even Cathy caught it.

They had turned a corner. The blame for Elijah's abduction lay in Cairo but not without the support of someone in London. Apart from the couple themselves, the airline and the taxi company, who else knew of Elijah's change of plan? That was the million-pound question.

A schedule was decided on for that day. The sergeant needed to track down the last of Catherine's friends on his list. After that, he and Cathy would attempt to re-check her movements for two weeks prior to her abduction, taking into account her dealing with Mary Simpson, her charity work and the details from off her credit card statement.

////////

11.05am

Matt watched when Andy returned and DI Spragg entered his office. Rebecca was also focused on them. And when DI Spragg returned to her desk, he was quick to catch Rebecca glaring in their direction before her attention returned to her computer.

There had been no reply to his previous four calls to Holly Wise. Fifth time around, his luck was in. The woman sounded breathless and explained how she had been discharged from hospital the previous day. Yes, she was a friend of Catherine Muscanna. She knew her from her college days.

With a touch of determination, she asked, 'Why are you inquiring about Catherine?'

'Her brother Patrick has filed a missing person's report,' Matt replied.

'Why did he do that?' She made it sound like he'd been a naughty boy. 'She's in Cairo, for heaven sake.'

Matt felt he was talking to someone who better than anyone else he'd spoken to knew the real Catherine Muscanna. For one thing, she hadn't balked at the mention of Patrick being Catherine's brother as the rest of her friends had.

He asked if he could call to speak to her in person.

'But why?' was Holly's reply. 'Have you spoken to Elijah?'

'We're finding it hard to track him down at present. I promise I won't take up much of your time.'

Holly agreed to a time of three o'clock and gave her address.

DI Spragg listened with interest in hearing of his conversation with Holly. She googled a map of Richmond to locate the residence and agreed to accompany him.

'I've got something,' said Ben who waited for all heads to turn towards him. 'I've checked through all calls to and from Patrick's mobile number, which I retrieved from the Missing Person's Report. I found the calls to him from a mobile number here in London.' He paused. 'Those calls weren't from Elijah Muscanna but from Omar Bakari.'

The attempt to drop that red flag on Patrick's involvement now seemed ill-founded. If Omar Bakari had orchestrated both abductions then linking him to Patrick was a real problem.

After considering the implications DI Spragg got to her feet.

'If Patrick were involved in this then why provide the evidence that would prove his guilt?' She didn't have to wait long for a response.

'Perhaps he figured we'd never have Omar Bakari's mobile number.' Rebecca was fired up.

Matt was surprised when Ben piped up.

'He could make out that he's a pawn in all of this. What's surprising is that there was no contact from Omar Bakari to Patrick in the week the Muscannas were abducted which you would expect. Omar Bakari only called him three times in all.'

'Precisely,' replied DI Spragg.

'Who's to say Patrick doesn't have a second mobile?' Rebecca wasn't giving up that easy.

'If that's the case any of them could have had a second mobile, Ali Defel, Andrew Palmer, even Elijah and Catherine,' replied DI Sragg.

Rebecca returned to her desk and noisily swivelled around in her chair.

Their report was almost completed. Matt had summarised receipts for the whole of the week prior to her abduction. Catherine had bought sandals, sun cream and after-sun protection. Moisturising cream for night and day. CDs, DVDs, a blouse, two pairs of trousers, a shawl and some jewellery. The only receipt missing from those itemised on the credit card statement was one from Marks & Spencer where she'd made purchases to the value of £50.90 on the Tuesday. It was the last piece of the jigsaw. He mentioned it to DI Spragg who suggested they call to the store for a copy of the receipt as it was just down the street from the station.

///////

2.20pm

At the customer services desk, Cathy gave the date the receipt had been issued as well as the credit card number used to pay the amount. Helen, the assistant, wrote everything down and went to discuss it with her supervisor. When they both returned, Joanna introduced herself and then asked for some identification.

'This is Irish,' remarked Joanna on handing back her ID card.

Cathy felt a right idiot. On phoning Andy, she handed her mobile to Joanna who rhymed off an email address to which an authorised request be made for the information required.

Joanna handed her back her mobile.

'He'll send it straight away. I'll contact you once I have what you're looking for.' Cathy didn't know the telephone number of the station. Joanna scribbled down Cathy's own mobile number.

They left the store with Cathy conscious of the trouble they'd caused over an everyday receipt for everyday purchases in such a high-level investigation.

The coffee at the station was trickling strong and after an agreeable cappuccino in a nearby café, they made for Holly's residence.

It was a redbrick house with a dusky pink front door. A blooming lace-headed hydrangea flourished in the corner and a deep pink Victorian scented climbing rose by the door scrambled up to the eaves. The scent from the roses perfumed the garden as far as the gate. Holly's sister Willow, a woman with numerous clips in her hair wearing baggy floral trousers and a brightly patterned jacket introduced herself on opening the door. They followed her into the front room with its faded wisteria wallpaper.

Holly, looking pale and frail lay on a sofa close to the window. Willow placed a light blanket over her knees telling her she might catch a cold although the room felt muggy and warm. A long pink scarf covered Holly's head falling over her right shoulder. Her clothes were more somber than Willow's and about two sizes too big. There were half a dozen beads around her neck and her eyebrows were lightly worked on with a tan to brown pencil. Her lips were glossed strawberry. She smiled on asking them to take a seat. Willow called out from the hallway that she would make some tea.

'We're twins you see. Willow lives just down the road. She doesn't like to think of me on my own,' said Holly. 'I'm so lucky to have her.'

Cathy imagined that their parents were either naturists or hippies from the sixties. Both Holly and Willow had a warm pleasant nature about them. It was obvious that Holly was recovering from chemo. Such a diagnosis left most patients viewing life with more of a moral compass than would previously have been the case. They looked back and appreciated their good deeds and regretted the not so good ones. Happiness was a clear conscience. For that reason, Cathy felt Holly would be honest with them. No holding back. No regrets.

Without any encouragement, Holly mentioned how she knew Catherine from their days in college where they studied science.

'I had enough of it after six months and switched to garden design.'

Unlike the housekeeper or any of Catherine's other friends, Holly also knew that Tess was still alive.

'Did she ever mention Patrick?' asked the sergeant, ready with pen and notebook in hand for her response.

'Yes, she did.' And then with eyes fixed on him, she added, 'She confided in me that he had raped her. As a result of that, she became pregnant and had attempted to abort the baby but when she continued to bleed, the doctor had to be called. That is why she hates Carrabhain. It brings up too many traumatic memories for her.'

Cathy watched his hand remain perched in the air with

pen in position. His mouth moved but words refused to come. Then he glanced at her with a look of disbelief. Cathy too was totally taken aback. She found herself rubbing her forehead hard on imagining how this had torn the family apart, perhaps the reason James Hurley had dumped Catherine. She watched the sergeant focus on Holly, expecting to find her expression suspect. It wasn't.

'Well, you asked for the truth.' Holly sounded frank.

No wonder Patrick didn't want the truth to come out. A rapist, dear God, how could you live with that label around your neck! How had Melissa handled the truth? If he hadn't been honest with her, was their daughter at risk?

'We were the best of friends back then.' Holly raised her eyes towards the ceiling. 'This was where I grew up. Catherine often stayed over when she wasn't studying or working. She had a job in a local café in the evenings. My mother found her refreshing and in need of someone to care for her.'

'But she had Tess,' Cathy found herself saying.

'They weren't close,' Holly held a look of sympathy but then she suddenly smiled when she added. 'Catherine could be such fun.' She made a clicking sound with her tongue. 'On the other hand, she could be a stinging wasp.' She made it sound as if it weren't a problem. 'I'm afraid lying came easy to Catherine.' The smile spreading across her features emphasised her gauntness. 'My mother believed it was her way of living her dreams and what was the harm in it after what she had gone through?'

'Do you know Elijah well?' asked the sergeant.

She nodded. 'Of course. It was a shame they couldn't have children. That majorly strained their relationship.' She was staring at the fireplace. 'What angered him most was that she never mentioned what had occurred with Patrick before they were married. Divorce had been discussed but they pulled through once she accepted that he would take a second wife.'

Willow arrived in and set the tray on the low table. She loudly stated how she would make up Holly's bed before she left.

Cathy acted as the host and served the tea.

'Offhand, would you know of anyone out to harm her?' The sergeant held that serious expression of his.

Holly lightly chuckled. 'Why do you think something has happened to her? I told you, she's holidaying in Cairo.'

Cathy changed tack by asking how Catherine had seemed recently.

A look of suspicion vanished as quickly as it had appeared. 'When I was first diagnosed with cancer, Catherine called three times a week. Both of us were angry women. I, over my cancer and she on having to share Elijah. But then she changed, became happier in herself and didn't have time to call around as much. Fobbed me off with the excuse she was too busy with her charity works. While I was in the hospital, she came just once to see me.'

'Any idea what caused this change in her?' This was more in line with what the sergeant wanted to hear.

'I put it down to her having an affair.' There was a trace of mischievousness in her voice. Then dropping her cup and saucer back on the tray she added, 'Willow saw her once coming from that lingerie store. She hadn't been to see me in a couple of weeks.' She paused. 'You have to understand Willow gets excitable at times. And that day she snuck up on Catherine, stepped in front of her and probably shouted something like *surprise, surprise*.' She smiled as if it was being acted out in front of her. 'The reaction wasn't what Willow had expected. Catherine almost knocked her over and told her to mind her own business. Willow was so upset.' Another pause. 'We expected Catherine to apologise when she next called or at least to explain herself. But instead, she behaved as if nothing had happened. Willow refused to make anything of it. I had to accept her decision. But Willow wouldn't hurt a fly and she can be so sensitive.'

If Ben had scrutinized Catherine's mobile as well as she imagined he had there was no evidence to suggest she was having an affair.

Holly admitted that the birth of Elijah's son had changed him. 'If I'm not mistaken there is another child on the way.' She sighed. 'I imagined Catherine had felt pushed to one side but she has come to accept it. Amazing really.' Frowning she said, 'I couldn't understand why she had breast implants at her age. That is another reason I believe she is having an affair.' She found some tablets on the table and washed them down with the remains of her tea. 'You have to understand there is a bond between herself and Elijah, yes, of course, he wanted children but breast implants!' She slowly shook her head. 'It will only prove to his family that she is a most unsuitable wife. That is another thing she will have to handle, which won't be easy.'

Willow returned to the room announcing how she would call again later in the afternoon to prepare a light meal. Holly remarked how she'd mentioned Catherine's treatment towards her outside the lingerie shop.

Willow hunched up her shoulders. 'You would have thought I was spying on her.' Her huge eyes opened wide. 'But you see I had just arrived out from the book shop next door. And there was Catherine with a large bag in hand. She was on her mobile and passed me as she told whoever she was speaking to that they were in for a surprise when they saw her in what she had just bought.' Willow giggled. 'She got such a shock when I jumped in front of her that she dropped her mobile and almost pushed me to the ground to retrieve it.' She gestured towards Holly, 'When we both thought about it later, we could never imagine Elijah discussing lingerie with Catherine especially when she was on the street for anyone to hear.'

Willow stood behind Holly and mimed the words *time to let her rest.*

Holly pulled the blanket up around her.

'You're Irish. I wonder, do you know Carrabhain at all?' she asked.

'I actually have a holiday home there and love the place. I also know Tess,' Cathy replied.

With the help of Willow, Holly pulled herself back in the chair and rested her legs on the stool in front of her.

'Catherine has no intention of ever returning there, even for Tess's funeral. Nothing will change her mind once it is made up.'

And yet that was exactly where she'd ended up thought Cathy. She rose from the chair when she noticed Willow standing by, waiting.

'It's time we were leaving.'

'As I told you, there is no point worrying over Catherine. She'll return when she's ready or maybe she's off with her lover.' Holly again chuckled.

Willow led them up the hallway and out the front door.

'They've always been the best of friends. I remember their first major argument was when Catherine dumped Ali for Elijah. Holly didn't talk to her for months over that. It seemed to all of us back then that Ali and Catherine clicked straight off. They lived here with us for a while.' She smiled. 'My mother was ahead of her time when it came to couples sleeping around, that's why Holly and I don't know who our father is. At least our mother was wealthy enough to be able to do her own thing and not worry over money like so many women these days.'

By now they were on the garden path.

'How long were Catherine and Ali a couple?' asked the sergeant.

'Oh, I think a year or more, I can't remember.'

At the gate, Cathy pressed Willow further on that relationship.

'Oh, we were sure they were meant for each other. But whatever it was just turned to dust after Ali introduced her to Elijah. She had a way with men. No matter how hard Ali fought to win her back, it was pointless.' She dropped the latch of the gate into position. 'I would be more annoyed with Catherine for not supporting Holly over the past months if Holly wasn't now free of cancer. But not many would tolerate Catherine's selfishness.'

Another of Catherine's friends who will forgive her of everything.

Just as they were about to part way, the sergeant asked, 'Can you remember anything about the day you bumped into Catherine on the street?'

Holly raised the palm of her hand to her forehead as if attempting to encourage her brain to recall what she hoped was hidden there somewhere. Her eyes widened and totally pleased with herself she replied, 'It was Saturday 14th February, Valentine's Day.'

'About what time?' asked the sergeant.

'Three in the afternoon. Yes, because I had just arrived on the street and collecting my book was the first thing I did.'

They parted ways.

Cathy walked deep in thought. Catherine and Ali lovers,

no one had picked up on that. Or that it was Ali who had introduced her to Elijah. Perhaps it wasn't all that significant but as her mother would often say, *hot coals are easily kindled.* If Catherine had a lover then perhaps it was Ali. If that were the case then she was the one in control – for a time at least.

The sergeant had headed up the road with such purpose that Cathy had to quicken her step to catch up with him.

///////

4.25pm

Back at the station, the sergeant had pulled his chair up next to Ben. They were checking out calls from Catherine's mobile for Saturday 14th February. Cathy made for Andy's office and unloaded what they'd got from Holly Wise. Catherine's accusation that Patrick had raped her didn't surprise him.

'If only we could prove it. It will be Holly's word against his.'

'I don't believe it.' She sounded convinced.

Andy shot her an inquiring glance.

She'd given it serious consideration on her walk back to the station. But she needed someone to challenge her way of thinking. No one better for that than Andy.

'Let's just presume that James Hurley was responsible for Catherine's pregnancy.' She slotted her hands into her trouser pockets. 'What if she attempted to abort the fetus and Tess found her bleeding and called the doctor. Now if she had admitted the truth it would have totally destroyed their relationship for Tess had warned her against having anything to do with James Hurley.' She could feel that tick of excitement rising in her. 'It would explain why she was upset around the time they broke up. But it was her pregnancy that worried her.' She knew from his expression that he was considering it. 'What were her options? Her father was dead. Tess would have been furious with her. But if Catherine successfully laid the blame on Patrick then she'd have sabotaged that closeness between him and Tess. They were both adopted and over the age of consent. If they had a relationship it wasn't a crime. It would have been her word against his. And if Tess felt aggrieved over what Catherine had gone through, if she viewed Catherine as the victim. If she felt partly to blame for not trying to understand Catherine better then Tess would have supported her in whatever she decided to do with her life.' She paused. 'Tess paid for Catherine to attend college here in London, but she could have obtained the same education in Ireland for a fraction of the cost.' That spike of enthusiasm had kicked right in. 'It's why Nancy had asked the sergeant if Patrick had explained everything to him. Everything meaning the honest truth. Nancy admitted she was wrong not to have said anything sooner. It's the reason Tess hasn't forgiven her.' She leaned against the desk. 'And discovering that Patrick was innocent from what Nancy had told her last year when she was in hospital, that was what inspired Tess to track him down and pay for him to return home.'

Andy focused on her as if soaking her in.

'So many leaps of faith with your theory?'

Disagreeing with her was fine but if he had nothing to stand in its place then it still remained a strong possibility.

She decided to dissect it from a different angle.

'If Patrick did rape Catherine.' Her mind took time to manage her thoughts. 'Then why didn't Catherine appreciate Tess for supporting her back then? No invitation to London for a holiday or to meet her husband. Instead, she barely kept in touch preferring to keep her secret in the past. She didn't want to be reminded of it, might even have felt embarrassed by it.' She took her time. 'If Patrick did rape Catherine.' And this was what really had convinced her of her theory 'Then why would Catherine have a twenty-year-old photo of the four of them in her office? If he raped her, she'd have burned anything to do with him.'

The silence between them settled for a minute.

'I'm not disagreeing with you but let's think it over some more.'

Even if he didn't fully see things her way, she knew she had just made a clinching argument that couldn't be ignored. Enough of an argument to halt Rebecca's determination to find Patrick guilty.

'What about Ali Defel's previous relationship with Catherine?' she asked.

'What about it?' Andy replied. 'If it's water under the bridge then there is nothing to tell. I mean he returned to Cairo after college and he's now married with a family. You said yourself that he's convinced she's behind Elijah's abduction. And according to the housekeeper, Catherine isn't too fond of him. His car wasn't in the Richmond vicinity on the day Elijah was abducted or the following day. Nothing points to his involvement.'

She stood to leave. Yeah, she was happy with what she'd discovered.

Friday - 10th July

8.55am

Eric was the only one at his desk when they arrived. He made room for her and the sergeant to view some CCTV footage of Petersham Road, Richmond.

'I'm just making sure we haven't missed anything. Nathan Warral's car was picked up close by just before midnight on that Wednesday night.'

Cathy moved in on the sergeant's shoulder to read what he was reading, the list of car registration numbers being checked out.

'The top two are Ali Defel's and Andrew Palmer's,' Eric said.

And then Rebecca called everyone to attention for a briefing.

Mark was first up to explain how he had attempted to pull the licence plate number from the CCTV footage of the Mercedes that had taken Elijah from Cairo airport.

'The number plate has been lacquer coated which prevents it from being read by CCTV cameras. But there is a clear enough shot of one of the men.'

Cathy explained the conversation with Willow Wise regarding Catherine's behaviour outside the lingerie store. Ben sounded disappointed in reporting that there were no calls to or from Catherine's mobile on the afternoon of Valentine's Day last.

'She must have gotten her dates mixed up,' Ben concluded.

The sergeant appeared to be in his own world. Ignoring

what was going on around him. He moved towards Eric and whispered something that Cathy couldn't make out. He then rummaged for something on the desk.

Her mobile rang. The call was from Joanna at Marks & Spencer with the list of items contained on the missing receipt. Cathy scribbled them down as Joanna rhymed them off.

'A swim-suit.' Pause. 'A scarf.' Pause. 'Two bars of chocolate, a carton of milk, a tray of stir-fry and a tub of prawns in sour cream sauce.'

Cathy's mouth fell open and, in a haze, she rhymed off an email address and asked Joanna if she wouldn't mind forwarding her a copy of that receipt.

It took her some seconds to remember where she was. Rebecca was explaining something but Cathy wasn't listening. She couldn't believe what she was thinking. But if it were true then she needed to prove it. She lifted her mobile from off the desk. She studied what she'd been looking for. When she glanced towards the sergeant, he smiled at her the way he would when he knew they were thinking the same. He too had sussed it out.

Andy arrived as Ben slammed the handset back into position. He moved to the centre of the office.

'I've been able to trace calls to and from that second mobile of Butrus Shalas. There are numerous calls made to him that were picked up from a satellite closest to where our Nathan Warral lives. I think we can assume that the mobile number was that of Nathan Warral. Then I checked all calls to and from that mobile number. There were numerous calls to and from an unlisted number. Guess who lives in the area covered by the satellite that picked up those calls?' He grinned at them.

She watched Andy inhale, anxious that this was the link that would break this case open. Rebecca impatiently lifted her head eager to know yet somewhat annoyed she hadn't a clue who he was about to name and that she had not found the connection herself. Eric bit his lip. Even Mark stopped what he was doing to hear what was about to be revealed. Ben, smugly satisfied that he had everyone guessing. Oh yes, Ben enjoyed making them wait, piquing their interest.

Cathy nodded to the sergeant.

He understood her.

'Ali Defel,' he whispered.

It had Rebecca throwing him a look of confusion. After all, they had nothing on Ali Defel. Even Andy gave him a quizzical raise of his eyebrows. Another leap of faith!

But Ben nodded and asked, 'How did you know?'

The sergeant glanced at her. It was her turn to take it from there.

She first explained the information she had received from Joanna of Marks & Spencer.

'If Catherine bought those prawns then she was out to sicken herself.' She stood up and lifted the pen from Rebecca's desk as she made for the case board. She felt pride in her stance as she wrote and spoke at the same time.

'Holly Wise and her sister suspected Catherine of having an affair.' She turned to write Ali Defel's name boldly on the board. 'But there is no trace of the call she'd taken on Valentine's Day last outside the lingerie shop. So, she must have had a second mobile.'

It was Ben who weighed in behind her. 'And why would Ali Defel contact Nathan Warral if he didn't want someone murdered. And he could have lied to Nathan over Elijah's involvement with human trafficking. Those to be charged with her murder are immigrants. They would have understood the horrors of that which made it less of a problem for them to murder her.'

She nodded.

'But we have no proof of this only that Ali's residence is within the location covered by that satellite,' Rebecca snapped.

Cathy clicked her tongue.

'Catherine didn't abduct herself. With Elijah murdered she would have control of his business and could remain in London, living the life she'd been accustomed to.'

'So, if Ali was involved with her on this, he double-crossed her,' said Andy, slowly.

'Yeah, perhaps Ali wanted control of the business himself instead of involving Catherine whom he knew from past experience couldn't be trusted.'

Cathy could sense her heart pounding.

'It was Catherine who insisted that the housekeeper stay away on the day they were to travel. That never happened before. Why did she do that?' That was something that had played around in her mind from the start. 'She was the only one in a position to stop Elijah from making that scheduled flight. He would never have left her on her own and she ill. And she couldn't have Mary Simpson fussing over Elijah making sure he didn't forget anything.'

Rebecca narrowed her eyes. 'But then something went wrong.'

Cathy nodded. 'Who gains from Elijah's death now that Catherine has been eliminated?' She answered her own question. 'Ali. And if he refuses to accept the conditions laid down by Andrew Palmer's mother then he can do an undisclosed deal with her to buy Andrew's share of the business in return for not having him charged with embezzlement. The last thing she would want is for her son to do time for his crime. And that would give Ali control of the business.'

She felt utterly buzzed at that moment. The icing on the cake was to see the sergeant's bunched up smile.

Andy checked his watch. 'If Catherine was having an affair, we need proof it was with Ali Defel. All we've got right now is the possibility that Catherine may have been involved in having her husband abducted.'

'No, we've more than that.' She wrote a registration number on the board. 'A car with this registration is what Ali Defel arrived in one morning to the Muscanna residence. It is not the car registration Ali has given Eric. I bet if you check you'll find this car was on Petersham Road sometime on that Wednesday evening. I bet his wife would never have disagreed with whatever he told you. And he knew to leave his smartphone at home as it would have so easily tracked his whereabouts.'

'How did you get this car registration? Asked Rebecca.

'Does it matter?' Cathy replied.

Andy knew that Cathy had obtained that registration number on her once only unofficial visit to the Muscanna residence. It was why he was quick to insist it be immediately checked out.

'I'll suggest for Ali to call here this afternoon for a personal update on the case before he flies out to Cairo. When he arrives, we'll need to have enough to bury him.'

Andy turned to Eric. 'Get warrants to search Ali Defel's office and residence and with support from uniform, I want you to personally manage the search of his office. And Mark, you take charge of his residence. Be in position. Once I text you both that he's arrived here, move in.'

'What are we looking for?' asked Eric.

'An unlisted mobile that connects him to Nathan Warral, Catherine Muscanna and Omar Bakari,' Andy replied.

Cathy didn't think a significant charge would stick if their evidence depended totally on what they gathered from mobile phone communications. The European Law regarding a person's human rights could be challenged. If Ali had a shrewd barrister then all could be lost. She felt panicked at the thought of it. The only way to handle Ali Defel was to extract a full confession. To do that they needed to convince him it was his only option.

She checked the time. It would take close to two hours for Eric to secure the warrants. It suddenly dawned on her what needed to be done.

As Mark passed her desk, she asked, 'Could you spare me an hour of your time?'

He checked his watch. 'For what?'

'Someone needs to be questioned and I'm afraid it can't be me.'

'An hour max,' he replied.

///////

10.25am

Matt stood alongside Mark as the door opened.

'Mary Simpson?' Mark inquired.

'Yes,' replied the woman wearing tight shorts and a skimpy t-shirt exposing her sunburned arms and neck.

Mark produced his ID.

'We'd like to have a word in private?' He stretched himself

to his full height. 'Inside perhaps.'

Mary looked bothered. 'How many times am I to be questioned? One of Catherine's friends called to the house on Wednesday when I was there.' She folded her arms. 'She gave me some crazy line over Catherine having a brother who'd reported her missing. He's a liar. When Catherine gets back, she'll make rubbish of him and I hope I'm there to see it.'

They followed her indoors.

In the kitchen was a slim man in his fifties reading the paper while sitting at the table wearing shorts and a vest. He looked up when they entered. His glasses enlarged his eyes to give them an owlish expression. He pulled a cigarette from the packet that was next to him but said nothing.

Mary leaned against the sink, arms still folded.

'This is my husband Tom. He'd pulled his shoulder last week on a job.'

Matt had doubted that Mary's husband would be at home. When DI Spragg had explained what she needed, he imagined he would be traipsing across London in an attempt to track him down, alone, as Mark only had an hour to spare.

Mark focused on Tom. 'Am I correct in thinking you are the Muscanna's gardener and handyman. that you are responsible for emptying their bins?'

'Yeah, that's right,' replied Tom before taking a pull of his cigarette.

With no offer of a seat, Matt remained by the door.

Mark's hands swept up in front of him, palms facing the couple. 'Now just to be clear we are not out to charge anyone with anything but it seems there is a mobile phone missing from the Muscanna's residence. Not anything expensive but we would appreciate if it were handed over to us or its whereabouts specified.'

Tom tipped the ash from his cigarette into the ashtray when Mary glanced towards him in total disbelief.

'No way did we take no mobile.' Mary vehemently shook her head. 'No way.'

Mark nodded. 'If this mobile is found during a search of this residence then one of you could possibly be charged with withholding vital evidence. We'd rather that didn't happen.'

Matt remembered some of what Ben had explained to him.

'We can trace the whereabouts of that mobile as well as the time it was last powered up.'

He was chancing his arm. They hadn't even the number of that mobile until they hopefully found what they presumed was an unlisted mobile of Ali Defel's. But it was worth a shot.

Mary glanced at her husband before pressing a hand on her hip and trusting her head forward as if out to provoke a fight. 'You have some nerve coming here questioning us over some poxy mobile. We have our own mobiles. Why would we bother with a second one?' Her head lifted off her shoulders with a sense of satisfaction. 'And if the Muscannas haven't returned yet then who told you there is a mobile missing?'

Mary Simpson was no idiot.

Mark backed back. 'Fine, but we will eventually track it down.'

Matt felt disappointed as they moved to leave.

But then came Tom's raspy voice as he said, 'I took the mobile.'

Thank God, thought Matt.

Mary glared at him. 'What are you saying?'

Tom stood and walked towards the back door. He then reached up above the cupboard and retrieved a bag that held the mobile.

'How could you have been so bloody stupid?' Mary slapped him on the arm. 'When did you get your hands on that?'

Tom handed it to Mark. 'I didn't steal it. I found it in the bin. It had been thrown away. I just took it.'

'When did you find it?' asked Matt.

'The day after they left. As I said it was in the bin, that's not stealing.'

Mark nodded at Tom. 'We never mentioned it was stolen and we appreciate your assistance.'

Matt checked the mobile, it was a small cheap thing with no GPS chip as a standard feature. He imagined Ali Defel's second mobile would be similar.

They left to the sound of Mary shouting as to how in all the years she'd worked for the Muscannas she'd never taken as much as a biscuit of theirs.

'But you heard him, I didn't steal it, I just found it,' Tom retorted.

///////

1.50pm

After answering her phone, Rebecca attempted to calm whoever was on the other end of the line. That followed a line of questions. *What was Lilly's temperature? Are you sure the rash isn't just hives? How long is she complaining of a headache? How often has she vomited?* It was after hearing the response to this question that Rebecca jumped out of her swivel chair and replied that she was leaving straight away. From previous phone conversations, Cathy had gathered that Lilly was Rebecca's young daughter. In Andy's office, Rebecca spoke at speed and probably didn't pick up on Andy's words of concern. Re-emerging, she grabbed her bag and was gone.

Eric and Mark, with warrants in hand, were in position waiting for the word to search the residence and office of Ali Defel while the sergeant appeared engrossed with Ben in checking communications from the various mobiles.

Of course, she hoped Rebecca's daughter wasn't seriously ill but she couldn't help feeling glad it would be Ben and not Rebecca who would accompany Andy to interview Ali Defel. Elijah's abduction and murder had nothing to do with their case of Catherine's murder. It would be impossible for her to be involved in questioning him, which was unfortunate. Proper police procedures would have to be adhered to on this. She lifted Rebecca's file off her desk and approached Ben. He would have preferred to sit and view Ali Defel being questioned rather than be the one firing the questions. The three of them ran through what was contained in Rebecca's file. She had the CCTV footage covering Petersham Road re-checked for all of Wednesday. The car matching the registration number that Cathy had posted earlier on the display board had been identified as arriving on the road at nine o'clock that night. The car was owned by a Barry Saunders who happened to be a neighbour of Ali Defel. There were also those details which Ben and the sergeant had discovered.

On being informed of Ali's arrival at the front desk Andy texted both Eric and Mark as he stepped out from his office. He buttoned up his jacket and then turned to Ben. 'Five minutes in Interview Room 1.'

She sat along with the sergeant and viewed the screen covering Interview Room 1 which Ben had set up for them before he'd left. They watched as Andy arrived into the interviewing room with Ali Defel. A flash of something crossed Ali's eyes when Ben entered.

'This is Ben Macken,' said Andy as Ben took a seat next to him.

Ali sat straight in his chair. He sounded anxious when mentioning that he was in a hurry as he had a flight to catch.

'Elijah has already been buried but this has been a cruel blow to his family. They need their close friends by their side on such a grave occasion.'

He was good; totally believable, she'd give him that.

Andy mentioned how Elijah could be seen at Cairo airport being escorted by two men to a waiting car. 'There is a clear enough description of one of the men. Most possibly Khafu will have it investigated further.'

'What about Catherine, have you found her?' Ali asked with surprising doggedness.

'We're working on it,' Andy replied. 'We have also made a connection with a man by the name of Omar Bakari. Have you ever heard of him?'

Ali bowed his head which made it impossible to observe his reaction.

'How would I know him?' He scanned the table, eyes remained downcast.

'When did you first meet Catherine Fowley?' Ben put to him.

Ali frowned but quickly regained his composure. 'Elijah and I were at college together. I knew her from back then.'

Andy was leaving it to Ben to continue and he did.

'But wasn't it you who introduced her to Elijah?'

Ali's eyes sat cold. 'Yes, I did and felt privileged to have brought them together at the time but I so regret it now.'

Ben was finding his feet and knew to play along in that game of deception. 'Were you not upset when she broke it off with you? I mean she wasn't just a casual friend. You had been a couple for some time.' He sounded so matter-of-fact, knowing it wasn't time to scare Ali off just yet.

Ali shook his head and replied, 'That was so long ago.'

Then Andy took over.

'Can you explain why you didn't answer your mobile when we tried to contact you via Elijah's mobile phone? I mean he was the senior partner in the business. You would have been anxious to discuss the matter of the embezzlement with him. Something you were concerned about. Why didn't you take the call or even attempt to call him back?'

Ali flipped his hand in the air. 'I can't remember. I was probably busy doing something at the time.'

No, not a good enough answer which allowed Andy straight in.

'Could it be that you knew it wasn't Elijah phoning, for you were already aware of his abduction?'

Ali's obvious shock was there in that firm line of his mouth, in the hardening of his jaw, in that quickening of his breath. Cathy could imagine that nervous inner voice of his telling him it was all about to come tumbling down around him. All that stack of lies and deceit. No, he needed to control that voice and remain strong. They didn't have enough on him.

'What is this? I've come here of my own free will as a favour to Elijah's father and you think it is appropriate to ask me such questions?'

Andy's response was to quickly ask. 'Do you know of any reason why Elijah was murdered?'

Ali could be heard inhaling. 'I did hear he was involved in human trafficking.' He lowered his head. 'It could have something to do with that.'

'Did you believe those rumours?' asked Ben.

'There could be truth to them, but I can't be sure,' he replied as his hands knotted tightly together.

He was playing it carefully, just giving enough of a detail to sow the seed of suspicion without actually pointing the finger.

'I'll ask you again, did you ever talk to or meet a man by the name of Omar Bakari?'

'No.' He was adamant.

Andy's mobile rang. He nodded as he listened to what he was being told. Nothing said apart from, 'Thanks for that.' It was triumph that lifted Andy's shoulders back. 'I need to inform you that your residence has been searched and a mobile found. Among your listed contacts on that mobile is one Omar Bakari. Now let's stop playing games. It is time you began to explain your involvement with this man.'

Ali sat as if his breath was stuck in his chest, refusing to allow him to breathe. He was obviously feeling trapped. He took his time to respond. 'Omar Bakari did contact me. He wanted my help to abduct Elijah but I refused.'

'Did you ever meet him?' asked Ben.

He nodded. 'Initially at his hotel.'

'Was that the only place you met him?' Andy demanded.

Ali attempted to search his mind for a believable answer while doubt stood by at every turn ready to trip him up as to how much they knew. In the end, he made no response.

As Andy went through his file, Cathy imagined Ali's heart racing, out of control.

'If you were not helping Omar Bakari then why did he call you four times on the day Elijah took that flight to Cairo? We will soon pinpoint the location of where you were when you took those calls. Your office perhaps?' Ali sat as if he'd been blitzed with a high voltage stun gun. Andy went on to mention how Catherine also had a second mobile which they had found. How there was only one number she contacted through that mobile and how they had made a call to that number earlier.

'Surprise, surprise, it turns out that call registered on your second mobile just like all the other calls from her, even one from last Valentine's Day around three in the afternoon when she called from outside the lingerie store to tell you about what she had just purchased. So, you weren't just *friends?*'

Full marks to Ali and Catherine on how convincingly they concealed their relationship thought Cathy. You had Mary Simpson adamant of Catherine's dislike for Ali. And Ali himself showing no interest in Catherine which was why it was easy to accept his belief that she was involved in Elijah's abduction. All it took was for a close friend to express her suspicions after her sister had been snubbed on the street. On knowing of the couples past history, Holly might not be surprised to discover the identity of her friend's lover.

The fight had gone out of Ali. He sat there possibly trying to decide what to do next.

Andy leaned forward.

'How do you think Elijah's father will take it when he is informed of your involvement with Omar Bakari and your affair with Catherine Muscanna? The woman you were out to convince us was responsible for her husband's abduction.'

It was then Ali asked to speak to his solicitor.

'I think that would be advisable.' Andy then stood and for a second, he hesitated. Then he said, 'Ali Defel I am arresting you on suspicion of your involvement in the abduction of Elijah Muscanna, ...' He rhymed off the arrest statement and cautioned him.

Andy then asked Ben to have the Station Officer brought in to take charge of Ali.

Cathy understood what Andy was up to. Once a witness crossed the line and became a suspect it changed everything. And before proceeding, the suspect had to be informed of why they were being arrested. The Station Officer then took control by completing a Rights Sheet and having the suspect sign it and allowing the suspect to make a call. The Station Officer's job was to ensure that the suspect's rights were protected. If a judge gives you the *don't buy it* look after you have stated when precisely your witness became a suspect then you're done for. The case is thrown out. The suspect walking free. All that hard work wasted.

///////

4.50pm

Matt focused on the screen as Andy and Ben re-entered Interview Room 1. He'd spent the last hour working with Ben on checking through all communications from Ali

Defel's second mobile while DI Spragg and Eric worked on tracking down Barry Saunders. Ali was already seated with his solicitor by his side. The solicitor watched Andy and Ben take their seats. There was no smugness in the solicitor's expression, no air of defiance just enough of a poker face to leave you wondering what was coming down the line. Ben gave the date, time of interview and those present. The solicitor was an Alan Crow.

He leaned forward.

'My client is willing to do a deal. He will name those involved in Elijah's abduction if in return you agree to charge him with abduction only.' He made it sound as if it were a reasonable request.

Andy looked from one to the other of them in disbelief.

'The only deal he'll get from us is a guarantee that Khafu Muscanna will not be informed of his involvement in this for twenty-four hours. That will give his family in Cairo time to leave before they're caught up in it all. As for his family here, I expect they'll be safe for now. It is his choice.'

But Ali didn't have a choice.

'Can you guarantee I will not be extradited to Egypt?'

On that, Andy gave him his word.

Matt turned up the volume as Ali began telling how Catherine and he were having an affair for the last eighteen months. Omar Bakari knew those whom Ali owed serious money to in Cairo. When Omar arrived in London, he tracked him down and agreed to have Ali's debts wiped clean but in return, he wanted Ali's help to abduct Elijah and he'd agreed to it.

'Catherine never wanted to live in Cairo and hated Elijah's second wife. She agreed to make herself ill so that Elijah would cancel his trip. Then, when she was feeling a little better, she pleaded with him to take a later flight. She knew to remove his mobile from his briefcase before he left.'

'So, what happened to Catherine?' asked Ben.

'She double-crossed me. This plan was hers. I don't know where she is.' In that clipped precise tone of his, Ali sounded believable.

'So, when did you last see Catherine?'

Ali shook his head for an answer. 'The Monday before Elijah's trip.'

Ben then went to explain how they had contacted Ali's neighbour Barry Saunders who at present was working in Saudi.

'He was surprised to learn that his car was more than once spotted in Richmond, in particular, close to Petersham Road. He suggested we speak to you as he'd planned to sell the car and had left you the key. Now we know exactly when you last saw Catherine so why don't you tell us the truth.'

Ali's steely eyes fixed on Ben.

'I visited her on Wednesday night after Elijah had left. We agreed to meet up on Friday but she never turned up. I don't know where she is?'

'And did you try to contact her when she didn't turn up?' asked Ben.

When Ali nodded Ben asked, 'From which phone or mobile?'

Ali shook his head. 'I cannot remember.'

'We can check all of them,' said Andy. He leaned further forward then. 'You never called her. For the same reason, you never returned that call we made to you from Elijah's mobile because you knew exactly where she was.'

Ali's solicitor sat there taking notes.

Andy asked about Ali's on-going communication with Nathan Warral.

Ali replied, 'Omar Bakari passed on his contact details in case his plan didn't work and a backup was needed.'

'What was the back-up plan?'

A flicker of hesitation before Ali replied, 'We hadn't decided.'

'Ali Defel, I would like to caution you on suspicion of your involvement in the abduction and murder of Catherine Muscanna. You do not have to say anything.......'

The solicitor tried to disguise his alarm at such a caution and whispered something to Ali who nodded but said nothing.

Andy was playing it by the book, Ali needed to be made aware of the fact that he had now crossed that line to suspect.

'Did you suggest having Catherine abducted and drowned far from here?' When no response was forthcoming Andy continued, 'Catherine's body has been found. Those responsible have named Nathan Warral as the man they worked for. So, you see, your involvement in this is pretty obvious.'

Matt felt himself smirk. Ali had never imagined that their evidence could link him to both abductions. Blaming Catherine for her part in it all would have weakened the case against Ali when she wasn't around to defend herself. His word against no one. And with a good barrister, he'd have been handed a minimum sentence.

'I'm giving you one last chance at the truth or our deal is off the table.' Andy turned from Ali to Alan Crow who by now was sitting further back in his chair.

It was all over for Ali. And he knew it.

'After we had agreed to the plan of having Elijah abduced, Catherine mentioned how she would be interested in running the business. That was her mistake. I knew how easily she would twist the situation to her advantage. It would never have worked between us. With me as responsible as her for our involvement in Elijah's abduction I needed to get rid of her.'

When there was silence, Andy picked up the slack.

'So, you contacted Nathan Warral but you also passed Patrick Fowley's number on to Omar Bakar and asked him to contact Patrick under the pretence he was Elijah. You were out to cover your tracks if Catherine was discovered. You expected us to check up as to when Patrick was here in London and then discover the communication between him and Omar Bakari. You were aware of the falling out between the pair from years back.'

Ali nodded, the fear was gone from him, his blank expression, similar to that of a statue's. 'Catherine had made a fool of Patrick once. I knew it would be easy to do it again.'

'Why did Omar Bakari want Elijah abducted?' asked Andy.

'He wouldn't tell me only that he would be well paid for it.'

'How did Catherine react when she realised that you had double-crossed her?' asked Ben, reading from what he'd written down.

'She never knew. When I arrived at the house on Wednesday, she was feeling better. We were both excited at how well our plan had worked. After she had showered and returned to the bedroom, I handed her a glass of wine laced with sleeping pills. She'd no idea what lay ahead of her.' He grinned. 'Because she hated Carrabhain. I decided it should be her resting place.'

The more Matt focused on Ali the more be believed that Ali was a true psychopath. He'd read somewhere how psychopaths were often successful individuals because of their ruthlessness, callousness and ease at which they could turn on the charm. It was impossible for them to consider the feelings of others. That was Ali, down to a tee.

It was Ben who asked, 'Why were you anxious to obtain Elijah's computer? We checked it out, there was no email from a solicitor to Elijah.'

'There was a file with all passwords to Elijah's bank accounts. I had hoped to withdraw money before he had been found dead.'

Andy sat with hands laced together in front of him. 'But he was your lifelong friend. How could you involve yourself in his murder?'

Ali sat there almost smirking. 'What, you think I should have regrets?' He leaned across the table. 'When we were kids, my parents felt honoured to be considered friends of Khafu Muscanna. And when Elijah came to play at our home, he would sulk until he was handed whatever toy I was playing with. So, I learned to play with toys that did not interest me and pretended to be upset when they were handed to him. And then I would pick up the toy I had wanted from the start and pretend I wasn't really interested in it. That worked. When we came here to college, I had presumed that Elijah had outgrown his selfishness. But when I introduced him to Catherine, he wanted her and won her. For that, I hated them both. And when my business in Cairo failed and I owed money to loan sharks I needed a way to start again. Elijah loved to boast over how well he was doing. He didn't have any friends here and insisted I come work for him.' He leaned back in his chair and paused for a minute. 'From the first day I started work I wanted what Elijah had and this time I was the one who would take from him. I knew Catherine would be unhappy over Elijah's decision to take a second wife and that I would win her back, even if I didn't really want her. All it took was for Omar Bakari to turn up and set my plan in motion.'

Matt watched as the interview ended. Ben, Andy and the solicitor walked from Interview Room 1. Ali was escorted to a cell.

//////

10.53pm

It was a balmy night. The pub overlooking the river stood smothered with flower baskets. The group of them were lucky to arrive early enough to bag a table out front. It was the first time they were totally relaxed around each other. They laughed, joked and sat surveying if not those passing then the fine river view. Eric and Mark had been there for the first round and possibly the second but they left soon after that. Now that Ben and Matt had finished their drinks they were moving to leave. Matt held the tabletop as he hauled himself from his seat. Never before had Cathy witnessed him drunk. She imagined not many had. Thankfully the pub was a stone's throw from their hotel and Ben was also heading in that direction.

A dog lay beneath a chair and didn't move when his owner went inside to buy a drink. Cathy didn't want to leave, to head to bed, fall asleep and wake the following morning with that day behind her. Nor did she want another drink. She was pleased when Andy pulled his chair in next to hers. No point being happy on your own. A little drunk, he began telling her of his first ever break-up with a girl called Janie. He was only eighteen at the time and had been so broken-hearted he'd lost a stone in weight in just a month. Cathy couldn't help but laugh along with him. When he asked about her first serious relationship, it sounded strange to admit it was with Dan.

'So, you haven't a clue of what it's like to lose your first love? Let me tell you it's not easy.' A hint of that knowing look of his was there.

'But I did lose him in the end.'

'Not the same. No way the same.' Some words slurred, head shaking.

The dog owner finished his drink and left. The dog followed with the lead trailing behind him.

When it came to closing time, Andy insisted on walking her back to the hotel. She thanked him when they got there.

'I thought we might spend the night together,' he sounded sobered up.

'What if your wife needs you?' She watched his reaction.

With a swing of his head, he answered, 'She won't.'

Did he imagine his charm would work on her as it had before? When he had arrived at her place for dinner, she had hoped they'd have time to talk things out, but Lucy's arrival prevented that from happening. And for the last week, things had been on a total working relationship footing.

'Andy, I don't need a repeat of what happened before.'

Whatever he was about to tell her would burst open that magnetic connection of theirs for better or worse. It was hard to remain stoical and she a little drunk. How often she had thought about this moment but what she hadn't reckoned on was that heightened sense of anticipation and disappointment all rolled up together. She was dreading his response.

Andy steadied himself. 'My wife and I have separated.' If he were expecting a response, he didn't get one. 'Our daughter Nina suffers from epileptic seizures. Anything can set her off. I'm talking seizures that can last up to five hours and scary as hell to watch knowing there's nothing you can do for her.' His mouth softened. 'My wife and I had agreed to separate a month before I first met you. We had broken the news to the girls, then Nina experienced the worst fit ever. That was what happened that last night I was with you, remember? My wife was phoning me from the hospital.' He caught her hand. 'We guessed that our break-up was what triggered it and we tried to make it work. But after six months, we knew it was a lost cause.' A second's pause. 'I know I should have contacted you before I did but I just didn't know how to tell you. When I did finally find the courage, you refused to answer any of my calls.'

She watched that look of concern in his expression and imagined what he and his wife had gone through. And she believed him. And yes, she'd have done the same, would have remained with Dan, put up with his affairs if the health of either of her daughters required it. No question about it.

He waited for her response.

She moved towards him, took his face in her hands and kissed him with every ounce of passion in her body.

Saturday - 11th July

11.55am

Arriving back at the house, Matt was tempted to take another two painkillers. He had already taken four since he'd woken at six that morning. Luckily, he'd made it to the toilet before throwing up on the flight. Checking himself in the mirror, his face was a greyish green. He should never have drunk so much the previous night. It was only that morning he had noticed a text from Jackie. Aine had agreed to drive her and the kids home. Thankfully he didn't have to face the drive to and from Cork. He took his second shower of the day and hoped the queasiness he was feeling would soon pass.

DI Spragg had seemed giddy on the flight home. There he was as sick as a parrot while she rabbited on about her father, her daughters and how she couldn't decide whether to head down to Carrabhain to collect Truman today or leave it until tomorrow. As they had walked from the plane, she took a phone call from Andy that had her beaming with a smile. She mentioned how it had been a pleasant flight and that she was glad he had called her. There she was with her all happy, girly kind of reaction he'd never have expected. He had noticed how she and Andy hit it off over the week. And then last night when he was leaving the pub, even if he were drunk, he remembered them laughing together and Andy's arm across the back of her chair. Ben too had mentioned how they both seemed close.

'So, when are you expecting him over on a visit?' Matt

had asked as they sat into the shuttle bus to take them to the car park.

She had grinned like a teenager. 'It hasn't been decided on yet.'

He had himself another glass of water before driving into the village. Pat Lynch was in the front passenger seat of his sister's car and waved as he passed. Matt knocked on the door.

Patrick didn't invite him in but stood with arms folded listening to what Matt had to say. He said nothing when Matt had finished.

'If you like I'll come in to help you break the news to Tess.'

'No,' replied Patrick closing in on Matt. 'You believed I was guilty?'

Matt took a step back.

'I'm sorry you feel that way. But I was only doing my job.'

Matt had made it his business to check up on the previous assault claims against Patrick from years back. It had been Rebecca who had initially contacted the Vancouver police. The officer Matt spoke to outlined how Patrick's previous girlfriend, Jennie, had since made thirty such claims against every man she had dated and had threatened to break up with her. The officer assured him that Patrick was considered a decent law-abiding individual.

Patrick's eyes narrowed. 'And if you hadn't got to the truth would my so-called past have come back to ruin me and my family?' His obvious anger was in his voice. His fear of being prevented from returning to Vancouver, of being arrested in front of those close to him, of being dubbed a rapist. A label that he'd always be associated with regardless of being found innocent at a later day, if ever. It was all there.

Matt felt his stomach churn. 'As I said, I was only doing my job.'

'If you honestly knew Tess then you'd have known I wasn't guilty or she'd never have welcomed me home.' Patrick was having trouble controlling the tremor in his voice. With a deep inhale of breath, he raised his hand to the door-handle. 'I'll tell Tess what she needs to hear.'

He closed over the door and left Matt standing there.

Friday - 24th July

1.05pm

Tess was flanked by Patrick on one side and Melissa on the other. Heather and Brandon walked behind them. They all headed up the centre aisle of the Church. The villagers came out in force. Andy had arrived over for a few days and Cathy was glad not to be there on her own. The choir was in attendance, encouraged by Nancy, a long-standing member. The largest wreath had no message. Everyone assumed it was from Elijah's family, but she knew they would be the last to send anything. Cathy suspected the sender was Martin Rodgers.

Beautiful as the priest's words sounded, they weren't altogether accurate. He focused on Catherine's positive side only which was what the congregation wanted to hear. There was no eulogy, no Patrick to proclaim her as a loving sister. And outside the Church, Patrick and Tess continually repeated, 'Thank you for coming.'

The previous day Cathy had a call from the artist, Maggie Williams. She apologised for not getting in touch sooner but she'd been on vacation. There was a trace of an Irish accent in her voice, which Cathy hadn't noticed when she'd phoned and left that message. Maggie was genuinely upset to hear what had happened to Catherine. She went on to explain how she was her best customer from when she'd first started buying her work ten years back.

'She loved my paintings and insisted on sending me what she believed the pieces were worth. I have a blood disorder and with no health insurance; if it wasn't for Catherine's generosity, I'd never have afforded my treatment.'

At least Catherine had done good for someone.

Cathy had asked Maggie if she were Irish.

'Sure am,' she replied, 'I lived across the street from the National Maternity Hospital there on Holles Street.' She chuckled. 'I think you know some close relatives of mine but we won't go there. I left all that behind me when I arrived here in New York.'

Catherine must have believed she'd found her sister, Margaret Rodgers now Maggie Williams, the artist living in New York. How would she have handled knowing that Maggie was only her cousin and that her mother was still alive? But learning that her father had disowned her would have done her no good.

Ali Defel's family in Cairo had left their home early that same evening he'd confessed. Pleading guilty meant no prolonged court case. Nathan Warral had turned up dead in an apartment in Lanzarote. Cathy wouldn't be surprised if Martin Rodgers had tracked him down. She was sure the suspects had supplied his henchmen with his name. And of course, the media stressed how those same men were remorseful over their actions and had co-operated fully with the investigation. Cathy didn't know if Omar Bakari had been found or who had paid him to carry out his plan, another one of those top secrets to be withheld.

Tea and sandwiches were served in O'Mara's after the funeral. Tess was as pale as paper and pained with grief. Heather was there by her side, attentive to fetch her anything she needed. Now there was a girl who would have a whopper of a story to tell her friends when she returned home. And how she'd relish the telling of what details she had been privy to.

Cathy had called to see Tess on Sunday when she arrived down to collect Truman. Patrick hadn't told her the full facts of the case. When she asked Cathy to be honest with her, she was to a point. Told her how Catherine was having an affair with Elijah's best friend, Ali, and how it was he who had her murdered and was also a player in Elijah's murder. After hearing that, Tess had bowed her head and sank back into the chair.

'There was a side to Catherine that was hard to understand, she had me thinking I wasn't a good mother and I didn't understand her. She never believed there was anything she couldn't do. And you just wanted her to succeed and then she'd be happy and see that I was only doing my best,' she said in a solemn voice. 'But to blame Patrick for raping her was unforgivable.' Then with a sigh she added, 'I hope she'll be forgiven for that.'

Cathy had understood how she felt.

With an attempt of a smile Tess had finished by saying, 'She was someone you'd remember or should I say, she was someone you couldn't forget.'

That too sounded true.

Cathy pulled herself back to reality in hearing Jackie mention how she'd decided to return to work part-time.

'With the amount of income tax I'd be paying and the cost of a minder, it wouldn't be worth my while working full-time.'

Sitting there among the locals eating sandwiches and drinking tea it struck Cathy how she knew the full facts on Catherine Fowley from when she'd been born. The sergeant knew more than most. Tess, Patrick and Melissa might have thought they knew everything but would have been surprised to learn of her close link to Martin Rodgers.

She watched Matt in conversation with Patrick, then Jackie interrupted them. And when they moved to leave, Jackie hugged Patrick. You could imagine her wishing him a good flight home and hoping he'll soon be back. Then Patrick turned to shake Matt's hand. Now that pleased her.

She and Andy also moved to leave. But Cathy stopped to chat with Molly. From her, she crossed to Tess and hugged her, saying she'd call the next time she was down. Melissa and Patrick were at the door.

'Thank you for coming,' Patrick said.

Their previous argument forgotten about.

'And thanks for all you did.' Melissa squeezed her hand.

'Don't leave it too long to return,' Cathy replied.

She walked towards Andy who was waiting by her car. On his suggestion, they had hired a cruiser for the weekend.

//////

2.55pm

Deegan seemed surprised when Matt entered the station. Over the past few weeks, between his trip to London and the time he'd spent with Detective Finnegan in Athlone, the place seemed to belong more to Deegan than to him. He was beginning to feel he was a stranger in the place.

'I thought you were heading off for the weekend?' Deegan asked.

'Yeah, but I just wanted to check in with you first.'

Deegan smirked and that had Matt smiling.

He was still on a high over how the case had gone. At the Media Press Conference, DI Spragg had insisted that he sit alongside her and Superintendent Clarke. There was no sign of Detective Finnegan. The message had been a simple one. They had arrested those responsible for the murder of Catherine Muscanna, formally Catherine Fowley, and had assisted the London Metropolitan Police in identifying the individual responsible for planning her abduction and murder. Matt wondered if Catherine's true nature would ever be revealed. It helped that Ali Defel had pleaded guilty as charged. No lengthy case where everything about her would be picked over.

Afterwards the Superintendent had sounded pleased to inform Matt that he was in the top spot to step into the next vacancy as a Detective Sergeant. In such a position, if he were to work with Finnegan and Reeves, they would be answerable to him. Finnegan had so many close contacts throughout the force it would be difficult to try and manage him. A transfer to another Division would be best.

When he sat at his desk, Deegan brought him a mug of strong tea.

'How did the funeral go?' he asked.

'As you would expect,' replied Matt.

It was Tess who had called into the station on Tuesday looking for him.

'I want to see Catherine's body.' She had sounded determined.

Without hesitation, he agreed to drive her to the morgue.

'What about Patrick, does he want to see her?' Matt had asked.

'No. He'll remember her as she was.' At the door, she had turned and said, 'But can Nancy come with me?'

'Of course,' he had replied knowing such an act of

generosity was sure to build bridges. Nancy had been devasted on hearing the news. For two days the supermarket never opened.

They had made the trip on Wednesday. He was glad Tess had Nancy for company. They cried together when they viewed her body. On the journey home, they talked about Catherine and the things she got up to as if she had never done wrong in her life.

He was surprised when Patrick approached him in the pub earlier.

'Thanks for being there for Tess, it was important that she got to see Catherine.'

'That's my job.' Matt had replied.

Patrick heisted before he said, 'It's just as Melissa said, you get paranoid when you feel you're being attacked. That's what I was feeling.'

Matt had nodded. 'I can understand that.'

He was glad things between them were now on a better footing.

Matt refused Deegan's offer of a biscuit.

Part of him felt sad about leaving Carrabhain Station. It would always hold a soft spot for him. And he had concerns over whether he could manage an investigation team without the involvement and support of DI Spragg. Time would tell he told himself as he rose from the chair.

'Right,' he said as he left. 'See you next week.'

Get in touch with me at:

www.rosaleenflanagan.com

Mailing List
From my website you can subscribe to my mailing list which will notify you of all updates regarding my books.

Contacts
www.facebook.com/rosaleen.flanagan.7
twitter.com/rosannaflan